D0392332

The Tin-Kin

THE TIN-KIN

Eleanor Thom

Duckworth Overlook

First published 2009 by
Duckworth Overlook
90-93 Cowcross Street
London, EC1M 6BF
Tel: 020 7490 7300
Fax: 020 7490 0080
info@duckworth-publishers.co.uk
www.ducknet.co.uk

Copyright © 2009 by Eleanor Thom

All rights reserved. No part of this publication
may be reproduced, stored in a retrieval system, or
transmitted, in any form or by any means, electronic,
mechanical, photocopying, recording or otherwise,
without the prior permission of the publisher.

The right of Eleanor Thom to be identified as the Author of
the Work has been asserted by her in accordance with
the Copyright, Designs and Patents Act 1988.

'One': Nilson, Harry (CA) © 1968 (Renewed) Golden Syrup
Music (BMI). All rights administered by
Warner-Tamerlane Publishing Corp.
'Sh-boom' Words and Music by James Keyes, Carl Feaster,
Floyd Mc Rae, Claude Feaster and James Edwards –
© 1954 (Renewed) Unichappell Music Inc. - All Rights Reserved –
Lyric reproduced by kind permission of Carlin Music Corp.,
London, NW1 8BD
'In the Hay' lyrics reproduced by kind permission.
Words and music by Chris "Dixieland" Dooks © 2008

Every effort has been made to trace copyright holders and to
obtain their permission for the use of copyright material.
The publisher apologizes for any errors or omissions in the
above list and would be grateful if notified of any corrections
that should be incorporated in future reprints or editions of this book.

A catalogue record for this book is available
from the British Library

ISBN 978 0 7156 3832 3

Typeset by Ray Davies
Printed in Great Britain by
MPG Books Limited, Bodmin, Cornwall

John Williamson

'Jock'

03 January 1902 – 14 September 1927

Mix Tape – June '95

The Midnight Hour – The Elgins
Walking Shoes – Tanya Tucker
What I Am – Edie Brickell and The New Bohemians
One – Three Dog Night
Sh-Boom – The Crew Cuts
I've Got Tears in My Ears from Lying on My Back
Crying Over You – Homer and Jethro
Three Cigarettes in an Ashtray – Patsy Cline
Labelled With Love – Squeeze
The Ballad of Patch Eye & Meg – Michelle Shocked
Road – Nick Drake
Creeps Like Me – Lyle Lovett

Dawn

They were somewhere between two signs, 'Welcome' and 'Have a Safe Journey', a row of two-storey houses not long enough to name. In windows the curtains were mainly drawn, the lights off. Maeve had quietened down in the back seat. She was whispering numbers to herself, as though she were trying to count stars but kept getting lost.

One. Two. One. Two. Wuntwo wuntwo.

What are you counting?

Maeve ignored her.

The drive was almost over. Dawn kept going, flicked a switch to put the beams on full, wound the window down a crack and lit a cigarette. She pushed a cassette into the player and hummed along. She liked country songs. They helped her feel warm, as if the sun was sitting in her belly.

> *I drove me fifty states away*
> *Now I'm the needle in the hay*

Short but cold, these summer nights! A strip of sky was starry between the pine tops, the road taking them north. In open fields she slowed to take the dips in the road, in and out of lazy pools of shallow mist. She passed the distillery with its fingery chimneys, braking hard round the hairpin bend cupped in its palm. She stopped singing now, listened to the engine and the spin of wheels. She was surprised to remember the twists and turns, the road's gentle inclines and swifter falls. She could drive as if asleep, an invisible reel pulling her in.

Midnight. Dawn parked in front of a house. It was split in

7

two, a flat at the top and a flat below. Until a week ago the top had been her aunt's. It was theirs now.

The house had plain, square angles, dusty orange in the streetlight. Nothing had changed since she'd left. Time had traipsed by with its mind on something else. She checked over her shoulder. Maeve was sound asleep and the street was empty. She'd get the cases inside before carrying her daughter to the strange bed they would share.

The gate grunted like an old woman and the garden was matted with creepers. The door to the top flat was around the back and the steps were gently bowed. Everything was slow, but crunching up the gravel path Dawn heard her own breath quicken before she felt it. Stirring the keys in her pocket, she remembered a game she used to play.

Inside was a cupboard that had never been unlocked. Peering through the keyhole, nothing but the deepest black. Tomorrow the clean-up would begin. She would pull the flat inside out, disturb dust particles that had been skulking for years and send them spiralling in the sunlight.

✳ VISION ✳

Bars on the window split the moonlight intae squares. The sky's far away. There's cold flagstone on the floor and a dark ceiling that folds in on me. I look for the door, get just a sense ae it, a solid blackness shut tight in the pit ae my stomach. The place reeks like a dirty close.

I shiver. Cold. But my jacket smells warm. It's smoke and spilt whisky. Pain circles the back ae my heid, pressing down, oil-like. I'm in a corner, one arm stretchin out so my fingers just stroke the light and turn silver at the tips. I try and sleep, pretendin it's summer and that I'm in one ae the caves near the beach, warm sand for a mattress. But it's too quiet. Nae waves crashing or gulls crying here. I'm swallied alive.

A chair scrapes the floor somewhere, metal, grindin like machines at the scrap yard. The sound rakes up my throat. I try and work out where it comes from but there's echoes in this place. Echoes and drips. Slether trickles cool on my cheek but I cannae lift a hand tae wipe it. My arms feel deid from the elbows down. Footsteps get nearer, stop, and someone keeks through the letterbox hatch. He grunts, drops it back so the hatch swings in and out, playing with the light from the corridor like a moth, showing up the flagstones. The cell flickers like the newsreel countdown at the picture house. Three, two, one . . .

BANG!

They're pounding on the door. I feel the solid thumping in my chest, my belly, the pain in my neck.

When I shut my eyes it's a ride on the dodgems so I keep them open and peer at a clarty black stain. It explodes against the wall, trickles down the plaster and disappears behind the tin bucket, same as what we use at home. The sight ae it clenches my stomach like a fist.

I think ae Rascal, pray they've nae hurt him. He was with me when I was lifted, I'm sure ae it. And there was a song playing. I can hear a hint. Even in this hellish place a wee snatch ae the melody's snuck its way in like a draught. I cannae remember the whole number. It gets on my nerves, a sneeze that's stuck.

> *Hello hello again,*
> *sh-boom and hopin' we'll meet again*

I can picture the jukebox, records lined up like liquorice wheels, waiting and hoping. Peter's Café will have been shut for hours, but I can see the place, clear as if I was in Cooper Park right now, strolling past the lake, looking in the windows. Moonshine glows all ghostie-like on the wiped-down table-tops. I have tae remember that song!

Then the penny drops, falls heavy inside. It was me chose the song. *Sh-boom. Life could be a dream, sweetheart.* She sat opposite me, tears runnin down her cheeks, while that stupid number went on turning.

Later I hooked up wi Tommy the Barra. We made plans. We're getting out ae here, soon as the summer comes. It's best tae head south for work, he says. My old ma'll be pleased, even though she'll miss me. Wee Betsy'll gurn that she wants tae come too, but there'll be no wee lassies. It'll be just the gadgies back on the road. Except now we'll be travelling in style. Nae tents. The Barra got himself a bus!

The rest ae the evenin's a blur.

> *Dat-dat-dat-dat-dat-duh.*

But that's the least ae my worries. Someone's unbolting the door.

'Get to your feet,' says a voice.

I cannae move but make out like I'm trying. He comes close, smoking a ciggie, a wee red glow crossing the cell. In the doorway the light's blinding.

'You deaf?' he whispers, close tae my face now.

The dull weight ae my heid thuds suddenly against the flags. Pain floods everywhere, my eyes, gums, deep below my foreheid, and it's a while before I realise there's a strange noise coming from my own mouth. I suck my voice back as he leans closer again. I'm sure he's lookin tae burn me with his fag.

'What's*ss* that you *sss*ay? *Sss*peak up!' he goes, his voice playful, a smirk.

My scalp tightens. I'd ken that voice anyday, that hiss like the wind whistlin down a cracked lum. Old Munro. He's a quiet one. Buys his smokes fae the booth on platform one, every day at four on the dot, just as the Lossie train blows *its* whistle.

'Capstan*sss*, packet ae twenty.'

Us station boys cry him 'Snake'.

He's diggin me square in the ribs with the toe ae his boot. I try and shuffle out ae reach, but he turns his heel and gies me a wee kick like he's giddyin-up a pony. Another toby arrives in the cell. This one keeps in the doorway, a drawn-out shadow that leans on the frame, hands in pockets.

'A Lady Lane lad?' the toby asks.

Snake repeats the words back like a wrong answer, a schoolmaster about tae gie you the strap. 'Lay-dee-Lane.'

'First time I've seen him,' goes the shadow.

Snake flicks ash on me.

'Well, they're all tink*sss*.'

I whisper a curse under my breath. Eat your mother's . . . and I've barely shut my gob when the pain hits me another time. Back ae the heid. (*Sh-boom*.) He hunkers down tae crank cuffs on my wrists.

Suddenly, a bell! My heart rises. Someone's come tae get me home!

11

But they take their time. The toby in the doorway puffs out bindweed smoke. It twists over the flagstones. His voice is slow, watchin. 'Nasty cut, that,' he goes, and it's a while before he straightens up and heads away down the corridor after the bell. He leaves behind him the fraying ribbons ae ciggie smoke and a square ae light in the doorway.

The cuffs are cuttin in. I'm trapped, cheek on the slabs, trussed up like a bird in the butcher's. There's a whistle as Snake sooks in his breath, gathering his strength, and I harden myself, expect what's coming. Any second now.

My brother's been here often enough. He's told me how it is with Munro. Snake'll go for the ribs, the spine, the back ae the skull, the –

ONE!

He sinks his foot intae my kidneys.

And TWO!

A toe-cap skims my ribs.

Everything inside goes hot, hunkered and dirty blood black. I cough and spit. When I've gasped a few lungfuls I start tae pull together again, remembering the outline ae my body, finding the centre ae the pain. I feel my breeks clinging tae my legs, hot and wet. Snake sneers over me. I'm nae better than a filthy animal. And again he beats his boot intae my side, hard, like he's kicking a sack.

ONE!

TWO!

And ONE!

And TWO!

I curl, drag my knees tae my chest, loll over. My insides knit together and my voice comes out in gulps, a crackly wireless. The noise makes him laugh. I better shut up before the joke runs dry so I squeeze my eyes shut and picture myself at home: my camp bed with the poky springs, my aeroplane books and the wee planes I've carved, the clicking ae Ma's knitting needles.

12

Duncan sits halfway up the dancers on the creaky step, polishing shoes. Curly and Jeannie cosy in round the fire. They're sookin on spoonfuls ae sugar and margarine, telling stories. Wee Betsy does her homework at the table. She squints at sums and chews the end ae her pencil.

Snake twists over me, peering down like I'm something he's stepped in. He plays a game, tucks dribbling kicks round my ribs and up ontae my face. I feel the tacks on his soles as he scuffs past my cheek. And then he brings his heel down. My heart goes crack.

My heart gets a kick start. I taste metal, choke the stuff up, but straight away more gushes in, gurgling mouthfuls ae soup. I cough dark and thick, and sobs jump out like soap suds bursting.

Later, Snake straightens my body on the floor. My insides groan and roll like he's tippin the world over. He grabs a fistful ae hair and hauls my heid up tae slip something under. And just then there's this amazing smell, so good I want tae drown in it.

Perfume! It's her scarf! She draped it round my neck after we left Peter's, and it's still soggy from the rain and sweet from her skin. The scarf's more than just damp, though. Soon it feels wet under my heid, drookit. The scent ae it's so beautiful. I could wrap it over my face, this wonderful thing. It could make me invisible. I want tae breathe it right intae myself. But I cannae breathe it in. I've no breath at all! And now I remember another thing. I was at the hospital tonight, lying on the fresh blue and white striped linen. It could be years ago but I ken it was just a few hours past.

Snake sniffs, spits a bit. Perhaps the dust gets tae him. He turns tae leave.

'My dog!' I want tae shout after him. But I stay quiet. Nae enough puff. Every breath's like sucking through a stalk. I cannnae get it back. Count! I think. Breathe! I wonder if I'm having an attack like thon manny at the station. We'd tae gie him a bag tae breathe with.

My wish comes true. I'm sinking intae the scarf, disappearing. But it hurts. I think ae a beetle on its back, screaming 'Wrong way up!', its legs frantic. I hold myself tight, tight, tighter, squeezing my ribs like ropes round bundles ae rags. A man takes each end of a rope, and they pull. The cloth gets compressed intae bails.

I've no breath left in me now. My insides are going tight. The bails ae cloth are thrown on the lorry and the men get their wages. The lorry drives off, down Lady Lane and up High Street. They watch it get smaller and smaller and smaller.

I'm still now, very still. The thoughts in my heid have folded up, like clothes going in a suitcase.

I'm gone! I was gone in a blink!

But I can feel something in my hand. My hands were empty, but there's something there now, real as rain, just like how I felt my watch strap days after I pawned it. Wide open space. A hundred thousand faces. A place that smells like the beach, and tastes ae peat and berries and pokes ae chips. Planes that fly over oceans.

A world so small it would slip through a buttonhole.

❋ WINDFAAS ❋

Auld Betsy, 1954

Ah met the Batchie Woman when ah wis ainly a young dilly. It wis the same summer ah met George, an ah wis already carryin oor first, wee Georgina. Ever since then ah've been sure the Batchie Woman's got the gift, an fer better or worse, ah aie heed her visions. They're fairly clearer than the few ah've had mysel ower the years. O ho!

Yesterday ma nephew the Bissaker came back fae work sayin the Batchie Woman wis needin a word wi me. 'A wee bit ae bother she's wantin aff her chest,' that's whit he cried it. That wis aw ah could get oot ae him, though, an since then ah cannae think ae ony ither thing. Ah've sat wonderin whit her 'wee bit ae bother' means.

The Bissaker cries the Batchie Woman's work 'auld wifey's footerin'. He doesnae tak ony ae it tae hert. Ainly believes in things he can sell. O ho! Ho! Ha! Rags an scrap metal are that loun's ainly faith! But the Batchie Woman foretelt his ain birth, years ago. She kent aw aboot his scrap yard, even then. She kent afore abody that he'd buy thon place an mak a winner ae it, an that a year later he'd hae jobs tae gie aw oor breed. Sure enough, within a year ae him takin oan the yard we were aw speakin ae leavin the camps, comin aff the road, shiftin intae hooses in the toun. When the Batchie Woman tellt his mither aboot that vision, she said she saw it aw happenin in the shadow ae Lady Hill.

Ah shout up the dancers tae Curly an the bairnies that ah'm aff tae see her noo, an closin the door ahint ae me ah look ower

15

the rooftops across the Lane. Risin above them's the brow ae Lady Hill, an this mornin mair than ever afore it nods tae me like it wis leanin doun tae whisper in ma lug. 'Whit did ah tell ye? The Batchie Woman's nae a circus act, right enough, an Auld Betsy's nae a bloody fool!' O ho!

Ah walk alang the Lossie tae reach her wee cottage. It's nae far, but the path's uneven an her hoose is easy tae miss. It's circled wi trees an high hedges so fowk cannae peer intae her windaes. She's nae patience fer interferin an nosyness. Fowk nivver see the Batchie Woman in toun. When she's got somethin tae chew ower wi ye she sends a message tae come tae her cottage. But even fowk who've known her a hale lifetime dinnae ken much aboot her ain story. Naebody's got a clue how auld she is. Ah remember bein twenty mysel, a fair whilie ago noo let me tell ye, o ho! But the Batchie Woman had somethin ae the auld wifey aboot her even then. The rumour is she's put twa husbands in an early grave, an ah can believe that. Ah've nivver seen her wi ony bairnies or grandbairnies, an she bides alane these days wi nae sae much as a cat fer company. There wis a time she kept chickens an a goat, but nae ony mair.

Fowk say beasts wilnae even enter her gairden noo. Jugals dig their paws in at the gate, an the closest the wee birdies fly is the trees ower the water. Some say her gift's turned wicked. Spoiled.

Oan the wye alang the path ah pass the place where George asked me tae be his woman. It feels a lifetime ago, an it almost is, ah suppose. Ah aie stop here onywye, tak a wee rest an remember him. That summer ma faimly wis travellin wi his, stoppin in aw the same places, an wan evenin ah met George oot alane, here in Elgin. Ah wis oan ma wye tae fetch Father fae the bar afore he drank the week's wages, but when George offered tae tak me tae the showies instead ah forgot. O ho! Mither wis horn-mad wi me later oan, wi Father in the doldrums ae the drink an nae a sign ae me. But they werenae harsh aboot it. It wis easy tae see ah'd been swept aff ma tramplers! O ho! Ho! Ha! An they were pleased. They'd aie liked George. It wis ainly a few months after that ah found ah wis haein his bairnie, an that wis enough fer us so we nivver bothered wi a weddin.

The Batchie Woman wouldnae utter a word tae me aboot Wee Georgina. She'd ae been oor eldest. Ah learnt aw sorts ae other things that first visit, though: that George would be a good man tae me; that we'd hae nine bairns; that we'd be happy. She wis right aboot aw those things. Except we ainly had eight bairns ae oor ain. Jock's the eighth. Ma good boy, Jock. After he wis born an a few years had passed, ma George counted aw the heids roun oor campfire oan wan haund, an aw the poor wee souls that should ae been there but werenae oan the other. Then he says tae me, 'The Batchie Woman wis wrang then, Betsy, we've ainly ever had eight.'

It did seem that wye fer a while, an aw the time ah felt like a goose wi a missin gosling. O ho! Ho! Ha! In a silly dwam, ah wis! But by faith, nae lang after that a terrible thing happened. Ma poor, dear sister, bless her sweet soul, wis taken by consumption just a month after her first baby wis born. A dreadful tragedy. But that's whit brought her wee Francis intae oor nest. The Batchie Woman nivver tellt a lie. We had oor ninth bairn.

Ah've lost mair bairns than a mither ever should. Francis, Peter, an Wee Georgina, ma very first. She nivver lived tae see a sunrise. Ah'm sure the Batchie Woman saw that sad night months afore it happened an didnae dare speak a word ae it.

Ah'm standin at her gate noo, wonderin if it's true aboot the beasts nae wantin in her gairden ony mair. There's a lone rook ower the Lossie crawin awa at me, an ah wonder if it'll fly closer if ah wait. But then the Batchie Woman's curtains twitch. O ho! She kens ah'm here afore ah've even chapped oan the door.

Ah tak a step an feel somethin soft under ma shoe. A ploom. Ah nearly squashed it. There's a hale apronworth ae the great muckle fruits oan the ground, dark purple an blue an juicy-

17

lookin. Windfaas. They come fae the trees at the top ae the Batchie Woman's gairden an must've rolled aw the wye tae the gate. Normally ah'd pick a few up, sink ma teeth intae them. Ah love plooms, straight fae the tree an still warm fae the sun, stewed intae jam, steamed in a puddin or baked wi sugar. They're grand. But somethin's nae right aboot these. They're too fine, perfectly roun like giant black marbles, aw the same size, an nae a bruise, nae sign ae a bitter, unripe side, or a single mushy, fusty bit atween them. So why's naebody been by tae pick or tae scrump them? The ploom skins are full tae burst wi ripe flesh. Ah can smell the sweetness. But they're nae hummin wi wasps or dusty like ye'd normally find them. These plooms hae a deep satin shine, like a greengrocer's sat polishin them wi a lovely clean white hanky aw mornin. Ah go doun oan ma hunkers an turn a few ae the fruits ower. By God! The underbel-lies are perfect an aw. Dirt wilnae cling tae the skins, an nae a wan ae the bonnie fruits is flawed by a single worm's hole, marked by fox's jaws or a beastie's sookin tongue. Not even a bird's peck. They're untouched, smooth as stanes.

Ah tak a deep breath, mindin ae the Bissaker's words. 'A wee bit ae bother.' Ah wonder whit it's oan. Last time ah wis in this hoose ah asked the Batchie Woman aboot ma Jock. Maybe it's somethin oan him. A wee bit ae bother. But Jock's a good boy. Ah'm sure if she had a vision aboot him it'd be a marriage wi a bonnie dilly. He's at that age. Twenty-one. Ah feel lighter as ah start towards the door. Maybe that's aw this vision ae hers is. A wife fer ma youngest son.

Ah'm nearly at the top ae the gairden path noo, but ah still cannae see the Batchie Woman's face. It's aw darkness inside the hoose. Jist afore ah reach the front step an the door opens wide, ah hear a thud. Anither ripe ploom falls fae the tree, unplucked an unpecked. It rolls past ma tramplers, makin fast fer the gate.

Dawn

One is the loneliest number that you'll ever do
Two can be as bad as one

The music made the task feel less endless. Sorting and tidying her aunt's possessions, she hoped she would come across the missing key – and open the cupboard. But there were so many places the key could hide. Her aunt's home was one of endless bits and bobs, jam jars rattling with different coloured beads and buttons, a jewellery box with a broken dancer under the lid, a brown plastic bracelet, used dress patterns, someone's war medals, a ring with a red stone, and a silver brooch that said 'mother'. Sleeping in a small box was a concertina that wheezed a groggy dischord when she lifted it. There were umpteen bottles of scent gone fusty, faded yellow like plastic cemetery flowers. Everything smelt of the golden perfumes, sickly-sweet as second helpings of syrupy dumpling. It made her treasure-hunting flustered and nauseous. Her fingers scratched at the lids of shortbread tins grainy with rust; inside every one, more lost or forgotten 'bonnie things' tucked away in no particular order, most of them bound for the dustbin. Still no key.

She picked up a dressing table mirror, mock Victorian with gaudy embellishments on the back. She spun it round to check her face and pursed her lips. Her features didn't suit the frame. She was a woman who only made herself up with lipstick but smiled timidly. Her body wasn't what it once was. Not that it was bad. She still got the odd compliment. Pretty face, folk said. But since having Maeve she could never find clothes that fit right. She needed a haircut. She could see that now, looking in the mirror, frowning at herself. But those salons were a nightmare, the sitting still, the questions, not least the cup of coffee they always placed just out of reach so taking a sip would always need an apology. She sung along to a couple of lines before letting the mirror drop.

Two can be as bad as one
It's the loneliest number since the number one

Dawn had strewn the contents of a small box onto the bed. Earrings, safety pins, shells from Findhorn, fragments and shards and pieces of grit. The tiniest grains were pushed along the wavy tufts of candlewick bedcover like silt washing down a hundred streams.

Maeve had no friends but Dawn didn't either. That was what happened when you moved house too often. All morning Maeve had sat with her, picking things up and chattering. Dawn had tried to second guess the objects that would keep her daughter interested, anything that wasn't sharp and couldn't make a mess. She'd handed over a pretty embroidered handkerchief, some old coins, a stuffed toy. She'd hidden the waxy-looking lipsticks and a rusty box of gramophone needles. The old concertina was Maeve's favourite. She was in the garden with it now, pulling and squeezing, the instrument braying like a donkey.

The cassette reached the end of the side and clicked off. Dawn thought about turning it over but decided against it. She liked this album. It would be a shame to ruin it by listening too many times. Instead she would concentrate on the task, turn keepsakes over like stones, looking carefully as though she'd left something hidden there. She'd made games of these things herself once; left small, clammy fingerprints on them.

Her aunt had told her what was in the cupboard was none of Dawn's business. Auntie Shirley's secrets. She'd always said it playfully, a finger tapping her nose. She'd liked to tease Dawn, wind her up to see what would happen. But this had been an uneasy game. Dawn had sensed the secrets, put her palms against the chilly paint of the door, pressed a cheek to a panel, tried to peek through the crack. She'd wished the secrets could whisper themselves out loud or peer back at her.

Shirley had everything recorded, evidence of a life stored willy-nilly. Her flat was dark, heavy with notes-to-self implying long forgotten appointments, outings and meaningful gestures, full to bursting with the tat she'd amassed. Now it lay in every drawer, unlabelled and unexplained down to the last scrap. Sometimes a few scribbled words would uncrumple in Dawn's hands and she'd hear Shirley's voice in her head. Dawn would miss her then; a pain like a hand pressing down on her breastbone. She hid those moments from Maeve. She'd say she had a snuffle, a cold coming on, and then she would push whatever it was that had set her off into the bin and go back to the search.

A key turned up in a cutlery drawer and Maeve found another in the pocket of a doll's dress. Dawn held them in her hands, weighing them. They looked too new, and she was not disappointed when they didn't fit the lock. The cupboard was old and whatever was inside, the secrets she imagined, suggested a key that was tarnished and heavy. She wanted a key with personality; something that couldn't be forged twice.

What's in there? Maeve said.

I don't know. Maybe nothing.

Maeve twisted her comforter, Blue Scarfy, giving it a Chinese burn. She was turning the soft, fragile silk into something hard and strong.

Don't worry, we'll open it, Dawn said into Maeve's silence. I want to find out. She felt suddenly ridiculous, the way she had when her aunt once caught her rummaging for the key.

She'd tried to pick the lock once. Dawn laughed. It was a strange noise in the emptying flat, so she muffled it with her hand. She ran her tongue over the tooth that had chipped. It was so smooth now you'd never know she'd damaged it once, not knowing how to pick a lock or what shape to make the wire. It was a coathanger she'd tried with, bending it into a vague key size in her mouth. For months after her tooth had felt rough, a shard missing; but it had been satisfying, feeling the splinter in the enamel with the tip of her tongue.

She could always use a crow bar. Would that be wrong? Shirley wasn't even in her grave yet.

The cupboard was in Dawn's old bedroom, but her aunt had re-decorated after Dawn married, and Dawn's room had become the good room. It was a room for entertaining, which had never been in Shirley's nature, so the room was never heated. After ten years it still had a new-carpet smell. It was full of best things, china ornaments, paintings, embroideries pressed and stretched behind glass, crystal decanters in display cabinets, family portraits.

Shirley had loved Maeve. The first baby photo Dawn ever sent had been enlarged and hung on the wall in here, and over it a more recent snap had been tucked into the corner of the frame – Shirley on a bench at Edinburgh Zoo with Maeve cuddled into her side. Maeve was a blur of black hair, red dress and bright green, slethery lollipop. The sweetie hovered like a flying saucer halfway along its trajectory to Maeve's mouth. Dawn remembered the few seconds after that picture had been taken, the lollipop crash-landing on the gravel, stuck with dirt, and Maeve's tears, the wail that went on till her eyes were dabbed with a hanky and a replacement lollipop was pressed into her hand. Then they went to see the camels.

Do you remember Shirley? Dawn had asked on the journey up. But Maeve had stared blankly the way she always did when she didn't know the answer to something and didn't want to say so.

Something beginning with 'Shhh', Maeve had said.

They'd just been playing I Spy.

Sheep, it must be. But Dawn played along and pretended not to know.

It was a year since they'd seen Shirley last, and that was too long. Maeve was still so small.

I'm going to see Granny and Grappa? she'd said when the game was finished. Grandpa was a new word for her. It always came out sounding like the Italian drink.

You'll meet your granny and grandpa soon, Dawn had told her, and then changed the subject.

At two o'clock Dawn and Maeve ate their lunch in the good room. It was the only place left that wasn't strewn with bursting bin bags. Opposite them was the mysterious cupboard. It was quite small, built into an alcove, a heavy lock sealed with a thick layer of paint. Shirley used to dust down the outside of the cupboard, but asked what was inside she'd always do the same thing – touch her nose and say it was her secret, tell Dawn to stop nosey-poking.

Keeps a tight ship, your auntie Shirley, Dad had always remarked. Dawn's father's real name was Gordon, but everyone had always called him Dad, even his younger sister Shirley and Dawn's mother, Wilma.

Dawn had been seven when she'd gone to live with Shirley. She remembered Mother insisting it was for the best, that Dawn and her aunt would be good for each other. Dad had been unsure at first but eventually he was forced to agree.

It's nerves, eh? New babbie on the way and whatnot, Dad had said. It's just for a wee while. And it's for the best, eh? pet? Ye ken how mammy worries. Daddy'll take everyone tae the pictures on your birthday. How's that? Ye might even have a wee sister or brother by then.

Dawn had been a lazy lump, a ditherer, a wee liar, always causing her mother Wilma worries. 'Wilma Worries' was what

Auntie Shirley had always called Dawn's mother behind her back.

Dawn hadn't shopped yet, so all there was to eat was cold chicken from the fridge. Maeve thought it was slimy. She grumbled and hunched over her plate, pulling with her fork at something stringy. Dawn took it away and began to cut the meat into tiny pieces, removing everything but the whitest flesh. As she scraped some of the meat off the drumstick and stared at it on her fork, she thought about Maeve's pickiness, and felt put off. A pink dot blushed in the meat, a broken blood vessel like the one over Dawn's left eyebrow. The food looked a bit dry. Shirley had always overcooked things. But it smelt okay. She pushed the plate back to Maeve, who stabbed a tiny mouthful and looked at it beadily. It was then, trying not get cross, that Dawn noticed her sister, Linda. The high school photograph sat on the mantelpiece, the smile fading in its tiny frame. She'd almost forgotten there was an auntie for Maeve to meet as well.

Maeve had just finished chewing her miniscule bite when she pointed at the clock on the sideboard and jiggled in her chair. The clock was an old digital one in a wooden case. The time was 2:12.

Look! Mummy, look! Two. One. Two. Two. One. Two, Maeve said, not taking her eyes off the numbers.

What do you mean?

The numbers flicked to 2:13.

Maeve's face changed. You missed it, silly! When can we go home?

You've not met Granny and Grandpa, yet. Or your auntie Linda.

Dawn's throat tightened round the words but it was all she could think to say. Maeve just nodded.

Is your chicken all right now?

Hmm.

Have a bit more.

Dawn turned to the window, which was trickling with raindrops. She was remembering the dingy city flat she'd been renting for four months. She'd been glad to see the back of it. And they'd have their own place now too, if it all worked out.

After lunch she wrapped the chicken bones in a copy of the local paper. There was a hole in one page where a story had been neatly snipped out. Dawn tucked the corners of the paper in round the leftovers, the smell of newsprint mixing with chicken fat and swimming in her head.

The ringing started as Dawn was washing up. She stood beside the phone.

Letting it ring.

Letting it ring.

She could hear Maeve in the living room, laughing at the afternoon kids' programmes. Lifting the receiver she smelt Fairy suds on her fingers, tasted them on her lips. The line was lifeless.

Yes?

There was an odd static pause. She thought she heard an intake of breath, or was it nothing but silence? 'Guess who?' it seemed to say.

Dawn slammed the receiver back on its cradle. She breathed through clenched teeth and the words she had wanted to say into the phone, 'Go to Hell', stuck and furred in her mouth like the overcooked chicken. She was sure it would be Warren, her husband. Husband. She'd always thought it was a horrible word.

The phone cable came free of its socket when she wrapped it round her wrist and yanked two or three times. Plastic lashed through her hand, the sting of it making her eyes water. The connector dropped to the carpet, wires ripped out of the wall. 'I'm a can of worms!' it laughed. Dawn wiped her eyes and pulled her favourite black cardigan tighter, linking her hands through the sleeves. The pulse in her wrist hammered against the tip of her index finger and she pressed down on it, feeling the vein and cartilage, the tapping like Morse code.

In the living room Maeve was cradled between the cushions of the huge armchair and Dawn threw herself into a corner of the sofa. She reached for her cigarettes, lit up and blew smoke towards the ceiling. On the television a hairy purple puppet was clanging a frying pan, laughing hysterically from its red gash of a mouth.

The living room was done up in an old-fashioned way. Very little light came through the window and even on a bright day this place would lull her to sleep. The sofa covers were olive green velour and its squashy cushions were well-muscled, pinned in with silky fringe and buttons. The hungry cracks were a good place to find pocket money, probably enough to buy sweeties for Maeve and a packet of cigarettes. She'd search them later.

From her corner of the sofa Dawn noticed the silver dog ornament. It had a stumpy tail which rang like a doorbell if you pushed it down, and he used to be her favourite thing in the house. Once her wee sister had tried to pinch him, but Dawn had seen her and told Auntie Shirley. The dog had been standing in the same place on the mantelpiece ever since.

Shirley had kept him shiny. Dawn smiled, remembering the care her aunt had taken with all the ornaments and pictures, spraying and wiping them one by one every weekend. She'd done it without a thought, making things clean, like an actress sweeping off face paint. Dawn sensed a sadness in the quiet that was settling on those things now.

She balanced her cigarette on the edge of the armrest and picked up the dog. It was ugly close-up. She shined its back across her sleeve before pushing down the tail and bringing the dog to life. A strangled buzz was trapped in its belly like a bee under a glass. Maeve climbed up beside her, nudging in to have a closer look, and Dawn pressed the tail down again.

Bzzz, went the dog. Bzzz. Bzzz.

Maeve cuddled into her and stroked a finger between the dog's ears, and for a second Dawn felt a little guilty for not surrendering it to Linda all those years ago.

Dawn's baby sister Linda was a good girl, Mammy always said. A wee lamb that turned folks' heads. She had blue eyes and springy blonde curls, always smiling, dressed up like a dolly in soft hand-knits and T-bar shoes. She was born in 1963, the very same day Dawn turned eight, which was old enough to remember the whole fiasco.

Dad had come round to Shirley's with news of the birth, sweaty and tired, still wearing his uniform. He said Wilma was fine. She was resting in hospital, and the baby was healthy, beautiful, and blonde. Daddy's eyes and Mammy's mouth.

They sat down to tea together, Dawn, Dad and Auntie Shirley. But celebrations were thin ice. Shirley was angry because Dad, in his excitement, hadn't remembered to say happy birthday to Dawn. There was no present or card for her. Shirley had baked Dawn's favourite cake and iced it with a giant number 8, but it was sliced now with good wishes for the baby.

My Lord! Born on the same day! Fancy that! Dad laughed, once the number on the cake had reminded him. Ken what your mammy'll say, eh? Let's hope it's the ainly thing they have in common! Eh? Eh? That's what she'll say.

Dad splurted his tea. A fat cigar was smoking in his fingers, and it was the happiest Dawn had ever seen him. He'd taken his hat off and put it on the table, and Dawn stared at it. It was the same hat she'd worn in dressing-up games, when her being silly had made him laugh. Now it was cocked to one side and rested on its brim, and it stared back like it was seeing her in a new, unflattering light.

Just wait till you see your sister, Dawnie, Dad said with a lullaby of a voice. She's a wee miracle! A wee Goldilocks!

Dawn scowled at the cake with its fancy icing. It looked too fussy next to the tall black hat.

What's that wet Wednesday ae a face for, eh? Come on, love!
Dawn kicked a chair leg.

What's the matter? Don't you love your auld dad any more?
No!

Slowly he began to change colour. Don't start, pet, he said, his tone changing. Especially if you're tae visit the hospital. Mammy's nae finding all this easy, eh? And you've a wee sister now! What do ye think, eh?

Dawn only whispered what she thought, almost to herself. But Dad heard. He stood up from the table and thumped his fist down.

Gordon, let her be today, Auntie Shirley said, using her brother's real name for once.

But before he got the chance to do anything Dawn ran from the table and slammed the door behind her. She went to her room and sat on the floor in the corner, picked the wallpaper round the cupboard that wouldn't open, and whispered it again.

Bloody baby.

She could hear the voices in the living room and wished she knew what they were saying. They'd not be going to the pictures like Dad had promised, that much was certain.

Shirley didn't come in till Dad was gone. Dawn was still sitting on the floor with an ear to the cupboard.

Were you talking about me?

We were talking about the baby, Dawnie. We can go and visit her tomorrow, if you like, eh, chicky?

When Dawn didn't answer Shirley came over and stroked her hair. She loved doing that. Dawn's hair was silky then, just like Shirley's used to be, except Shirley was blonde like the new baby, and Dawn, unlike her name, was dark.

I kept your birthday cake for you.

I don't like that cake any more, Dawn said.

A birthday was all she and Linda did have in common as it

turned out. Folk said they were like chalk and cheese, those two. The sun and the moon. Angel and the Deil. Dawn was still living with her aunt when she turned nine and Linda had her first birthday, and by then there was no mention of it being just for a while any more.

Mother loved to boast about the new baby whenever they bumped into her out with the pram, and all the town marvelled that wee Linda was the spitting image of Shirley Temple. Aunt Shirley always laughed to hear that, a funny kind of laugh she kept barred behind her teeth.

But that's who *I* was named after! Isn't that a strange thing?

Those meetings left Dawn feeling sick, and perhaps Shirley had felt the same way, because she'd always held Dawn's hand a wee bit tighter on the way home.

The best thing about living with Shirley had been the rasps, three rows of canes that produced sweet, fat berries every year. They'd eaten them with yogurt and ice cream and Dawn would mash hers with a fork to a creamy pink mush. She still missed the taste of those summer afternoons with Shirley.

It was a stroke that had taken her aunt. A neighbour had found her in the garden, on her back between the raspberry canes, hands tucked neatly in the pocket of her apron, a little red pip on her chin.

Dawn left Maeve in front of the telly, slipped on her shoes and went outside with a bowl. On her way she selected a few ornaments and dropped them into a box by the door, ready to go to auction: a glass figurine, a ceramic cottage, the Victorian mirror, and a strange wee clog Shirley had always kept on a windowsill.

Shirley had been cold when they'd found her. Down on the ground she'd been tucked away from the gaze of the nosey parkers who might have seen her sooner. The thought of it made Dawn want to lie under the rasps. It had been sudden, unexpected. The earth beneath the canes was dry and dusty, warmed by the sun. Dawn sat and pulled her knees close. The untrained leaves were tickling her arms and she reached over for a clutch of berries, which she stuffed straight into her mouth.

Dad had written to Dawn with news of Shirley's death. He wouldn't have had her phone number, she supposed. It was a strange letter and she'd folded and kept it. He'd never written to her before, not even four years ago when he'd become a grandfather, but he did send a card for Maeve signed 'Granny and Grandpa'. Shirley had told him Dawn's little secret. 6lb 5oz. No one had ever told Warren. He'd know about Maeve soon enough, though. Surely he'd guess.

Dad had signed off his letter saying he hoped Dawn would come back, maybe even think of living in Shirley's place now that it was all hers. The local schools were good, he'd said. He'd written something about himself and Wilma getting old, how Shirley had been his much younger sister, after all. He and her mother might not have that long themselves. And he'd love to meet the wee one, he'd said, because they didn't have much to look forward to any more.

Dawn lay back, tasting the fruit and the soil, watching the sun glow yellowy green through the leaves. She'd thought for days about the funeral, wondered if she should go at all, whether it was safe. And now that she was going, what she would say to them? The letter made them sound different.

Dawn was licking juice from a fingertip when she heard a cough. She jumped and sat up, leaves sticking to her back and jeans. But no. Thank God it wasn't Warren. Christssake! The man took a step back. He was just a neighbour. He could have been the one that had found Shirley's body. In the sun's glare it was hard to see what he looked like. His thick blond stubble glittered like sand, was almost blinding.

Um, I've a parcel for you in the house, he said. It was a nice voice, the accent of someone who'd probably left town and later come back. Ally. I live below, he said, gesturing round the front. Can you come round tonight? I'm just away out.

There was still a sour taste on her lips from the rasps, but she tried to smile. She said she'd see him later.

Twelve steps led to the porch and she sat on the fifth, looking at the sky. The clouds had formed like breaking waves, a shoreline of them one after the other, the curling surf of Norse pictures. She'd often seen waves in the clouds here, loved to watch them form and disperse. They rose and fell like tides. She decided to have another cigarette. She would sit and smoke, waiting and watching the crest of the waves being blown away, the sky wiped clean. After that she would settle Maeve for a nap, unpack her cassettes and listen to country music, and tomorrow they could take some of Shirley's things to the auction. She'd make up another box of assorted. It was good. A clearing-out and a fresh start was just what they needed.

She always kept a small pack of matches in her pocket, and she took them out now. She liked to give them a shake first. A picture of a bridge was on the front, and she would have kept it once because it was a perfect place to hide things; small jewels to leave in a hurry with.

A sudden sickness rose at the thought of Warren's phone call. Maybe he'd tried again. Again and again. The connector was pulled out of the wall so there was no way to tell. She'd been stupid. She'd panicked.

There was only one matchbox left from her old collection, an empty one, Scottish Bluebell brand. There was nothing inside now but a good feeling, one she wanted to keep. It flickered when she held the box in her hands and very occasionally Dawn would allow herself to do that. A small pleasure. There were other more harmless things, cigarettes, her music, tucking Maeve into bed, kissing her tiny palms which always smelt of playtime, a mixture of sweat and the sweetness of petals, sugared rhubarb.

She lit a match, loving the scratch when it caught, the tingle in her fingertips, a hint of phosphorus in the air. She had the promise of a few quiet minutes before the day moved on. She had to keep herself together. And somewhere she would find the key to the cupboard. If there was a secret, maybe it was supposed to be discovered like this, only after Shirley was gone.

It was late in the evening, after Maeve's drawn-out bedtime, when raised voices in the flat downstairs reminded Dawn of the parcel. She waited till it was quiet before going to knock.

Ally opened the door. At some point he'd had a shave and changed into a long-sleeved shirt that was brilliant white against his clean, freckled face. He probably worked outdoors, near the sea or on a rig, because his skin had that stung look that comes from salt and cold wind. He took a slow look at her before he went back in, and for a moment she imagined they were going somewhere together and he was fetching his coat. When was the last time she had a night out? God only knows.

She leaned on the wall beside a window overlooking the pavement. The door opened again. She turned round, expecting the man, but it was a wee boy in pyjamas. He stood staring, sucking chocolate milk through a straw for what felt like too long. It looked like he'd been crying and the drink was some kind of comfort.

Hello.

He was quiet, eyes wide on an unlit match she was twiddling in her fingers. A nervous thing. Over the street an old woman appeared between the curtains of an upstairs window, her stern expression framed with lace. Dawn met her gaze and flicked the matchstick into the gutter.

Mum says do you want a cup of tea?

The boy was almost smiling now, and Dawn saw he had a missing front tooth. He could drink chocolate milk with his mouth completely closed by placing the straw in the gap.

No, thanks. Has the tooth fairy been yet?

The chocolate milk slipped back down the straw. He shifted it over with his tongue and started to bite it flat.

Do you want a cup of tea, Mum says? he asked again between bites.

I've my wee girl upstairs.

The boy stared for a bit longer and went back in the house.

You've met Kyle then, said Ally when he came back. I've another one – Kirsten. She's younger. The parcel was in his hands, a soft rectangular shape wrapped in brown paper, an official label on the front.

Sorry to hear about your mother, there, Ally said in a hurry, nodding behind him towards Shirley's house and handing over the parcel.

She was my aunt.

Oh? He shuffled his feet and glanced at his front-room window, where Kyle was watching them talk. The chocolate milk was gone. He was holding the curtain back with one hand and the other he was holding out, making an eff-off sign with his fingers.

Kyle!

The boy only smiled and stuck the two fingers closer to the glass. He shoved them in Dawn's direction.

Dawn smiled behind her hand.

Ally banged on the window.

Stop it!

The boy lowered a finger. Up yours. One finger. Two fingers. One finger. Two fingers. And then he jumped down and was gone.

Sorry, Ally said, starting to laugh. He's just learnt that trick.

Dawn said it didn't matter.

Come and ask us if you're needing anything. Feel free.

I will, Dawn said, turning to go.

It's Ally, by the way, he said, half holding out a hand she was too far away to take and then lowering it again, tucking a thumb into his belt loop.

I know. You told me before, Dawn said.

Oh. Are you Dawn? We read it in the obituary.

She nodded.

They shouldn't have put my name.

She went round the back. It was a late July evening and the neighbours had their windows open. Teatime noises filled the gardens, a television squalling, cutlery clinking, a kid whining. Ally's door didn't slam straight away. Maybe he was listening to the same sounds, and Dawn's footsteps crunching on the path.

She left the parcel on the kitchen worktop and checked on Maeve, who was still allowed to sleep beside her in the big bed. It was a habit Dawn didn't mind. The room was quiet and the duvet was still. Maeve's curls fanned out round her sleeping face, a deep-sea halo. Blue Scarfy was beside her on the pillow and she was dimly lit by the clock on the bedside table.

It was ten past nine.

Dawn left the door ajar and went to run a bath. She looked in the mirror as the steam gathered. A wry smile had appeared on her lips. It seemed to sit there all the time now. When her mother saw her at the funeral she would probably say, 'Why are you making that soor face, Dawn?' But it was just her normal face nowadays. The way the lines fell. Imagining herself back at Ally's door, she wondered if he might have found her unusual-looking, like Warren and the few before him had. He'd seemed to take a good look, maybe making up his mind. She laughed at herself. Who was she kidding? He was a married man.

She used Shirley's coal tar soap. The same brand had been in the bathroom since she was wee and the smell made her feel like bedtime, completely relaxed, no prospect of that sudden chill when the latch clicked late at night and Warren was home.

Dawn. You in, hen?

Was he still around? Very likely. On the way back from the supermarket she'd pushed Maeve right up High Street in the buggy. It had been risky, but she'd been hot and exhausted and

34

it was a short cut. Folk had been hurrying round the shops, weighed down by bags, irritated by heat, traffic and narrow pavements. Cars had been coming and going from the new garden centre and the DIY superstore. They'd been at a standstill on the roundabout by the leisure centre, drivers and passengers all with long faces, some of them sucking on sweeties or slurping fizzy drinks from the petrol station. A busier place than the one she'd left behind.

Warren would have been somewhere amongst it all. He'd have heard she was back, especially if there was a death notice. His mother had always scoured the local rag from cover to cover. No wonder Dawn had already got a phone call. The bastard wasn't going to let her get too comfy. After her bath she'd check again that the chain was on, and only then would she relax, listen to music for a while. The songs got stuck in her head sometimes, especially the silly ones that made Maeve laugh.

I've got tears in my ears from lying on my back
In my bed while I cry over you

She was humming by the time she got out the bath, pulled the plug and rubbed her hair in a towel. She checked the chain was on the door. She tippy-toed into the kitchen, her feet making tacky prints on the red lino which Maeve would have hopped into, playing stepping stones, if she'd been awake.

Look how tiny my feet!

Dawn thought she might as well take a peek in the parcel. Drips from her face soaked into the brown paper while she tore it. Inside were Aunt Shirley's clothes in a plastic sack.

She put the kettle on. It was a whistler. It took ages to boil, but Shirley had never wanted to change it for a new one. Maybe she was right. There was something soothing in the sound of the

35

steam building, water gradually beginning to bubble. All the mugs were dirty. Dawn opened a high cabinet on the wall to look for more and found the shelves crammed. Another hiding place? A plate fell out, skimming past her cheek, shattering on the worktop. Shit, she whispered, hearing Maeve's drowsy moan in the bedroom and praying she wouldn't wake up. If she did, it would take another hour to settle her back.

But Maeve slept. She was good at sleeping, lovely to watch. Dawn adored that. She sat down and went through the pockets of Shirley's skirt and apron, hoping she might find a tenner. The skirt pockets were empty apart from a balled-up paper hanky. Everything smelt of talc and dry-cleaned tweed. The apron pocket seemed empty too, but when Dawn checked it she found a bit of paper inside, the article cut from the local paper. It was folded neatly in four. On one side were things for sale, nothing circled, on the other side a news story.

    Travellers do Battle to Stay Put

Below the headline was a photo, a disgruntled woman leaning against a fence, and behind it a scrubby patch of land. At the end of the story a meeting was announced in italics. Dawn assumed her aunt had intended to go. She threw the cutting in the bin and went back to the remaining things on the table. A pair of spectacles, a packet of sweetpea seeds and a half-eaten Toblerone, Shirley's favourite.

Chocolate was Shirley's small pleasure, but she'd only ever eaten half a bar at a time. It seemed a shame now. Dawn had a sudden pain, an inkling of doubt. She wondered if someone may be watching. Usually that feeling meant she had to check again, the question not leaving her alone. Was anyone outside? Was the chain on the door? Was Maeve tucked up in bed? She double checked, just to be safe, but the feeling didn't go away. She sat back down and turned the Toblerone over and over, pushing the feeling down every time a wave of it rose up. If Shirley was here, they'd have been watching television now, dunking digestives into tea, reading *Take a Break*, which Shirley had delivered each week. She would have to remember to cancel the subscription with the newsagents.

At the bottom of the parcel sat a pair of beige shoes. Someone had tied the laces. Dawn put her fingers inside. Whenever she packed a suitcase she always stowed little things in her shoes, socks and jewellery. Sure enough, stuffed into a toe was a white envelope and inside it was a pair of gold earrings, a chain and a pendant. The last time Dawn had seen the pendant it was hanging round Shirley's neck. She'd never taken it off except to have a bath.

Now, holding it close, Dawn could see a tiny crack. She lifted the pendant to her ear and shook it. She looked again. There was a tightly pressed seam and in the centre was a notch just big enough for a fingernail.

In the garden the birds were falling asleep one by one. It was getting darker. The clock ticked in the other room and she heard raised voices again in the downstairs flat. A car started and then drove away at a pelt out the front. But Dawn's attention was on the pendant.

It needed a little coaxing, but soon it lay on her palm, split open like a walnut. Inside was a single lock of hair bound with old thread. Dawn looked at it for a long time, admiring its sheen in the darkening kitchen, and inside a feeling danced around her. A tiny searchlight on a wide sea.

✳ SHOE ✳

Jock, 1954

Nancy's coxcomb is the pride ae the close. A bonnie golden curl hanging like a crescent moon over her wee forehead. But right now she's bawling murder. There's a great gummy knot glued tae the coxcomb, still wet from her big sister's gob. We'll have tae snip it off.

'Uncle Jock,' Wee Betsy swears tae me, 'the gum fell on Nancy's head *by accident*!'

So what I saw coming round the corner wasnae Wee Betsy clartin the sticky mess down intae the hair, but trying tae get it out. That's the story? Gum. How did she get her hands on gum?

'CURLY!' I shout up the dancers. Where the devil is she? I've the door tae the Lane wide tae the world behind me, nipping wind at my back, Baby Nancy stuffed under one arm, my free hand trying tae pull Wee Betsy inside, and there's nae sign ae the woman. These are nae even my bairns!

'CURLY!'

While all this goes on, the pesty Bissaker's waiting in the Lane tae ask about a job. Last thing I want is him seeing me like this, hanging on the kinchins like an old fishwife. He's the boss, even if he is my cousin. This place! So much for a welcome home from work.

Thank Heaven. The door at the bottom opens and here's my old ma.

'Oh, Jock. Would ye look at ye? Ha! Yer a good boy. Where's Curly? An thon brother ae yours? Will they nae look after their ain bairnies?'

Her voice is low and creaky like the floorboards.

I press my lips together and nod at the baby, who's about tae wipe snotters down the lapel ae my uniform. Curly's likely tae be up the drying green, and who knows where bloody Duncan's got tae. Down the yard maybe, or away drinking his wages. With a swing, I propel Nancy right intae her granny's arms and she stops wailing. Thank the Good Lord.

When Ma spots the gum in the coxcomb she's dumbfoonert. She takes the clay pipe out her mouth and her lips make an '*Oh!*' shape. No sound comes out at all. If it wasnae for the ruined coxcomb I'd think she was trying tae blow a smoke ring.

She whispers, still gasping in her breath. 'Oh, me! Oh, no! Oh, but that's a shame. By faith, whit-a-shame!'

What else can I do but nod and breathe 'Aye' a few times as Ma mourns the curly coxcomb. Wee Betsy's half hidden behind me, peeking at her granny from round the side, trying to wipe her gummy fingers. Ma looks up from the baby.

'Oh, shaness, Wee Betsy! Whit-a-shame!'

'Aye,' I say, kickin my boot against the loose board. 'But an accident, I'm sure ae it, Ma.'

She snaps back quicker than a swatch. 'Oh, you, Jock, jist like you tae be sayin that. Ye've aie been a saftie wi her. Thick as thieves, the pair ae ye.'

Wee Betsy and me follow her down the hall and intae her room. She opens the drawer for a comb and scissors and ignores me trying tae defend us.

'It fell out her mouth, Ma. I was watchin.'

But there's no arguing with the old woman, so I take the easy way out.

'Tell your granny what happened, Wee Betsy. I'm away for a drink with the Bissaker. See yous later.'

I push my niece in front ae me. A secret wink, and I get a wee smile off her. 'Aye,' she's sayin. 'Granny, it's God's honest truth.'

Wee Betsy's a toughie and I am too soft, Ma's right about that. But she's a good girl and most ae the time I dinnae mind her hanging about my room or helping her with homework. It's the school that teaches her tae be so canny. She writes already, left-handed just like her granny. Nae that Ma can write, mind. I'm the one that writes her letters, and she just signs her name with a cross.

I hurry intae my skivvies and the Bissaker winks as I come outside with the dog following at my heels. Some help the Bissaker is! He's still chuckling tae himself about all the commotion.

'Rascal, go on, lad,' I say, ignoring my cousin.

We're turning intae the High Street at the bottom ae the Lane when suddenly there's an almighty screech. Nancy's gurning again. Ma must be tugging at her with the comb tae see if there's anything tae be done about the curl. If you ask me, the poor wee thing would prefer scissors.

We go tae the Vicky. The landlord's nae a bad sort. He sees us most evenings. The Bissaker cries a couple ae screwtops and rakes in his bag for change. He wears the leather shoulder bag when he goes hawking round the doors. When folk hand him smaller bits, anything takin his fancy goes straight in the pouch. Duncan does the same when it's his turn and the Bissaker doesnae mind. A few times my brother's even had Wee Betsy along with him on the cart. Folk are more generous if they see you've bairns tae feed, and she aie comes away with a pocketful ae biscuits.

'Ah've somethin here fer you, Jock.'

'Oh?'

We take a seat at a narrow table near the back. It's a bit unsteady on its one leg, could do with a tighten up. I lean down and push my fingers intae Rascal's long grey hair. He lays on the floor like a good jugal, a good boy.

'A bonnie wee thing,' the Bissaker's saying, 'nae use tae me. Fer that dilly ae yours maybe.'

41

He raises his voice and gies me one ae them looks. I go red at my secret. My dilly. She's country folk, nae from travelling stock like us, and Ma's nae been told. Nae by me any road.

The Bissaker footers round in the bag, then lays something on the table in front ae his bottle.

'There, that's fer the dilly. Dinnae say I never gie ye anythin.'

It's a child's slipper, velvet, patterned with emerald triangles, a fur ankle trim, and a wooden heel that clip-clops on the table-top when the Bissaker trots it over tae me, a twinkle in his eye. The wee thing's already got tae be a hundred years old, and it looks so delicate in his big hands! She'll love it. I nod thanks and drop the slipper in my jacket pocket without a word.

We talk about the yard and the horses. I call two Double Centuries and kind ae hope Duncan will get here and liven things up. I delve a hand down beside the tiny slipper. The Bissaker's blethering and I hum and haw, nae really listening. I'm thinkin about Lolly, our meeting at the Playhouse the other night after it closed. I arrived early tae stand outside and spy her in the booth, behind glass, counting the evening's takings. *Seagulls over Sorrento* was on the bill with *Mexican Manhunt*. Lolly tidied her curls, smoothed her powder-blue cardigan, bit her lower lip, threw worried glimpses at the clock. All this cause it was me walking her home! At the door, 'CINEMA' blinked in lights above me. They sparkled on Lolly's nail polish, on her pearls, in the look she gave me.

When she finished work we went the dark, back road where naebody would see and nae tobies were likely tae be nosing round. We've our own quiet place, near the hole in the river where Ma's got the wee kinchins believing the Devil stays. Devil try and stop me! I feel like Mister Magpie with a diamond in his nest.

Beneath the table, my hand keeps goin back tae the pocket. My fingertips travel round the rim ae the slipper. This was a thing ae luxury and riches once, warm fur, silk, soft velvet. I slip two fingers inside, right up tae my knuckles, down tae where the toes should be, and stroke the lining.

'Dae ye nae think?' the Bissaker says.

I nod at whatever it was, take a quick gulp ae my Double Century, and call a half gill.

At the back ae nine the door tae the bar flies open and hits the wall. Rascal sits up, panting. Duncan's here, leanin on the doorhandle, letting all the heat out and the wind whistle in, flapping past the tails ae his coat. When he pulls a stool up next tae me I feel the chill coming off him. His cheeks are rosy, but nae just fae the weather. Got a few drinks inside him already, I'd stomach a guess.

'Aye!' he sighs as he sits, reaching over tae pat the jugal, who's keen tae greet him.

'Aye!' the Bissaker nods. He lifts a finger tae the barman and another three nips are on their way. Duncan offers round smokes. I can guess what the first thing is he'll ask, and I'm right. He puts it tae me, just as I'm watching the wee flame catch on the end ae my cigarette, when I'm nae looking him in the eye. He laughs.

'Well? How are ye? My jingies! Yon Lolly, eh? Country han-tle, ken, Wullie? Could ye nae have done better fer yerself?'

Of course, what he means is the opposite. I couldnae have done better in a million bloody years! Duncan nods, winks tae the Bissaker, who's laughing soundlessly with his mouth open. Catching flies.

'Lolly,' goes the Bissaker, playin with her name in his mouth. 'Lolly. Lolly. Maks you a lollipop, eh?'

They laugh at their ain joke, couple ae comic geniuses.

'Ach, keep it down!' I say. They're birling round on their stools, nudging at me, one on each side.

'He's haudin his wheesht, eh? Will ye nae tell us how ye got taegether?'

The Bissaker and Duncan are nae interested for a second in

how we met, only if Lolly's let me have a go yet. I laugh through my teeth and wait for them tae get bored. Inside my pocket I caress that lovely wee slipper.

I wonder what a girl like her can see in me. I might not be bad-looking, at least that's what Ma says. I've a proper job at the station, and I wear a suit and tie. But come on! Folk werenae born yesterday. They ken the family I'm from! Loll's a nice dilly. She wears pretty frocks and styles her hair like the stars on the posters at the pictures. Her family bides in a council house on a proper street. What her da would do if he kent I had my mucky tinker hands on his daughter. He'd be pure horn-mad! He's a butcher by trade, ae all things, and her brother's a bloody toby as well.

Loll's aie asking about my family, mostly questions I dinnae want tae answer. I'm the youngest ae three brothers and the only one that's nae got himself a wife yet. Three sisters have married and flown the nest. Duncan's married tae Martha, who we call Curly. They've got the three kinchins, Wee Betsy, Rachel and the baby, Nancy. Jimmy Jugs is the eldest ae my brothers. He lives just out ae town, more like the old ways. I cannae tell Lolly about that. Six ae a family he has with the wife Annie, and they're all lassies an all. 'Damn us bloody Whytes!' Jugs and Duncan say tae folk. 'We're nae use at makin laddies.'

Wullie the pesty Bissaker, my cousin, he's married tae Jeannie and they bide in the house with us. They've nae kinchins ae their own but they adopted Peter, years ago when he was just a baby. He came off ae the cart like a bit ae scrap metal, but he was spoiled rotten by them, coinneached tae death, that's what Ma says.

Peter's away at National Service now, like I should be. I never went. A stroke ae luck, according tae Ma. They ruled I had gammy feet and didnae want me. I couldnae tell Lolly about that either. It's nae fair. All the lads who've gone tae service would rather have stayed. They'd have found jobs and married local girls, everything the easy way. But I'd ae done anything tae learn tae fly. Sold my own neice! Instead I'm left at home like a bairn. I carve wooden planes and watch them swing round in circles from the ceiling. What a bloody hero!

Service is boring anyway, by the sound ae Peter's letters. Only the toffs get tae fly the planes, and folk like us just mend them, maybe nae even that. All some lads get tae do is sit outside the hangars watching grass grow. We're better off at the yard, Peter says. Nae that he aie felt that way. He wanted tae go just as much as me.

'Put yer feet up, Jock!' he said the day he went, a train ticket in his pocket, all pleased with himself. I was left behind on the platform, so jealous that for a second I wished he'd stayed on that cart as a baby and I'd never laid eyes on him. There's nae a thing wrong with my feet. One day I'll learn tae fly and I'll prove it.

Anyway, with Peter gone it seems I'm the only unmarried gadgie in the land. And with Father in his grave, God rest his soul, I'm the apple ae my mother's eye. It would be fine, but that naebody keeps out my affairs these days. Aunts and all the gossips come tae see my ma and they mutter and match-make, get themselves hot under the collar.

'What'll we dae wi' thon Jock ae yours, Betsy?'

'Ma Mary's in toun next week. *She's* nae courtin, ye ken?'

Now we're really talking in bloody opposites! Are they blind? Heaven forbid I end up with my wee cousin, Big Mary. When I got the job at the railway, Ma was moaning that now I was all respectable I'd be looking for a wife among the country folk. I told her nae tae be daft, but that was before Lolly. I never expected a dilly like her tae mang a word tae me. It's nae normal, really. Her folk look down their noses at us, especially the lot in the council houses. And folk from these houses have different habits, or so it goes. I'll tell you one thing I ken for sure, though, the dillys are nae so feart ae going tae Hell.

The Bissaker and Duncan have given up botherin me and they've gone back tae blethering about horses. I still help out with the family business sometimes, when I'm nae at the station. The Bissaker keeps a pony and cart stabled near the old mill, and the lads take it in turns going round tae ask for rags. Duncan's a good woollen-sorter. He'll do it wi his eyes shut. We collect metal as well, tons ae it. Most ae the scrap goes tae the yard, but if any can be mended we keep that back and sell it. Some bits we keep for ourselves. It's jaw-droppin, what folk think they've nae use fer: toys, heaps ae clothes, even old silver, valuable stuff.

We do odd jobs too, general labour and farm work when we can get it. There used tae be forestry, sometimes fishing or shipbuilding. But we're nae able tae get those jobs now, stuck in the Lane. My wages fae the station are decent, though, and the yard does well. Folk off the road bring in rabbit skins and we send them tae Belgium. They end up as fur linings in posh girls' gloves and boots! I imagine those gloves on the hands ae rich dillys, moneyed folk in London and Paris. Loll got upset when I told her that. At first I thought she was jealous, but it wasnae that. She had a pet go missing when she was wee, and her Mammy blamed the tinkers, said my people stole it. It's just the kind ae stuff the country hantle dream up about us.

'Jock. Eh, Jock?' the Bissaker's saying. He's just finished his drink and I guess he must be wanting another soon. It'll be my round.

'Aye? What?'

'Yon manny fae Forres's wantin some harness fer his pony. Will you tak it tae him by the end ae the week?'

I nod.

'Look at the state ae him!' the Bissaker goes tae Duncan. 'Awa wi the fairies! It must be love!' And they burst out laughing.

'Aw, would ye fuck off, the pair ae ye?'

There's going tae be hassle. I ken the minute Fat Munro

46

comes in cause the man owes us. Duncan did a job for him more than a month ago now. He did it in good faith and charged way less than the going rate. Curly has new pencils and books tae buy for Rachel, who'll be starting school soon, and that bastard'll hold ontae his money as long as he can. Tae make matters worse, he's fae a police family. His snake ae a father's in the force, a real evil bastard, Duncan tells me. If we're doing jobs for toby families like this one, times fairly are hard.

I cannae even think ae the tobies these days without getting a lump in my throat over Lolly. The lads dinnae ken her brother's in the force. I'll be keeping that quiet.

The Bissaker nods tae the bar. Duncan's telling a story but he stops short when he spies Fat Munro, and we throw each other those looks. Like there's a plan. Maybe this time, with the three ae us taegether, we'll get something out ae him, at least whatever's in his pockets. It's nae a fortune, ken? That's what we're all thinking. If we play our cards right.

But Duncan's nae very good at controlling a temper. He goes over and taps the man on the back. Munro glances over his shoulder, then turns away tae scan the whisky bottles. You'd think he'd never met Duncan in his life. And this is all it takes. Duncan makes a fist, and with the other hand he gives Munro's jacket a tug. The daft bugger cannae help himself.

Folk sense trouble. Voices go quiet, and it's all eyes on my brother. He's still got a fist up and everyone can see he's longing tae mar Munro. Even the dog kens something's up. Munro rocks forward and back, and for a minute I think his stool's going tae tip him on the floor or buckle under his weight.

The problem with Duncan is he likes a drink, and he's a wild animal when he's had too much. Even I'll admit that. It takes three men tae get him in the toby wagon when they take him tae the quad, which is where he's endin up tonight if he's nae careful.

We aie stick by him and bail him out when we can. Duncan's

a hard worker. He never misses a day. Heaving scrap makes him strong, and Munro might be heavy, he's round as a bloody balloon, but there's nae muscle on him. Duncan could easy do him if he wanted, send him intae next week if he was stupid enough tae dare. But he's got a brain in there somewhere. At least I think he does. Wouldnae be that stupid.

I'm looking really hard at Duncan's fist getting tighter and tighter, ready tae mar this bastard toby right in the teeth, when the barman's hand clamps down on his arm. I go tae try and break it up, but there's already someone round my shoulders, hauling me tae the door as well. All three ae us are huckled out the Vicky, the barman shouting 'Okay, lads, okay, we're no wantin any trouble.'

The barman looks down at us from the step and he actually apologises under his breath before going back inside.

'Sorry, boys. Understand, though, eh? Police family. Ye ken that.'

Duncan's tripped over the Bissaker in the confusion and now he's flat out on the road. He's like that with the whisky. One minute you're there having a chat, and a nip later you're carrying the crater home. We pick him up, and there's Fat Munro, watching through the leaded window. His fleshy cheeks press close tae the glass, all golden, the flicker fae the fireplace glowin on the end ae his ugly snout. Mean, tight-fisted bastard right enough. The door opens again and someone kicks Rascal intae the street. He yelps loudly, and there's laughter in the bar.

The Bissaker takes one ae Duncan's shoulders and I grab him at the other side. He shouts out cause he's hit his head and maybe he doesnae ken who we are for a second. Maybe he thinks we're the tobies carting him tae the cells.

'Eat your mother's shit!' he shouts, and I cannae help but laugh.

'Good work, Duncan!' the Bissaker says, talking opposites again. He's no really angry. Duncan derserves every penny he's worked for. He's got three bairns and a wife tae feed. We help him back tae the Lane and he stops every few steps and says, 'Haud up a minute. Haud up, there.'

Back home, I lay Duncan on the sofa in the room where his family stay. I creep out, hoping nae tae wake them going down the creaky dancers tae where I sleep. My bed's directly below, in the small bit at the back ae the Bissaker and Jeannie's place.

Ten minutes later I turn out the Tilley lamp. I've put the bonnie wee slipper the Bissaker gave me on top ae the pillow. Lolly. She's who I think about before I go tae sleep. Beneath the sheets I unbutton my underwear and wriggle my hand in. When I start getting intae it the rickety bed'll rattle, and next door they'll probably ken what I'm up tae. I try and keep it quiet, though.

We're used tae hearing everything. Ma haughs her chest out. The bairns play and squabble and greet. The men's boots stamp up and down the dancers. We've tae piss in a bucket since a lorry on its way tae the rag store crashed intae the outhouse wall. And that's nae the half ae it. It's filthy in a house. It cannae be healthy. Ma says we're living like the clartiest ae the country hantle. Cats howl and flech themselves, dogs bark and whine, chase the cats, who flee up the lum and fill the room with soot. Curly and Duncan up the dancers, and Wullie and Jeannie next door'll be rumbling about with each other when they think the bairns are asleep and dreaming – making the bedsprings go squee-eak, squee-eak. If ever it was quiet at night I'd be petrified. I'd think I was the last man alive.

But I can block out all the noises and think about one thing. Lolly. My Lolo. I smell dust on the slipper. I'm almost there. The back ae my skull is pushed intae the mattress with the pressure, and pleasure pulls at me like it's coming from below the bed.

But suddenly there's a wrong sort ae noise. A THUD. And another.

THUD.

It gets me right in the gut and I open my eyes. My carving ae a Sea Hawk jet's swinging on its thread from the ceilin, backwards and forwards like it's been hit by an enemy bomb. Mayday! Mayday!

THUD.

Duncan's boots on the boards. I should've taken those clodhoppers off. He starts bellowing like a bloody foghorn and Rascal barks. He gets feart when Duncan's drunk, daft jugal!

'AH CAN FUCK! FIGHT! AN' HAUD A CANDLE TAE ANY MAN!'

The echo ae Duncan's words, heard a million times, gies me an empty feeling, a twist inside. Curly's lighter steps make their way over tae Duncan. She's barefoot, cautious ae gettin skelfs, wary when he's taken a drink too many. The wee kinchins'll be awake too. I hear the rise and fall ae Curly's voice, the relief in it as she talks Duncan quiet again.

I yawn. He'll have woken half the Lane, the great drunken eejit. And here's me lying in bed with my hand in my breeks, jingies the size ae Jesus!

❊ SPACEDUST ❊

Wee Betsy, 1954

Monday is the best night of the week. The wireless stays in Granny's room, but tonight we've shifted it cause she wants a bit of shush. Uncle Jock has heaved the old thing into his room and we'll sit on the bed and listen together, just me and him. When Uncle Jock fiddles with the dials he gets creases in his forehead, but Jock's wrinkles don't stay there all the time. He can wipe them off with a hand, not like Granny with her mashed-tattie face.

'Not a peep, pet,' Uncle Jock says over the buzzing wireless. 'Maybe it'll nae work here.'

I'm already on the bed waiting, and I fold my arms over my chest and kick a heel into the mattress. But he hasn't stopped trying. He twiddles away and I watch the wee orange marker sweep left and right over the dial. It crosses names of places we only hear of in the news and at the picture palace: Paris, London and Rome. There's a strange one, Bud'p'st, and near the middle is Scotland, where *Journey into Space* should start. But all that's in the box tonight is a swarm of bees.

We've never missed a single episode. The music at the beginning makes my ears screech and I always hold my breath till the voices start. That's what it's like when you're flying in a space machine. Everything's fast and screaming loud, and the air is funny. Special words are used up there which I didn't know before, but Uncle Jock explained all the hard bits. He knew what Mitch and Jet meant by 'Over' and 'Check' and 'Earth Control'.

Now I know the right words, I sometimes play The Space

Game. I say things like 'Hello, Lunar 142. Landing Control, please.' Wee Rachel gets in a huff cause she can't join in. But it's her own fault. She can't sit still long enough to listen to the wireless.

'Aha!' Uncle Jock says all of a sudden. The box makes a pop and then goes clear. He's fixed it just in time. The posh voice is doing the introduction.

'The BBC presents Jet Morgan in *Journeeey intoooo Space*.'

The music starts. I clap my hands for Jock. He kicks off his shoes and jumps on the springy bed beside me so I bounce. We pull a coat over us and Uncle Jock reaches to turn the volume up, which makes the wireless crackle again but not too badly. There are mannys shouting in the Lane and we don't want to hear their racket. I lean my head on his chest and he kisses me, pulls the coat higher over my shoulders. A space suit.

This is the best feeling in the world. It's just us, our breathing, the smell of soot that's in our hair and clothes and bed sheets. Our Mission Control. And them. The voices in the box that come from the future in the clean, cold sky.

Dawn

The music in the church was leaking from a keyboard set on Wurlitzer and an old lady swayed plumply at the piano stool. The minister was standing nearby, nodding in time. He couldn't have met Shirley. She hadn't set foot in a place of worship in years, Dawn was sure of that. Aside from family there were about twenty friends and neighbours at the funeral, which seemed a lot considering. No one would have paid attention to Dawn if it hadn't been for Maeve.

They were sitting on the same pew as her sister and parents, the building impressing a strange silence on them after their five years apart and the stiff welcome acted out at the church door. Her mother kept peering over, a confused expression on her face as though she were searching for the right words to sum everything up, to find some kind of bond between them all. Later she might make them stand in a line for a sombre family photo. When would she next get the chance? It wasn't like they spent Christmas together. A few times she whispered harshly to Dad, who was smiling in Maeve's direction whenever he could catch her eye.

Well, then, Dad had said when he saw them arriving outside the church, and he'd bent down to speak to Maeve. Dae ye ken who I am?

Dawn had been about to whisper in Maeve's ear that this was her grandpa, when he'd suddenly blurted, 'Aren't you a bonnie wee thing? Just like your mammy was as a bairn!' Dawn had swallowed her words. Instead she'd kissed Maeve's fine, shiny curls, breathed in the smell of the baby shampoo. No More Tears.

Now Maeve was scuffing the toes of her new red shoes into

the tiled floor. She'd pressed herself close to Dawn as they'd come in, wary of the strange wrinkled hands patting her shoulders and smoothing her hair. It was the first time she'd been inside a church and here she looked so small it was terrifying. So small a person could be too easily torn away. One single swipe of God, if there was such a thing.

Linda had been less friendly than Dad. She'd briefly placed her arms round Dawn but they'd touched only by accident where Dawn's tense shoulder blades met Linda's wrists and could not be avoided. The perfume on her sister's neck was so strong and sweet it had stung Dawn's nose. Breaking apart, Linda had waved a pen and held out a tiny card for a wreath, blank and waiting.

There was something insincere about writing messages to the dead, like the stories Dawn told as a girl, when sometimes she hadn't known, even herself, if they were real.

Dawn was full of excuses, her mother used to say. She'd always found reasons to wander to places out of bounds, and in shops she'd been an embarrassment, putting things in her pockets and forgetting they were there. She'd always been off fighting somewhere, but of course it was the other kids who started it and Dawn never admitted any blame. Her stories had gone on for ever.

Years later Dawn heard herself telling another story, how she'd had a bit too much to drink and walked into a lamppost, given herself a black eye. And that time everyone had believed her, except for Shirley, who had always kept her doubts to herself.

Staring at the blue Biro poised on the wee card, in the end Dawn had settled for 'Thank you for everything.' She'd scribbled the words, trying to keep them neat and hold her shaking hands steady. Her sister had hovered, sniffing at Maeve, who'd been uncomfy in the heat, itching in a blouse with a tickly label, wriggling and stuffing her hands down the back of her skirt.

Linda looked nothing like Shirley Temple these days. She'd bleached her hair too many times and it had gone a strange shade, a minty paste, ironed paper-straight. She wore it long and Mother obviously liked it. When she'd come over to say hello to Dawn and Maeve, it was Linda she'd petted, stroking her hand over the flat, milked-out tresses.

Mother had said hello to Dawn, and then she'd looked down at her granddaughter. 'And what's *your* name?' she'd said, pretending.

Maeve had hidden her face, and Mother turned to Linda with a whisper.

Maeve Dunn by name and 'may've done' by nature, I suspect, if she's even a wee bit like her mammy was.

Linda only commented after they'd sat down in the church with Maeve between them.

How old's she now? Four? Four and a half? And it's true, Dawn. There's only you in her. No clues there. Shirley said she didn't know who the F.A.T.H.E.R. was. She spelt it out and raised an eyebrow, the skin beneath it eye-shadow white, gleaming against the fake tan.

Linda had been seeing Warren for a while after Dawn left. 'Seeing him' was how Shirley had put it. At the time Dawn hadn't cared. But now the thought of them together floated in front of her eyes, flesh pink and cranberry red, their mouths black and open like the holy singers on the stained glass window. Dawn felt a stab. She didn't know what to believe.

The minister faced the crowd and the keyboard music stopped. Everyone waited. He gave an introduction and pointed to a board with a list of hymns. He announced the first one. Hymn number 121.

Maeve tugged at Dawn's clothes, and when Dawn didn't look down she poked her hard in the belly.

One. Two! One. Two!

Shhh! Dawn quieted her, but Linda heard.

What's one two? she whispered.

Angels.

Oooh! Like that one? Linda said, pointing to a painting, a milky white scene of Heaven and a glowing woman with long caramel curls. She looked like an advert for conditioner.

Maeve frowned.

Dawn had never heard about the angels before. She looked down at her daughter, who was whispering again.

One. Two. One. Two.

Angels, Linda said. That's nice.

The minister had a hard job summing up Shirley's life. All he had to go on were the dry facts Dad had offered up, Shirley's simple, sensible tastes, which everyone knew about already. Dad's memory didn't seem up to much either. He couldn't mind what his sister's first job was (and even Dawn knew that), why she'd briefly gone to Aberdeen, or what she was like as a child. He probably didn't know if Shirley had ever been to a rock and roll concert or had a boyfriend. But to be fair, it was hard to imagine Shirley being young, dressing up, doing the twist, falling in love. She'd never mentioned those things herself.

After a single sob at the mention of Shirley Temple, Linda squeezed out a few tears. She dabbed her eyeliner and snuffled into a tissue, then tucked her hair behind her ears. It didn't seem right that Linda was the one to cry, but Dawn had always been so much the stronger one. She could sit through the weepiest of films with dry eyes. Warren had called her an Ice Queen, and sometimes she'd wondered if there was something wrong with her. A blockage. But here, next to her snivelling blonde sister, Dawn was pleased she could lift herself above grief, up to the rafters where the hymns echoed.

Dawn's curls were black like Maeve's, a natural jet black with just a few grey hairs these days. She was born with it, black hair reaching right down her neck. It was one of those stories Dad had always told the same way.

I said, God Almighty! That's nae a babbie, that's a black craw! That's what I said the second I laid eyes on the bairn!

He joked about it.

Would you ken something about this, Wilma? Been seein some Italian feller? Naebody in my family's got beetle-black hair like that!

Dad wasn't mean, though. He'd never wanted to upset her. If she looked upset at him he'd pull her close and swing her through the air in his arms, telling her she was bonnie.

Every beetle's bonnie in its daddy's eyes, eh?

When Maeve was born with that same beetle-black hair, Dawn thought she was the most beautiful thing in the world. She'd been pleased to have her all to herself.

Linda looked over with watery eyes. She held out a clean tissue, as if being without one might have been holding Dawn back.

I could have lent you something from my wardrobe, Linda sniffed. You didn't have to come like that.

Dawn was still wearing the black cardigan. Cigarettes in the left pocket, matches in the right. She sucked air through her teeth as if she'd just lit up. The day she starved into Linda's size it'd be her own funeral. She looked past Linda to Dad. By the looks of things he'd barely sung a note or mumbled an 'Amen' despite Mother's niggling elbow in his side. He was like Dawn. Since the service had started he'd sat rigid as the plain wooden cross he'd pinned his eyes on. Dawn couldn't imagine him writing the words in the letter she'd kept. She'd not even known his handwriting. It was full of flourishes she would never have suspected, curly tails and loop-the-loops.

Mother sat on his other side, knitting needles poking out her handbag like antennae, and her hair-do set like crinkle-cut crisps. She'd given Dad's hair a tidy with water before the service began. Dawn could see the wet grooves from the comb's teeth and his scalp below, salmon pink beneath the silver.

It's your own sister's funeral, Dad. You have to look present-able. That's what Mother would have told him. Or folk'll talk.

Dawn had overheard her mother boasting before the serv-ice. There may not have been many people there, she'd said, but the *right ones* had showed up. That teacher from the West End school was there, the *West End*, mind, not the East End. And there was that manny who used to live over the road from Shirley. Everyone knew he'd inherited, and now he had a big second home in Spain. It *meant something* for such folk to turn up.

When the minister said 'Let us pray' for the second time, Dawn scooted along the pew and made quickly for the door. She could feel the eyes at her back and heard her mother's long suck of disapproval, but she ignored it. Her fingers were secretly rolling over the papery smoothness of a cigarette in her pocket, and she didn't have to look over her shoulder to know that Maeve was following behind her.

Outside it was pouring. Long blades of grass were bending with drops of rain which swelled and swirled. Dawn watched the torrents from just inside the church. She leant against the sturdy wooden doorframe and watched Maeve play at spinning and hopping. It was better to remember Shirley like this. She'd always enjoyed nature. And now she'd go into the ground herself, become part of the earth. Dawn had never believed in Heaven and Shirley had never spoken of it. Maeve was still too young to understand, but Dawn hoped she did believe in some-thing. Perhaps not God, but something, at least for now, even if it was angels or some other silly idea.

Maeve was whispering.

One. Two. One. Two.

The new cemetery squelched and oozed under their feet, and there would likely be a puddle at the bottom of the grave. It was still spitting. Dawn followed behind Dad, who linked arms with Linda and Mother. She hung back, and it wasn't till now that she noticed Ally, her downstairs neighbour. He was casually dressed in jeans and a black jumper. The young woman by his side had come without a coat and he'd given her his. The sleeves covered her hands. Ally reached out to take her arm but she was too busy adjusting her umbrella and didn't seem to notice. Dawn wanted to watch them for longer, but she had to keep hold of Maeve, who was desperate to jump in the muddy puddles. Dawn tried to distract her, showing her the gravestones.

The new cemetery was organised into a grid, long neat rows of wet granite slabs like cut-offs from kitchen worktop. Tough! Chip- and scratch-proof! They would never weather, crumble and rot, not like the bodies beneath them. Dawn read the names and inscriptions out loud, pointing to them. 1972, 1985, 1965. To Maeve that might have seemed a long time, but the graves in the old cemetery had been there much longer. Some were leaning over now and almost all had worn, the sandstone inscriptions rubbing gradually away to nothing. Dawn used to go there as a teenager to meet her pals and drink shandy from tall brown cans.

Shirley would share a grave with Margaret, 'Beloved Aunt. At peace since 1968.' Shirley had only ever mentioned the aunt in passing. There were a few years spent with her in Aberdeen. Dawn reckoned this must've been in the mid to late fifties because she couldn't remember Shirley ever not being there. She only remembered her coming back, and getting a present from her 'new' aunt. It was a stuffed panda, or maybe it was a black and white cat. She couldn't remember now. Dawn was wondering where the toy had gone when Linda, who'd taken Maeve's hand, snorted with laughter and leant over to whisper in Dawn's ear.

Imagine the two of us side by side in the grave.

I'm going to be cremated and you'll rot on your own, Dawn said.

Linda's face tightened like a shrunken cardi and Dawn realised she'd hit a nerve. She hadn't meant to. It was only a joke. Even so she felt a pinch of guilty pleasure and imagined it, her own glee, locked up tight and festering. But Linda wasn't going to let her get the last word.

I'm still the youngest, remember? I'll get to watch you burn.

Linda smiled like a cat and Maeve looked between them and giggled, thinking something funny had been said.

Her sister had grown a sharper tongue. Dawn slipped her right hand under her left cardigan sleeve, drawing her fingers along the scars. Burns Warren gave her. They were less angry than they used to be, faded and gone smooth, shiny, pinched in the middle like snowflakes.

A sign at the church hall said 'Bishopmill Knitting Circle. Cleanliness is next to Godliness. Wipe your feet!' It was the circle Mother knitted in, and Dawn wondered if she'd written the notice. It was the kind of thing her mother would do, and Dawn felt sick at it. Her father's father had been the last chuchgoer on either side of the family. God was a long-dropped stitch.

Someone was going to make a speech and a microphone was being tested, which seemed extravagant, given the few people that had bothered to show up.

Testing testing, one two, one two.

Maeve looked at her mother. See? she said.

Ahhh! said Linda. Sweet. And she turned to Dawn with a worried look.

Has she always done that angel thing? Is it normal?

In spite of the rain, the hall was stuffy with a funny, nursery-school smell, disinfectant and sawdust. Two girls stood behind a table laid with coffee, tea, sausage rolls, sandwiches and short-bread, and they poured from tall flasks. The cups provided were too small to hold more than a few gulps, and the drinks went cold quickly. Folk stayed close, but not too close to the food, nervously stirring in sugar lumps. There was a tape player but no tapes except for a children's story collection and a country music compilation of Dawn's, which they couldn't use. It began with George Strait's number, 'Gone as a Girl Can Get'. Shirley would have laughed till her falsies fell out, but Dad and Mother certainly wouldn't.

Maeve was starting to get crochety, sitting under an empty table with a cloth over it, refusing to get out and kicking away the plate of food Dawn set down.

She's a fussy one, like you were, Mother said.

Dawn bent and swept up the crumbs. She didn't want to argue, afraid to make a scene. She took Blue Scarfy from her handbag and passed it under the tablecloth, hoping Maeve would curl up and be quiet.

When someone in the kitchen shoved a first load in the dishwasher the noise was welcome. Crockery shook and clattered in plastic trays, echoing off the walls, and it encouraged people to talk. So, Dawn overheard, how did you know Shirley? And another loud voice was asking, what Varsity did you go to? She looked round the room for an empty chair or a friendly face, a seasick feeling in her head. The tea in her cup was stewed and already lukewarm. She was hoping to see Ally, but he and the woman had left, and Dawn found herself wondering when she would next get a chance to talk to him. A few times she'd tried picturing his expression, the way he'd looked at her the evening she'd gone round for the parcel. Something about it had been hard to bring to mind, but seeing him in the graveyard she'd remembered his face that night exactly, his motley suntan so human against the flat white shirt and his eyes dark in the evening light.

Dawn picked the thread of a conversation. Dangerous folk they are, dumping their rubbish. Violent, aye. The council is totally inept . . . Well, it's nae wonder people do! Threatened my nephew and his pals. Can you believe it? Disgusting. Using the field as a *toilet*!

Dawn wanted to get Dad alone. She waited till Mother was

out the way, fussing at the table with the young waitresses, arranging empty cups on saucers and pushing the dirty ones aside, ushering them away.

How are you, Dad? Dawn asked, her first chance.

Ach, fine, fine. Where's our Wee Maeve? he said. His face brightened, eyes casting round for her. How's the flat? Any ideas for it? Eh? It's a good size.

This was a habit of his, asking too many questions, or the same question more than once, never asking the question he really wanted to at all. There was something he couldn't cough up.

Maybe I could gie you a hand with the clearing up? he said. It is quite a job. And ye don't want tae take stuff up tae the tip at the moment, not by yerself. It's right by thon gypsy site.

They were interrupted by the minister bustling up. He was halfway through a piece of finger food, crumbs down his black robe. Dad adjusted his posture, trying not to stoop. He wasn't sure how to talk to these people. While he tried to make polite conversation, Dawn dragged Maeve out from under the table and they made their escape. Seeing them head for the door, Dad gestured across the room, lifting a pretend telephone to his ear. Dawn nodded, but she knew he wouldn't get through, not with the wires hanging out of the wall.

Outside Shirley's front door, Dawn shook her handbag upside down, littering the ninth step. Maeve was tired and Dawn was rattled, hot like the crockery coming out the dishwasher in the church hall. She'd gone and locked herself out. A Chapstick rolled over the edge of the steps and disappeared into an overgrown rhododendron never to be seen again. There was an open packet of travel tissues, her Walkman with its tangled headphones, a sticky, empty sweetie wrapper, a dozen chocolate raisins covered in grit and hair, ninety-two pence in small change, a tatty wallet, a lipstick, two biros, a small pack of broken crayons, a ratty-looking cheque-book, and a ticket for the

Glasgow Underground. 23 March 1992. The ticket was rolled into a cigarette shape, which probably meant that on that particular date she'd been trying, failing, to quit.

Dawn chucked most of the contents back in the bag, swept the chocolate raisins over the steps, wiped her brow and sat down.

Mummy's locked us out.

'Fishinfe,' Maeve whined through several folds of Blue Scarfy. When she was grouchy she always sucked on the comforter and Dawn could never make out what she was saying. Dawn held back a scream. One of the raisins hadn't quite made it to the edge. She flicked it and it sailed into the air, landing somewhere in the flowerbed. Maybe it would grow into a magic beanstalk and she could get the hell away.

Try the hanging basket! a voice shouted.

Dawn looked round.

Anne, a woman said. She was standing at the back door of the bottom flat.

We never had a chance to talk this morning.

Ally's wife had changed clothes since the funeral. She'd put on too much green eyeshadow and a pink top with a slogan that read 'Me! Me! Me!' She came out into the garden followed by Kyle, and clipped him lightly over the ear, telling him to keep his new jeans out of the dirt. She was carrying a younger child, who started to cry. Anne looked up.

Kids! Bet you're glad you stopped at one.

Something was smeared over the front of the baby's dress. It looked like peanut butter. New on a half hour ago, Anne said, pulling roughly at the clothes. It's just constant bloody washing.

Dawn remembered Maeve at that age, hours spent in the laundrette. There were bananas squished into pockets, jammy handprints, mud and slether and sick, and a tube of toothpaste half eaten and half smeared into Maeve's hair, all over her clothes and up the wall. Much worse besides. But maybe enduring the torture of the laundrette so early in life, the sweat and steam and constant roll of driers, was what made Maeve almost obsessively clean now. She worried about mud on the soles of her shoes, picked and pawed at her clothes at the sight of even a tiny stain or spill, and cried if her nose needed blowing. Blue Scarfy was the only exception. She wouldn't allow it to be washed. Not after the terrible fate of Scarfy the Original, who had disintegrated in the machine. The only traces of it had been the iridescent green threads Dawn Sellotaped off the rest of the washing.

It didn't take long to find the spare house keys. They'd been pushed deep into the compost under a clump of wilting ivy. There were five or six on the ring, all different shapes and sizes. Dawn cleaned each one in turn, Maeve wrinkling her nose and blowing on them for fun before they got a quick wipe with a tissue. Dawn would separate the two Shirley had used, the Yale and the Chubb, and then they would be through the front door again and she could make herself a cuppa.

It was in the middle of all that, before she even realised, that the key to the cupboard was finally in her hands. She was holding out the cold metal nib of it while Maeve pursed her lips and blew breath warm over Dawn's fingertips. Dawn turned the key over. It was heavy given how small it was. She looked. Not a fancy thing, just like any iron key. But it was old. She had that strange feeling again, as if someone might be watching. She hurried to get into the house. She didn't stop to take off her coat or worry about Maeve's stiff new buckles. She went straight to the cupboard, still flustered at locking herself out but feeling something else now too. Sparks in her fingertips. She'd almost given up on finding the key. She'd been thinking of asking Ally for a tool to force the door, but now she didn't need to. She knew this key was the right one, even before she slotted it neatly into the dark lock.

There was a splintering as the thick paint round the frame

began to crack. Yes! it seemed to say. Yes! She placed her other hand on the wall and pulled. Part of the door dislocated itself from its seal and Dawn got a first scent of the chill air captive inside. For several seconds she stopped, afraid of disappointment. Maybe Shirley had just been having her on, and the cupboard would actually be empty.

In that same moment a sharp gust of wind whooped down the chimney, the windows were pelted with a sudden rainfall, a gull shrieked from somewhere over the rooftop, and a car alarm went off. A girl in the street screamed, then laughed, and in the flat downstairs something was dropped or thrown. It shattered. With a bit of whingeing, Maeve had just managed to get her shoes off by herself, and now she crossed the hall.

I want fish fingers! she was shouting.

But the cupboard door would only take one sharp tug.

A black and white photograph fluttered free and landed at Dawn's feet. Two wee girls with curly hair, dark as treacle. One of them was shy and pulling down the hem of her skirt. The other held her head high, not afraid to look straight at the camera. On the back was a message, a Chinese whisper in carefully placed letters. Dawn traced her finger along the words. 'Dearest Lolly,' she read, 'xxx.'

Maeve was opening and closing the kitchen door, swinging it on its hinges.

She was moaning her numbers with each swing forward and back.

One. Two.

Dawn's eyes filled with tears she couldn't explain. The slope of the handwriting pulled at her like a road in an atlas, the lie of the land and the lives connected to it. These small faces were not ghosts. They were not make-believe.

❋ BRUISES ❋

Wee Betsy, 1954

When Daddy lifts me off the ground, Jugs grabs my hands and pulls me high onto the wooden seat of the cart. There's just room for the three of us, me squeezed between the two men. We put the blanket across us to keep warm. Daddy takes the reins and we move off with a jolt, past the old mill and the stables where the road's bumpy. My feet nearly touch the bottom of the cart now, but not quite, so I let my legs swing. To, and my toes scrape the slats, fro, and my heels do the same.

I love riding up here, and it'll be even better once the cart starts to fill. Then I can look over my shoulder at the jumble of things and wonder what's in the bags and where it will end up, whether there's anything in there for me or maybe something for Uncle Jock. I watch the pony's haunches as we go the windy road, over the hump-back bridge, heading for the posh houses in the West End. The Bissaker called the pony Hughie after a friend from the war. His coat's greasy-feeling when you stroke him, and from up here the hairs glint in the light as he shimmys back and forth with the trot.

Daddy and Jugs talk about something boring till we come to a stop, and then Jugs stays with the pony. It's me Daddy takes to the door.

'Can I say it? Please, Daddy?'

'Aye, course ye can,' he says, and pounds on the big blue door. The knocker is a brass bull with a ring through its nose. Soon footsteps are coming from the other side and I swallow. I hope it's someone nice opening the door. If it's a nasty sookyface old wifey or an ugly brute I'll be too scared to ask and Daddy'll have to do it.

Today's my lucky day. The lady who answers has a bright yellow cleaning frock and plump cheeks with a flush like an apple. My mouth waters at the thought of apples. I'm sure I'll get one from someone today. Now it's my bit. I stick my chin out.

'Any old rags?' I pipe up.

She nods, aye! The lady goes back inside her house to fetch them and I look at my Daddy, who's smiling. He puts his hand on my curls and strokes down to my collar. His hand is rough but warm. We don't say anything while we wait.

We go to lots more houses. Some folk say no, not today, or no, they've not got a thing, but others have piles of things they're not wanting. I'm just starting to feel sure of myself when a woman on the corner of Grant Street takes one look at us and her face curdles. She slams the door shut before I can even say my bit, and the slap of it against the frame makes the words go lumpy in my throat, like trying to swallow when you have a cold. Daddy picks me up and carries me back down the path, straight onto the next doorstep. But it doesn't feel like a game any more and I don't want to ask the question.

I cheer up, though, as soon as we get to Darkie Smith's house. He gives me a biscuit. There are lots of old plates and teacups for Uncle Jugs, and Daddy gets a great pile of wheels and cogs from off of something. There are so many bits and bobs that Jugs has to steady Hughie and help load them on the cart too. With all this metal maybe Uncle Jock could make us a rocket. We could have our own journey into space!

'That'll dae, then, eh?' Jugs goes to my daddy, and we head off in the direction of my school.

Daddy must be reading my mind cause he says to tell Jugs what I've been up to at school, only he calls it 'that place'. Jugs teases me for going to school. Now I'm learning about the world and reading and writing, he says I'm one of the Bread and

Margarine Gentry. That's not a good thing. It's a tinky who's getting a bit bigsy. Uncle Jock is one of the Bread and Margarine Gentry too, cause he wears a fancy uniform for his job at the station. Jock hates being cried that, and for a while I pretend not to like it either. I pull a face at Jugs and fold my arms over my chest, but actually I'm pleased me and Uncle Jock are called the same thing.

'What else is it you telt me you liked at that place?' Daddy says.

'Roly-poly pudding!'

Daddy and Jugs both go 'RohwlEE pohwlEE pudding, is it?' They say it in a funny voice, a posh, English sort of way, and we all start laughing. For a while I just can't stop myself from saying 'RohwlEE pohwlEE pudding', over and over under my breath.

The best thing about school is my teacher, Miss Webster. All the other teachers in the school look the same and talk the same, and when you see them up the street they just nod and say 'Good morning,' or 'Good afternoon.' They don't stop to ask you how your day is. But Miss Webster's different. She wears pretty, bright dresses and has bonnie curly hair like mine. Most exciting of all is that sometimes instead of sitting behind her desk, she perches like a bird on the edge of it. When she does that she looks like a singer or an actress in a film, not like a teacher at all. Secretly I want her to marry Uncle Jock. Then we'd all be related.

The only thing I don't like at school is the wee break. Mammy gives me a slice of bread to eat, but the others in my class have nicer things, apples and sometimes cakes. I eat my piece in the lavvies, where Miss Webster and every one else won't see, and when my wee sister comes to school I'm going to make her do the same.

But today I've done so well at the doors I might have a proper piece for school tomorrow. My Daddy's got everything folk have given me at his feet. So far I've collected three pokes of biscuits, a liquorice stick, two apples, and even a copy of the *Beano*! Of course, Rachel will have the half of all this, and wee Nancy likes to suck on the biscuits. I wonder if Daddy would be angry if I asked for the liquorice now, so I could eat it all myself.

When we get to the end of the High Street I'm expecting us to go left and back up the road to the stables. The pony leans that way out of habit. But instead Daddy gives the reins a sharp tug to the right and we turn towards the shops.

'Where are we going?'

He doesn't answer me, or maybe he doesn't hear. Him and Jugs are speaking through their teeth, cursing about someone. Daddy looks serious and Jugs rubs his prickly chin in his hand for a while. Their eyes are narrowed at the road ahead, right through the gap between Hughie's ears. I try again.

'How are we going this way, Daddy?'

Daddy tells me to shush, cause we'll be home soon. He's got a job to do and I'm to just sit tight, like a good girl.

'Can we fetch Uncle Jock from the station?' I go, cause I know he'll be off work soon. Jugs makes a sucking noise and Daddy says that would be a very bad idea. I don't know why Uncle Jock isn't allowed, and I'm angry with Daddy and Jugs for always making fun of him.

When the pony stops, we're on a street with lots of identical wee square houses, a part of town we don't normally go. Daddy and Jugs get down together. This time I'm to stay in the cart and keep out the road.

Daddy chooses a house and opens the latch on the wee garden gate. Him and Jugs walk up the path to a white door. On the other side of the street a lady comes to her window and pushes back the net. She stares across at me for a few seconds, and I stare back at the Nosey Parker. The lady's eyes darken, and she swipes the curtain closed. At that exact same second there's a loud voice shouting something I don't understand, or maybe I just don't want to.

70

Daddy begins to shout back, but before he's even finished the man's screaming.

'CAUSE YER A BLOODY USELESS PACK AE DESPER-ATES!'

The man is so fat he fills his whole doorway. He looks like Big Fat Joe in the *Beano* and he can't be wise, roaring like that at Daddy and Jugs. He tries to close the door but Daddy sticks his boot in the way and it opens wide again. I hear him shout something about his wee girl being in the cart. Then Jugs reaches in and grabs the man by both arms, pushes him up against the porch. He forces him still, holding him tight till the big fat man looks like Baby Nancy when she's bawling to do something and Mammy won't let her. His face changes pink to purple while Daddy comes back to the cart and picks up a spade. He doesn't look at me at all. He won't see me. For a second I think he's going to hit the man and maybe kill him.

My throat feels all tight and I can't breathe cause I'm too feart. Jugs has clamped the man's neck in the crook of his arm, trapped his head like one of Rascal's fleas about to be squashed between my fingernails. The man's purple face is growling back, coughing, and croaking that Daddy's a 'damn tinky who'll not get a penny oot'a my pocket' .

But instead of the man's head, Daddy brings the spade down on a sapling in the garden. He does it four times till there's a snap like a broken rib, and with each blow my whole body jumps. Why would my daddy hurt that poor wee tree? Then there's a different noise, a clattering hard blow to the wall, almost as loud as the sounds from the scrap yard that we hear when we play up Lady Hill. The man's latch falls off onto the ground. Daddy goes up the path, dragging the spade behind him, letting the blade make a terrible scratching noise on the paving. When he reaches the door he holds it up to the man's chin.

I have to turn away now. Behind me are the rags and wheels and cogs, and down the hill there's the corner. I feel sure the toby wagon's going to putter round it any minute with a siren going, and we'll all be quadded. I wish they'd left me at the station with Uncle Jock.

I peep back. Daddy and Jugs let go of the man when his wife runs to the door from inside and starts screaming. Set free, the man bends over double, holding his throat, and Daddy and Jugs come striding back to the cart. They're wiping sweat from their brows and can't close the gate behind them cause the latch is in the gutter. Daddy's rattling some coins in his hand and shoves them in his pocket. He throws the spade into the back, where it makes another clank. We're lucky Hughie doesn't bolt. He's a good pony. Thinking of that now, looking at his chestnut mane shining in the sun, makes me want to greet. If it was me and Hughie all on our own I'd take him on a long journey.

As we move off I notice the lady behind the net staring again. She looks like a ghost.

We pick up Uncle Jock just past the station. 'Here's oor dear brother, Lord Snooty,' Jugs says, as Uncle Jock takes a jump into the cart behind us, ready to tickle me or make me laugh. But then he sees Jugs and Daddy's faces, changes his mind and keeps quiet. Daddy holds Hughie by the reins and I hold Daddy on the sleeve. Jugs just smokes and rubs his chin some more. I'm the only one that says anything on the way back to the Lane.

'You can have my liquorice, if you like, Daddy.'

He doesn't answer, and I look over my shoulder at Uncle Jock, who doesn't say anything either, but he pats me on the back.

It's nearly dark by the time we're home and Mammy's out-side with Granny looking to see where we've got to. Just the sight of Daddy's face and she knows something's not right. She asks him if he's been marring again, and he doesn't answer. He jumps down from the cart without even saying hello. He puts a hand in his pocket, takes out the coins, and pours them from one hand into the other, letting her hear the sound of them. Then he puts them back in his pocket and he's away. We watch him leave with a sack slung over each shoulder, disappearing down the alley to the McPhees' place.

'Down you get, Wee Betsy,' says Uncle Jock. The little parcel of goodies I won gets handed to my mammy. She unfolds it at the corner and says 'Ooh!' She sounds pleased, but I can tell she's worried cause of Daddy.

I give Hughie a pat, and Jugs and Uncle Jock wave goodbye. They head off to the yard to unload the rest of the scrap and rags. Jugs will take all the old broken and chipped china to repair and sell, sometimes back to the same people that gave him it. That's how he's called 'Jugs'.

When we get inside I tell Mammy about the man, how Jugs grabbed him and he turned funny colours like a gobstopper. When I reach the bit about the spade she pulls back a chair and sits down with her head in her arms on the table. I stop telling the story. She doesn't say to go on, and when she lifts her face she's not greetin, but she looks dead tired. Mammy unfolds the napkin another time. She just stares at the treats and traces the hem of the napkin with her nail.

I get a beautiful red apple! I can eat it right away cause there's no tea tonight. I don't care. Not when I've an apple. I take it down to Granny's house, where the fire's really burning bright and I can read my *Beano* beside it.

Big Ellen's come to stay cause she's having a baby soon. Her and Granny are sitting on the edge of the bed, and they're chatting in the funny language so I can't listen in. I coorie up on the little seat right by the grate, so close I'll get red spidery marks crawling on my shins. The *Beano*'s open on my lap, and my apple is cupped in both my hands. I watch the blurry dance of flames reflected on its waxy skin. There's a bruise from where the cart was bouncing. I hide it under my thumb and press down on the damaged part a wee bit. It feels like a person's flesh with bone underneath.

The first bite of the apple makes a crunch like chopping wood. My mouth fills up. It's bitter-sweet and watery at the same time. All the little grains tickle my mouth. It feels like the tiny bubbles that fizz off my arms when I wash in the sink. The skin curls and twists round my tongue so I can't say a word, but there's no word for how good it is anyway.

When Ellen hears my teeth splitting the apple she stops talking to Granny and stares at me really hard. I was enjoying the *Beano* and the taste of the apple so much, their whispered mumbo jumbo had just become a blur in the background. I could have forgotten they were there at all. Now Big Ellen blushes a bit and blurts out, 'Oh, Wee Betsy. I'd love a bite ae apple. Dae ye mind?'

Of course I do, but I can't say so with Granny there, especially when Big Ellen has a baby inside her. Granny would tell me 'shaness' a hundred times if I did, and I do understand what *that* word means. I finish chewing and go over. I watch Big Ellen's hand taking the apple from mine, how she wraps her jaw right round it.

CRRRUNCH.

I imagine the juice running over her tongue. A shiny rim of it appears on her lips as she says, 'Oh, it's good. Thanks, pet.' She passes me back what's left of my red treasure.

There's a half finished game of cards lying on the bed between Granny and Big Ellen, and instead of playing they're looking at photies from Granny's tin. Big Ellen hands me one.

'Look! Thon's Duncan, yer daddy.'

He's standing at the side of a big horse, reaching up to its mane, patting it. Another man's in the picture too, riding in the saddle, but you can't see who it is cause that part of the photie's all foggy. Daddy looks happy.

'We were still oan the road then,' my granny tells me. 'Must've been the last month ae summer travellin we did. A tourist took that een at a horse fair, up near Muir ae Ord. Yer daddy nivver wanted tae go back intae a hoose fer the winter. Oh, me! Whit a temper he'd get oan him when the winds started tae blow. O ho! Ha! Ha! That wis him jist afore ye were born, nae lang after him and yer mammy first met.'

'Was I born here?'

'Aye, yous were aw born in the hoose, bairn,' Granny says. She makes it sound like that's a pity, a terrible shaness to be a tinker born indoors.

I bite my lip and turn the picture over. There's a message on the back, written in lovely handwriting. My daddy can't write so it must've been the tourist that put it there for him. I stroke a fingertip over the twirly ink.

'Can ye read, bairnie?' my granny asks. Granny never learnt to read or write. I can, though.

'It says, to my . . . darling Martha from . . . your . . . ever-loving Duncan.'

My darling. Ever-loving. Those words keep going round and round in my head. Even after I'm back upstairs and I find my sisters asleep and Mammy at the table with a face like she's looking out to sea, but it's just the empty pot on the hook over the fire that she's staring at. I still can't forget the words, the look of them written down like that; inky letters that curled like my mammy's hair, and like her by-name! No one ever calls her Martha in real life.

To my darling Martha from your ever-loving Duncan.

Dawn

A small black album lay open in the cupboard and the photograph of the two girls had fallen from inside it. There were other pictures, all the same size and held in with sticky corners that had come loose. The corners drifted to the carpet, a trail of confetti as Dawn walked to the kitchen. She was thinking about the picture, how an empty matchbox is never really empty, how a pendant is always a locket if you look close. Maybe Shirley had been telling the truth. Perhaps there were secrets in the cupboard.

Dawn poured some vodka into a china cup and took a gulp. She turned on the grill and got fish fingers from the freezer to feed Maeve. She kept turning to the photo as if she risked missing an explanation from it if she looked away. Whoever had been behind the camera when the picture was taken had said something cheeky and put the wee girls just on the edge of laughter as the shutter clicked. They were pretty, but their clothes didn't fit quite right. The elder one was squeezed into a kilt and cardigan, the sleeves and hem a wee bit short, and a dress, probably a hand-me-down, hung baggy on the other.

In the next picture there was a much older girl, long blonde hair, make-up, painted lips, a smile. She was only half covered, dressing or undressing in the dunes like a fifties beachwear beauty, shoulders bare except for two spaghetti straps. Tall grasses tickled the image. The photographer had taken her by surprise. Maybe he (because it would be a he) had been hiding in the long grass, waiting to capture the exact moment she spotted him.

Dawn turned the picture over for a clue but the back was blank. The strange energy she'd felt before had gone and the tapping of the rain on the windows had stopped as suddenly as it had started, leaving only a strange silence. Maeve was playing quietly.

Elgin had once had a pipe band. It had marched every weekend, deep-filling the town with warmth; rich and heart-stopping as gulps of Christmas pudding. But when the music stopped no one in earshot could get their day back in sync. The silence had pounded deeper than the great drum. Dawn felt like that now. The clocks in Shirley's house were ticking too loudly. It was an odd, uncomfortable feeling, one she usually only had late at night when Maeve had gone to bed and she was alone.

Where are you? she called.

Maeve mumbled something back. She was playing at swimming pool in the bathroom sink. She made a splashing noise, as if to prove she wasn't fibbing.

You'll have to stop when food's ready, Dawn said.

There were a couple more pictures she only glanced at. The blonde girl with her back turned, barefoot on wet sand, waves splashing up her legs. And then a close-up, a long scarf hung loosely round her neck, tassels blowing in the wind and a pattern like snowflakes falling down it. It must have been freezing, but the girl didn't seem to care. Her delight was as clear as written down.

There was a knock. Dawn's chest laced up tight. She hated it when someone unexpected came by. Couldn't control the nerves. Once she'd opened the door to a man selling shoes, a harmless wee fellow with salt and pepper hair and a red necktie, like something out of a fairy tale. He was holding a black women's shoe in his hand, a sample of his wares, and maybe it was the way he held it or the way the patent leather caught the light, or maybe she'd just been watching too much telly (her favourites were the thrillers and the spy flicks), but whatever the reason was, she believed he was about to shoot her. A stiletto heel aimed point-blank at her stomach. She tried to scream but her throat felt robbed, emptied with fear. It was several seconds before she managed to make any sound at all. And then she had nightmares for weeks, cause if she ever opened the door and there was a man with a *real* gun, by the time she made a single sound the trigger would have been pulled.

So she never opened the front door without checking who it was. Just in case. She couldn't forget to be wary. Sometimes in the city whole afternoons had gone past without her thinking of Warren – but not here.

Another knock.

Dawn ignored it. Maybe it was Ally from downstairs. But so what? She turned quickly to the next picture. It was the blonde girl again, further away this time, with someone stood by her side.

There was a third knock, louder than before, and this time Maeve stopped splashing in the bathroom sink and came into the kitchen, a drenched Barbie suspended in an upside-down dive in her hand. Dawn told her to wait in the bathroom.

Who is it?

Me, Dawn. It's Dad.

It had started spitting again. Dad had backed away and stood several steps below her, slowly getting wet. He peered behind her at Maeve, who'd toddled through when she heard his voice. Hello, lovie, he said, and she waved back with the wet doll. Dawn opened the door wider and Dad followed into the kitchen, looking round Shirley's flat as though he hadn't been there in a long while. I've just got Maeve's tea on. Drink? She started laying the table.

Dad didn't answer. He'd sat down where the album was lying open and was trying not to pry, brushing it away. His hands were older than Dawn remembered; thick, stiff fingers, Marmite-stain speckles that wouldn't wash. They still looked strong, though – good hands to hold. She still remembered him throwing her into the air and catching her.

Hmm? he said. Oh, aye. Tea.

I found those pictures in a cupboard in the good room, Dawn said, nodding at the album. Dad wasn't listening. He'd taken a wee box wrapped in bright paper from his jacket pocket and was beckoning to Maeve, who stood in the doorway sucking on the Barbie's wet hair. When she saw the box she looked first to Dawn

Go on, then. Grandpa's got you something.

He lifted her onto his knee and helped untie the shiny parcel ribbon. Inside was a gold chain with a heart and a tiny ruby swinging on the end. Dad's big fingers stumbled over its delicate thread.

You shouldn't have, Dad. She's only four.

Nae too young fer jewels, eh, princess? he said, lifting Maeve's hair and fastening the necklace beneath it. This was yer great-granny's once and now it's yours. Let's see! There. Is that nae bonnie?

What do you say, Maeve?

Thank you, Grappa.

Maeve was so pleased she let her tea go cold. She sat all the time with her chin pressed to her chest, admiring the wee gold heart with a red stone at its core.

Is it blood? she said.

No, pet, he told her. Not real blood. It's a ruby.

Dawn sat between Dad and Maeve in awkward silence. He tapped his fingernails on the side of his chair and watched Maeve. Dawn noticed the small photograph album had been closed and pushed out of sight. She poured herself another small measure of vodka and reached for it. It held only one picture to a page and she leafed to the last two photos, ignored Dad clearing his throat, a hacking, raking sound. It had bothered him for years. 'Dad's haughing' was what Mother called it.

The first photo she turned to meant nothing: a bleary shot of a strong-looking old woman in a cleaner's apron. Her mouth was parted and her eyes were closed, the lids crinkled: two dates. She'd have looked like an old-fashioned widow if it weren't for the sprigs of flowers printed on her apron and the way she'd placed her hands. She rested them either side of her belly, elbows jutting out as she laughed.

The last picture was another one taken at a beach. It showed a couple, and behind them a row of huge wooden posts that crossed diagonally from the sand into the sea. Dawn searched the horizon for a lighthouse, sure this was the beach she'd played on as a child.

Dad was half-heartedly whistling now and she had to try hard not to let it irritate.

The couple in the photo was the blondie from the other photos and a young lad who held her lightly round the waist. The boy was the same height as the girl, but while she was slight, he had broad shoulders, a casual stance. It looked easy for them to stand like this, side by side, each with an arm round the other. A strand of the girl's light hair was blowing loose over the bridge of the boy's nose and up towards his black cow's lick. It didn't seem to bother the boy cause he hadn't lifted a hand to sweep it away.

There was no name on the back and no date. Whoever's sweetheart this was, time had forgotten him. He wasn't in the other photos.

Do you know who these pictures are of, Dad?

He took the open album and made a show of holding it in an outstretched arm before telling her he couldn't say. He would need his glasses to see it properly. Eyesight wasn't what it used to be.

Maeve had finished eating and disappeared back to the bathroom with one hand clasping the doll and the other pressed over the necklace. Dawn looked at her father and took out her cigarettes. She pushed the pack around on the table-top.

You could have come down to the city to see us, she said.

He sniffed, looked at his hands. I nearly did, he said. Mother said ye'd want tae be left. She insisted, pet.

Dawn took out a cigarette.

Have you heard from the bairn's father? Dad said eventually. Dawn knew he meant Warren. It was there in the lift in Dad's voice, the nod to the window, to Elgin.

Later, after Maeve was asleep and Dad had left, Dawn did the dishes. She filled the sink with water and washing-up liquid and soap bubbles flew from the bowl up to the evening light. Oily rainbows swirled on their surfaces. She dropped the first of the dishes into the sink and more bubbles drifted free. When she tapped her fingertip against one it seemed astonished, blinked and vanished. A big one escaped her and sailed across the worktop, crash-landing and dying. It left a circle of wetness that said O!

She stood for a second looking at the ring from the burst bubble. The middle was dry, untouched like the eye of a storm or the centre of a bruise. At the centre of her bruises there had been a part that never went blue or black, yellow, red, or any other bruise colour. The middle of her bruises had gone shock white. A blind spot. It was the part of her that had said '*I never saw that coming*'.

Dawn wrung the tea towel, a tug of war. Hot water made the scars on her wrists blush. Every time she did the dishes or took a bath the old burns flared up, a reminder of Warren. Those weren't the worst moments, though. It was the good memories that could pull her apart, make *her* feel guilty, make her wonder if she had done everything wrong, not just for herself but also for Maeve. She put her inability to heal down to her fair skin.

Dawn pulled her sleeves down and her hands delved into her cardigan pockets to find the usual. Cigarettes. Matches. She checked the chain was on.

First thing next day, a man came to collect two armchairs, a nest of tables, a chest of drawers and a hefty dresser. There was nothing remarkable about the man except his hair, which was wiry and such a bright orange it reminded her of wild grass. It grew in tufts over his ears and bristled out of his nostrils as if fighting for light. The man was sullen. Dawn sent Maeve into the garden so she'd not get under any feet, and it wasn't long before she was joined there by Ally's wee son. The two of them disappeared into the flat downstairs and Dawn wondered if Ally would be home, if she should go down there later.

The man lifted and manoeuvred the old furniture down the steps and round the front to the pavement. Outdoors it looked timid, ashamed of its own cumbersome weight. It was like those documentaries on the clinically obese, folk who'd stayed inside for half their lives being wheeled out on trolleys and paraded across sun-bleached driveways to waiting ambulances. When the furniture was huddled in the back of the van the man slammed it shut. From the window Dawn watched him climb into the driver's cab and put the van into gear. As he pulled away she blinked at his number plate. Maeve would have liked it.

JW02 ONE

Dawn listened till the van had driven away and then looked around at the new space she'd made. The patterned carpet had been there for ever. There were islands of brighter colour on it where the furniture had sat, and for a while she would continue to walk round those patches, sidestepping ghosts. The room could have blended into any decade in Dawn's lifetime, and the smell had always been there too: roast tatties, dust, pot-pourri, cardboard. Only the television was different.

What a lucky girl you are, Dawn, everyone said when she'd first moved in. Your Auntie Shirley has a television! Shirley owned a middle-of-the-range set then, one with a black and white picture and a wooden trim. Her aunt had saved her wages for weeks and bought the television especially to make Dawn happy.

She switched the new telly on now. She could watch the breakfast news and try forgetting where she was, the velour settee that bristled if stroked the wrong way (like a cat), the dreary light filtering through a small window, mug mats of idyllic country scenes piled neatly on the table, and the clock always ticking like a headache on the mantelpiece. But the television was full of bad news and that only made her nervous. Planes were taking off. There were familiar replays of jets, dark angles cutting through clouds of sand, bombs sown like seeds over beige cities, fiery red flowers in the grey dust, shouting and whooping in the cockpit, the camera shuddering.

She turned it off and thought about fetching Maeve, then changed her mind. She could hear the children playing, enjoying themselves. Dawn was fidgeting, biting her nails. She'd always been a bag of nerves. A fidget-fodget-foo! Shirley used to call her that. It was true. You could always tell when something was getting to her because she'd have to start pulling her split-ends, chewing her cuticles, biting the inside of her mouth, the fleshy seam where the top and bottom teeth press together. Those were her bad habits, her wee things. You could always catch her at them when she couldn't settle to something.

She loved flicking through her music collection, the tapping sound, the way the cassette boxes clung to each other, fitted into place. They stood each one identical to the next. She could run a finger along the top of the smooth black edge and the pattern was regular as a railroad track. Clickety clack, clickety clack.

Clickety clack, don't look back.

Her house with Warren had been near the railway track. She used to lie next to him at night and listen for the goods trains pulling themselves through the night. She would close her eyes, feel the rhythm of the wheels in the empty space that was growing inside. Clacking and rolling. CLACKING AND

ROLLING. There were words in the noise of the carriages clattering by.

    GETTOUTFROMMUNDERIM
    GETTOUTFROMMUNDERIM
    GETTOUTFROMMUNDERIM
    GETTOUTFROMMUNDERIM
    GETTOUTFROMMUNDERIM

The day Dawn left, Shirley pressed a handful of notes in her palm and said exactly the same thing. You've waited a long time for that baby. You fly away, if you know what's good for you both.

✳ BURNS ✳

Wee Betsy, 1954

Some heelabalow! Mammy mutters that she's not waiting up for that drunken lout. She has a sore head.

'Why can yer daddy nae be mair like yer uncle Jock?' she sighs.

His dinner's left out, though, like always, and the fire's still hissing in the grate when we go to bed. Rachel and me curl together at the bottom end, under our own itchy blanket. Mammy and Nancy sleep the normal way. I lie wide awake, listening to the rain. It's soft except when the wind blows, and then it's like seeds scattering. It leaves long spitty droplets on the window – posh ladies' earrings. I've a pain in my stomach, wishing I could eat some biscuits, but I don't know where Mammy put them, and I'd be in bad trouble if I ate someone else's share. There's a dry crust wired into the mousetrap, but I'll not go near that. That's dirty. I roll over and stare at the ceiling.

You hear the mice scrabbling as soon as everyone shuts up and stops rumbling about. So the trap's set in front of the fire each night, and usually it's been tripped by morning. You'd think they'd learn, wouldn't you? They never do.

We're studying a poem by Robert Burns at school called 'To a Mouse'. I'm reading a couple of verses at the public speaking contest. I'm sure Miss Webster thinks I'm the best in the class, cause she keeps saying it sounds like I really care about the wee mouse, but I'd rather do a different poem. When I read this one out, all I can think of is Daddy setting the trap. And I think of the mornings, him wiping mouse guts off the wire.

The trap goes SNAP! Almost cuts the mousey in two. Other mornings it's still wriggling when we get up. Sometimes you think it's dead and then it moves its tongue or a paw, sad-looking, like it knows. Daddy beats the live ones with the poker and I have to turn away. When I look back he's swinging them by the tails, lifeless as bootlaces. He slings the dead bodies on the fire and the flames dart up and eat them, like in Hell, where the Hornie lives.

Daddy's boots come pounding up the stairs, back from the McPhees'. I know there's a mouse already caught. The spring released just now. CRACK. Same sound as the heidie's belt spitting down on Bertie Topp's palm.

We don't get hit at home. Granny says the men can pummel their fists and mar with each other all they like, but they'll no put a hand on a bairn while she's still got a breath in her body. Daddy tries to get me when I'm cheeky, mind, if Granny's not looking. He can catch Rachel, but I'm too fast.

My heart starts to beat heavy in time with Daddy's footsteps. I know there's going to be trouble. We had the tobies round after him. Granny whispered *shaness!* She had to lie. She said he was out of town, and no, we hadnae a clue where he was. Of course, *I* knew, but I kept my gob shut tight. Not a squeak when that lot come a-sniffing.

I snuck round the back. Daddy was there with the McPhee men. We cry them 'Spotty McPhees', and they cry us Whytes 'Plugs'. I don't know why, it's an old thing from the days when they all lived in tents. The men were chortling and snorting and pink with laughing, like a sty of spotty, pot-belly pigs right enough. I never talk to the McPhees. Daddy was taking a swig from a bottle, and no one even noticed me in the doorway till twice I said, 'It's the tobies, Daddy,' and one of they McPhees said, 'Aw, fuckin Hell,' and another told me to 'Get away back.'

Maybe they hid him after I was away, but they needn't have bothered. The stupid tobies only searched Granny's room, emptied the contents of her press onto the floor as she watched, wringing her hands on a shirt she was mending. They tipped the table and broke a mug that was set there. Warm tea splashed onto the floor, and like Granny said, there was no need for that. There was no need at all. Not when you could see fine that Daddy wasn't under the table. Not even a cloth on it. They smashed a bowl against the wall and it shattered right by Big Ellen's head. Granny said it could have brought her baby early with the fright.

His footsteps are uneven, like he's planting his feet in a snowdrift. That means only one thing. He's drunk. I pray, please! Let him just collapse onto the wee sofa! Sometimes he gets fired up at Mammy for no reason at all and sends her out to the landing, where it's freezing, no letting her in and crying her bad names.

The door slams. Mammy sits up. She must've been lying awake too.

'Duncan, keep it doun! You're makin a hell ae a noise.'

I close my eyes till I'm just peeking through the lashes and keep as still as I can, playing dead lions. Mammy gets to her feet and the two of them pace round and round the table where the Tilley lamp's set, glowering like they're in the ring, each eyeing the other, sizing for a fight. Can Mammy no see he's in a bad mood? Why can't she leave it till morning?

'We've had the tobies here again, that cursed Munro family that's aie on our backs. Are you proud ae yersel? The bairns have barely tasted food and you're out gettin peevie. I can smell it on you.'

Daddy struggles to rip his coat off, and when he gets his arms free he throws it. The coat scoots over the floor and I hear a button skiting, a noise like a rolling marble. The coat hits the door and crumples, the cloth ruching up, as if it's run away from Daddy and now he's got it cornered. There's nowhere for it to go, except press itself into the wall. That's how Mammy stands when he scares her.

He shouts now, but Mammy shouts back, things that I don't understand. It's questions Daddy asks mostly. No one ever gives the answers.

'Think you can gie me the lick ae your tongue?' Mammy snaps at him. 'You're no better than the bloody racheries.'

'Yer an auld bitch tae me, Curly,' he growls at her, and I almost start greetin.

'Drunk the bairns' dinner money, haven't you?'

'Shut yer fff . . . or ah'll fuckin murder you!' Daddy slethers.

But Mammy's still horn-mad and shouting, so he raises his voice above hers. 'Ah'm nae deif! you want the hale bloody world tae be listenin?'

This makes Mammy even wilder. She slams the table and Rachel jumps. I hold tight onto her in the bed so she won't get up and make things worse.

'The hale bloody world can put their lip in my stummel!' Mammy screams.

It goes quiet for a while, like Daddy doesn't know what to do. She must have said a really bad, dirty thing. Big Ellen said my Mammy's got a filthy mouth on her, terrible bad and typical of her breed, and that Daddy could have done better if he'd just waited. Mammy and Big Ellen don't like each other much.

Daddy stumbles to the fireplace. I wonder what's coming. I open my eyes wide, and through the shadows I see him pick something up. The mouse dangles by the tail, still alive, still caught in the contraption. Daddy brings it level with his face, fixes it there, laughs. The mouse twitches and its paws race hopelessly at the nothingness of the air. Daddy takes the poker. With each swing, a curse word.

But he doesn't get the mouse. It's flying back and forth like a pendulum, and every time the end of the poker comes towards it I think surely it'll be goodbye, wee sleekit cowrin beastie this time. But Daddy tilts sideways with the motion, off target. Misses every time. He tries a couple of swings again, more concentrated, making an animal kind of groan. First the poker goes too far to the left, then just below. His whole body's off kilter.

'Put that poker doun, Duncan! The bairns are watching.'

Mammy's begging scared now. She doesn't like him having the poker in his hands. But I think he looks funny. I'm nearly giggling. Daddy wobbles back, like he's going to fall over his heels, and the poker drops from his fist. On the uneven floor, the handle starts trying to get away from the pointy end. It turns nearly a whole circle.

Daddy puts the hand that held the poker on the wall. Quietly then, he holds the wee mouse an inch over the hot coals. It takes me a while to stop smiling, like my mouth doesn't know which way to go. Part of me wants to grin, bare my teeth. My eyelids peel, wider and wider as the mouse hangs in the red glow. It tries to get back from the heat. I hate him then. I hate Daddy for doing that to the wee mouse. I imagine the raw burning on its nose, the fairy thin paws, dry pain in its eyes. And I've my own pain, wanting to greet but my eyes too skinned, too watching.

'This is how ah feel, Curly. Look. DEEK!'

But Mammy's *not* looking. She covers her eyes, and Daddy finally kills the mouse, swinging it with an eeny meeny clap against the hearth. He prods it with a finger to check it's dead.

Now there's nothing except Rachel and Nancy snivelling. Daddy slumps into a chair. That's it, I think. Mammy will come to us now, and he will stay there a while before crashing onto the sofa. I start greetin. Big tears fall from my cheeks and into Rachel's hair. She's tucked her face into my neck and I hold her tight. It's gone quiet. Why doesn't Mammy come?

I look. The pair of them are cheekie-for-chowie, him still sitting in the chair, head bowed like we do in assembly, face in his hands. Mammy stands, wrapping her arms round his shoulders, stroking his hair like she does ours.

More tears run down my cheeks. Big raindrops on the window. I gulp and press my face hard into the mattress while Mammy takes his boots off, undoes his trousers and puts him to bed on the sofa. She sighs as she kisses him goodnight.

You'd think nothing had happened the next morning. No one mentions anything except for the fine we've to pay that Munro manny, even though he owed *us* money. Granny says we'll all pull together. She tells Mammy not to worry. 'Watch yon daddy of yours,' she says on the way to school with me. 'No better than a kinchin hisself, needs someone lookin after him. Pity Duncan's no got a heid on his shoulders, like Jock. Oh, me!'

At wee break, Sandra comes over. 'Betsy, are you wanting ma apple core?' I've not eaten a bite since yesterday, except for one of the biscuits I got off the cart, but I swallow and say, 'No, thank you.' She shrugs, kicks the apple core, and I watch it bounce and somersault over the ground to near my feet. Gravel sticks into the flesh and it looks like a grazed knee.

I watch Sandra skip back to her friends in her lovely red shoes. They look like the ruby slippers in the *Wizard of Oz*. If I had a pair like that I'd click the heels together three times, just like in the film, and say 'There's no place like home' three times over.

After school I find Rachel sitting at Granny's table. No one else seems to be around. She wants to play.

'Okay,' I say, thinking hard. It's funny having a wee sister sometimes. She'll do daft things just cause I tell her to. Once I got her into the shop asking for cinaminaminamin balls.

'Let's pretend to be Daddy,' I decide. I make my feet go 'clomp, clomp, clomp' on the floor and bash my fist on the table, making as sulky a face as I can – 'A mou ye could tie a string roun,' Granny would say. Rachel laughs. Daddy's boots are by the door.

'I've got an idea,' I say.

I twiddle the end of a lace round my index finger, the boot hanging down.

'Look,' I go. And I lift it over the fire.

'That's cheeky, Betsy. You shouldnae do that.'

'Shut up, cowardy.'

The boot smokes and a foul smell comes off it. That'll teach you, I think to myself. The flames dance around and lick at the toe part, which soon goes all black. I pull it out to inspect. Rachel wants a look too. She peers at it over my shoulder. A bit of the sole's gone crispy and the stitching there's come loose. I wonder if it's really going to hurt him, me doing this to his boot. Granny would think so. I hope he stubs his toe. A wee tinker's curse.

'Okay,' I say, flinging the boot down. 'It's your turn.'

'AH CAN FUCK! FIGHT! AN' HAUD A CANDLE TAE ANY MAN!'

I belly laugh just like Granny to hear my wee sister shouting that over and over. She stomps about the room with one foot inside the other boot, the unburned one, and she's facing me at the fire, shouting it one more time, loud!

'AH CAN FUCK!'

When suddenly the door opens. Daddy.

Rachel spins when he slams the door, and she almost falls over. I see his hand grab her wrist, and I plant myself on the burnt boot, looking for somewhere else to hide it. I think she's going to get a smack, cause Granny's nowhere to be seen.

But Rachel's laughing.

She's got her hand in his, spinning round and round like a windmill. And he's being stupid. He pretends to reach over to skelp her, lifts his foot like he's giving her a kick up the arse. His toe disappears under the hem of her skirt, but she just squeals, lowping forward, spinning and spinning till they're both exhausted.

'What about my other bairn? Is she no playin wi me any more?'

'Daddy,' I mumble, 'we had an accident.'

I can't look him in the eye as I take the horrid charred thing from under me. Rachel, who I think had forgotten cause of all the fun she was having, goes very quiet. So does Daddy for a while.

'Oh, dear,' he goes at last. 'These are nae mine. They're your Uncle Jock's boots. You'd better find him and say sorry. Tell him I'll fetch another pair fae the rag store. Don't look so glum, ah'm sure we'll find him some struds.'

It's God's honest truth. Daddy's wearing his boots and they're identical brown ones. I feel rotten. I hold the burnt boot really close, like it's a wee animal itself, and I can hardly look at Rachel cause she knows it wasn't an accident at all. My lovely Uncle Jock! The boot's a part of him. It's like that with people's things, especially their clothes.

I start sobbing when I see Jock, sitting on his bed and reading one of his fighter plane books. He's wiggling his toes, not knowing at all that I've doomed him! And he seems nicer than ever. Granny's right! There *is* a curse over him. And I've made it worse!

'What's got into you, Wee Betsy?' Uncle Jock says. 'Crying like that for an old boot! Look at your munty face! Have you lost your senses, darlin? That can be mended, don't you worry. You ken I'm pals with the sooter at the top ae the Lane? He can sort this in two ticks. Dinnae be daft. Dry your eyes, you silly bam. There, don't munt.'

I start to feel better. Just a wee bit better. And soon it's fine as long as I don't look at the cursed boot. I put my arms round Jock's neck and pray for him to be saved so that one day he can marry Miss Webster, just like I've planned.

When Daddy comes back he's got shoes. Not new ones, but they're fine. Sort of slip-ons with no laces. While Uncle Jock is trying on the shoes, I stroke Rascal's ears and make him roll over and rub his belly.

'That's me,' Jock says. 'A wee bit on the large side, but no matter.'

'You can wear two pairs ae socks,' Daddy goes. If I had money I'd buy Jock a good pair of socks, and a nice bone for Rascal.

It's peaceful that night. Daddy stays in and plays with us, which makes Mammy happy. She sings to Nancy, who gurgles, and in between she does nothing at all but sit and watch. I get shunted onto the sofa to sleep and Daddy takes my place in the bed, beside Mammy.

Late at night, and there it goes again. CRACK. Another poor thing in the trap. As I listen for signs of life, the poem starts up in my mind.

> Wee, sleekit, cowrin, tim'rous beastie
> Oh, what a panic's in thy breastie!

The voice won't hush. So quiet and ca' canny as a wee mouse myself, I tiptoe over the boards, two by two to the trap.

I go down on my hunkers. The fire's dead, and the cold makes all my wee hairs prickle. I tuck my chin inside my nightshirt, up and over my nose, and blow warm breath on my chest. My eyes peer over the top of my collar, watching the mouse. It's alive! Caught only by the tail. Just like the night before. You'd think they'd learn, really you would!

I pick up the mouse and the trap like it was a hot cinder, go to the blocked mouse hole, and pull the fistful of cloth away. My hands wrap round the creature, making a wee circle with it in the middle. Light streams through the boards from Uncle Jock's room. He must be reading about his planes again. Holding the mouse near a crack, I can see the panic it has taken. Its tiny ribcage shudders. Its wide eyes are black, shiny as wet liquorice drops. The ears are stiff, and the skin inside is smooth and bluey-thin, like drowsy Nancy's eyelids. I even feel the fluttering heartbeat.

I keep myself steady, trying not to shiver, and whisper a verse of the poem. As my legs go numb I feel more of what's between my hands, the whiskers tickling my fingertips, the sleek surface of the tail, the nose trembling like a tiny pink flower.

I free the trap.

Like a shot, the mouse darts from my hands, straight into the hole. He's away to his warm nest. But I sit there a while longer, smiling so wide it's like my lips are tweaking my lugs.

Dawn

She flicked through the paper. What would Shirley have have cut out? A large Dalmatian from Rothes was the star of the stage at the town's summer production. There had been a drugs raid in a house in Llanbryde, and there were lots of stories about the rain. It had been coming down for days. The gutters were rivers and folk were worrying about Lossie bursting its banks, the paper reminding them of previous floods right back to 1755. The only difference it made to Dawn was the view from the window, slates shining brightly on the rooftops opposite. It also meant she hadn't taken that trip to the coast. She'd found the photos a week ago and had taken them out a few times, particularly the one of the couple on the beach. She felt like going there when the weather cleared, just to stand on the exact spot where she thought it had been taken. It was more to do with her own good memories than anything in the picture.

She slept through as many hours as she could, letting Maeve watch television or play in the garden with wellies on. Maeve had become friendly with Kyle, and the two of them were spending most of their time downstairs, watching videos and playing with his toys. Dawn had seen Anne from downstairs a few times. They would bump into each other but she never knew what to say. She didn't like to ask after Ally, afraid to sound too interested. It was pleasing to know he was there, and she'd caught herself brooding over which room he slept in. Stop mooning, Dawn, that's what Shirley would have said if she were here. He's taken, chicky. It'll end in tears.

The weather had turned colder and she'd put the heating on. Awake, she shifted round the flat, staining her teeth with cigarettes and strong black coffee. Listening to music felt disrespectful to the silence. She stared out of the window, envious of the clean, wet pavements that were empty, blank. She stared at the walls and stared at her face in the mirror when brushing her teeth. She could study the reflection as if it belonged to someone else altogether. A noticeable face, the kind certain men would say things about. Unusual. Foreign. Cheer up, hen. It might never happen. There were dark circles slung under her eyes.

She watched television without really following. When the programmes ended and the pictures turned to snow, she let the buzz lull her to sleep again. She dreamt of messages from the dead but could never remember them later. She didn't believe all that nonsense, voices in the white noise. It was the stuff of horror films, not real life. She'd wolfed down the remaining half of Shirley's Toblerone, sharing it with Maeve. Sooner or later she'd have to do another shop. She kept expecting to run into Warren, wondered that he still hadn't been round.

She woke with a bolt, a dry mouth, the flat roasting. She had a swollen sensation as if she'd swallowed her tongue. It wasn't just the heat. There was someone inside the flat. Heavy footsteps. Knocking. The carriage clock said it was just gone three.

Maeve?

No answer. The noise stopped. Dawn waited. She got up from the sofa. It started again, a chock-chock of wood on wood. She got to the door of the living room and peered round the frame.

There was a woman standing in the hall, her back half turned. Maeve must have let her in. The woman was wearing a huge mohair jumper in streaky shades of grey, wisps of wool full of tangles. Her feet were in an old, wet pair of patent black slip-ons, with the toes bent upwards into snouts. Her mismatched socks were soaked and muddy. She looked like she'd been traipsing along the path by the river. The woman was waiting, leaning against the sideboard. One toe was sliding nervous circles on the carpet as if she were stubbing out a ciggie, and the knocking was coming from something she was chipping against the wall. She started humming along to it in a tuneless way, still unaware she was being watched. She studied the photographs on the wall and the ornaments. She picked up Shirley's unopened post from the sideboard and then placed it down again, carefully, as though she were dealing a hand of cards.

Dawn was surprised to see Blue Scarfy abandoned next to the letters. It was the first time Maeve hadn't taken it with her to play. The woman gathered up Blue Scarfy and sniffed it deeply, drew back, put it down.

Hello?

She jumped.

Oh!

The woman laughed and put a hand to her chest. Ah'm fae the auction. Yer wee girl let me in. What a cheek ye'll think ah've got!

They've already been from the auction, Dawn said. A man came.

The woman took a step back. She looked up and her left eye flashed blindly. It was as if the shock had imbalanced it, set it rolling like a cat's-eye marble.

The auction man's already been, Dawn said again.

But the woman's one good eye was looking at Dawn. She hadn't come to collect anything. It had something to do with the small slipper she was waggling in her hand. The toe was clasped in her fist and she'd been using the wooden heel to hammer on the door, woodpecker-style. Ratatat-tat. It was the same slipper Dawn had put into a box the other day and taken to auction. She'd had no use for it. It was child-sized, green velvet patterned with triangles, the fur trim mostly disintegrated.

The woman was about five feet tall, and an inch of that was the knots in her hair. A funny sort of Fairy Godmother. Dawn got a strong smell of wet yeti jumper as the woman came over and offered up the old slipper. She balanced it with two fingers on each side like a precious exhibit. Heel and toe. Christssake, what did she want?

This was in the box ye sent us, the woman said, smiling. Her teeth were straight but dirty, streaked brown like wheat kernels. Was it yours? she asked.

Dawn didn't take the slipper.

Everything here was my aunt's.

The woman considered this, one squint eye wandering round the hall all goggledy-gawk. Dawn wondered if she could see in two directions at once. She took her cigarettes from her pocket, slid one out of the packet and stuck it between her lips.

Shirley died last week. Smoke?

The woman's mouth twitched from side to side. Squirrel-like, she took a cigarette, snuffled at it, then dropped it into a wet, woollen pocket.

It was a stroke, Dawn added. She struck a match. The woman was caressing the wee shoe now as if it was a pet. Smoke. Stroke. It sounded like a gentle way to go. She hoped so anyway.

The shoe was old but nothing special, definitely nothing of value, not in that state. It had lived in Shirley's house for ever and its partner had always been missing. Somehow it had seemed to belong on its own. It was a strange colour. The velvet triangles were a deep emerald on an even darker background, but the fur round the top was a dusty shade of lime. Inside was a moth-eaten pink lining, and there was a frayed hole on the front where the pink showed through.

Are ye wantin it back? the woman said suddenly, holding it out again. It didnae sell. Here. Her face was starting to flush, mottled red like raspberry mush.

Dawn shrugged.

Ah thought it looked auld. Ah thought maybe ye'd sent it by mistake. Ye've nae idea faraboots yer aunt got it?

A van honked in front. The woman looked disappointed. She put the slipper back in her handbag.

That's me away.

Dawn watched her bustle down the steps. The sun had broken through the clouds and the woman's jumper was twinkling with trapped raindrops. She looked up into the sky and mumbled something.

Funny weather. I'll see you, then. It's Maggie, by the way, if you need me.

At the front window Dawn looked down at the van.

JW02 ONE

Strange pair of angels, Dawn thought to herself.

The driver was the same man who'd picked up the furniture. She recognised his tufty red hair and the flat cap on the dashboard. She thought she'd seen the woman before, but couldn't remember where. How would she have forgotten a face like that?

Ally's door opened and slammed shut, and she moved so she could watch him from above without being seen. He was wearing a tracksuit and running shoes. He did some stretches: calves, thighs, arse. Really gorgeous arse. Christssake. What was she thinking that for? He fiddled with his laces and headed off towards the park.

The windows of a house opposite were thrown open, the sashes rattling, still dripping. She could hear a piano player practising now, some famous piece they used on telly adverts. The player was stuck on one bit, missing a note, going over the same phrase again and again to get it right. Dawn listened harder, irritated for him. She started to gamble. If he got the tune right this time, Warren would be the next to knock at the door. Nah. That was daft.

Folk believed in all sorts of superstitious rubbish. Warren had been a bit that way himself. He had a notion about red being good luck. He mentioned it when they moved into the house. They'd just got married. It was a place not much bigger than a rabbit hutch, and it was in a mess, left empty for a while. But he loved it. There was a red doorstep, freshly painted. A good omen! he said, stepping onto it like a podium.

Come to think of it, they had lived at number twelve. So much for Maeve's theory! But it was hard to forget the good days like that. Some things would resurface, no matter what.

The slipper wouldn't be forgotten either. It came back again, abandoned this time, presumably by the strange woman with the yeti jumper and the rolling eyes. What did she say her name was? Maggie. The shoe was left like a foundling on the doorstep and Maeve rescued it coming in from the garden. It fitted her wee foot perfectly. She cobbled across the kitchen, the wooden heel going clop, clop, clop.

Look what I found, Mummy!

Maeve took it off and Dawn looked more carefully at it now, standing at the sink, turning the wee thing over in the light from the window. The fabric was rough as moss and burrs, maybe from age, or maybe it had always been like that. She put her fingers inside. Part of the lining was loose. It wrinkled under her fingertips like a sock slipping down inside a boot. Dawn lifted the material and rubbed beneath it. There was something tickly there. It got under her nails like the crumbs in the bottom of her handbag. She tilted it and saw something sparkling. Fine blonde sand. Maeve was watching.

What is it?

She told Maeve she was just thinking. She took the slipper with her and went to fetch the photograph album, flipped a few pages. It was just a hunch, probably nothing but silliness. What old thing didn't have a bit of grit in it?

But there was the slipper. It wasn't at the beach, which was the first place she looked. Instead she was surprised to see it clutched in the hand of one of the wee girls, held back so far it was almost hidden by the folds of her kilt. It looked deliberate, as if she didn't want the treasure to be seen. Fate had lent her a helping hand. A flaky white crease the length of a fingernail just scraped the girl's hip and the sole of the slipper, almost obliterating it. But it was the same one, or at least one of the same pair.

Maeve was beside her, reaching up. Scarfy was back in her fist. Dawn held out the shoe, and Maeve took it and pressed it to her chest. She smoothed the fur of the shoe with the silk of Blue Scarfy.

Dawn normally left her daughter's hair loose, the way she'd worn hers as a child, but today Maeve had stood infront of the mirror, brushing diligently, knitting and twisting it into two bunches. Now there was a tangled zigzag parting held with shiny bands and pink clasps. It would have to be teased out later, and Maeve would wriggle and cry, but Dawn hated to cut it.

✻ NITTIN AN SPEENIN ✻

Auld Betsy, 1954

Fammels fat as sausages, like ma George's haunds were. Aye. But they're nimble. Even as a young quine they were strong. They wanted tae be, wi the brood ah had, that along wi ma sister's bairnies an now the grandkinchins.

Ma eyes screw up tight, peerin at ma fammels tickin ower the cloth that Jock brought me. Ah'm pleatin, foldin, tuckin, gatherin, stitchin ower the folds, keepin them in place. Auld cloth. Some aither woman had pleated an gaithered it afore me. Faded, aye, but nae all ower. Ah found bonnie hidden colours unpickin the hem, colours bright as the day they were woven, like times ah remember fae years afore an nivver spik aboot.

If ah'm thrifty wi the cloth, there'll be enough tae mak a skirt fer Rachel startin at the school after Christmas. Curly's awa there now tae meet the teacher an the school nurse. Doubtless they'll be pokin an proddin the poor quinie, makin sure she's no starved. Whit a cheek these country fowk hae when they get it in their heids they're doin ye a favour! Oh, me! Ah ken bairnies in the fairms more wantin than ours, up at the skreek ae day tae walk tae school, nae food in their bellies, nae shoes on their tramplers, bairns whose faithers gie them the belt, bairns wi naebody carin fer them at aw. But that's fae whit they call decent homes. Shaness! It maks the blood run cal, the things ah ken an hae tae bite ma tongue ower.

Ah nick ma finger on the needle an, wi a tut-tut, sook at the sore bit. That's enough stitchin fer now.

Nivver waste whit someone's a use fer! Ah wind whit's left

ae the threed roun ma fammel an put it back in the tin wi the photies an the sewin things. The lid's got a picture ae Castle Grant where ah stayed ain time wi George after the weddin, jist the two ae us. We were camped back at the burn there when ma Peter wis born. Bless his wee soul. Oh, me! Poor wee thing passed. That wis in Ardclach, seven months after. Bronchitis.

Ah nivver name Peter oot loud. Nivver speak ae those days. Shaness!

Ah've no photies ae Peter. But ah keep this picture ae the castle. Nearly died when Jock tried tae change this tin fer another. A better wan, he said. Wan wi a lid that fits, Ma! Ach, but it's nae his fault. Ah nivver tellt them bout their brother Peter or ma wee girl Georgina either. Ah'm jist fond ae that lid, ah says tae him. Oh! Ah can be stubborn as an auld bull when needs be! Ho! Ha! Ha! Aye, poor Jock. He ended up takin the Castle Grant lid an fittin it ontae a new bottom fer ma. Now aw ma wee things are safe inside. Oh, me! He's a good boy, ma Jock. If ainly he could find hisself a nice dilly.

Nancy an Big Ellen are both asleep otherwise ah'd play a tune on the organ or sing a canterach an try tae get Nancy kickin those wee baby tramplers. An thon bairnie inside Big Ellen! It'll be a great muckle boy, that een. Jigs inside her when ah play! Boom, boom, boom! Aye. Jigs till Big Ellen's beggin me fer a rest! Oh, but that gies me the belly laughs. Ho! Ha! Ha! Ha! Ha! Oh, me! Ah love music. Love playin. Ah'll teach the wee lad the chanter when he's auld enough tae haud it. Every wan ae ma brothers were pipers, the best stummerer coulls in the North East. They taught me afore they left fer the war, an ah remember their pipe tunes tae this day. Aw in ma heid. We jist had the feelin fer it in oor family.

Pity Jock wis nivver mair interested in the pipes. He's the ainly wan ae ma bairns ever played. His granddad gied him a real piper's hat once, but wee Jock jist wanted tae look bonnie wi the thing oan his heid. 'Never mind those old tunes, Mammy,' that's whit he used tae say. He liked the young fowk's stuff, nae that ah blame him. There's some affae good modern music ye hear oan the wireless.

Ah get oot the chair an ma skirt falls heavy on ma hips. The fire's gutterin a bit low again sae ah throw on mair coal. The flames hiss, spittin a curse at me. If we were outside ah could mak this fire burn brighter than the sun in an autumn wood. Ah loved the campfires. On settled nights we'd sit roun singin, tellin tales fer hours, me wi the aither women, shoulder tae shoulder, each wi a bairnie or twa asleep at her bosie, a jam jar ae warm tea in her haunds. George would tak a drink wi the men, who sat aside maistly, an the twa fires, ours an theirs, would set the world beneath the trees glowin like those rosy red country scenes painted on moneyed fowk's dinner sets. O ho! Ho! Ha! Ha! Oh, me! We had good times in the camps.

George. Some mornins the wind blows in fae the sea an ah swear ye can taste the salt. That's whit he tasted of maistly. Fowk tellt me he wis the man who put the last rivet in the very last ship built in the Geddie yards in Garmouth. A steam drifter. *Blithesome* wis its name. Ah mind that, an oh me, oh do ah miss that man!

Well! Ah've worked mysel intae some dwam by the time Duncan an Curly get back an come bargin intae the room. Now, ma door's aie open, don't ever let onyone tell ye otherwise, but by faith, the pair ae them are at each other's throats like a couple ae bairns. Rachel's greetin, an that wee Betsy's got her arms folded ower her chest, makin a face that screwed up ye'd mistake it fer a lump ae dough the baker had stuck his fammels intae. Well seen it's nae gone very well at the school. Big Ellen wakes up in the midst ae aw this stew, an cursin the lot ae us she grabs her coat an storms across the hall tae lie doun on Jeannie's bed. Duncan hauds his haund oot tae Curly, who's bickerin awa, an then he turns tae me, bawlin his heid aff.

'Ma, would ye tell ma wife there is no wye on this earth, no wye, that we're gonnae cut oor lassies' hair all aff jist tae please some bitch nurse ae a burker's daughter? They'll look like bloody scaldies.'

Wee Betsy interrupts him, runnin up tae me an clawin at the waist ae ma skirts. She points at poor wee Rachel.

'She's got fuckin beasts crawlin in her hair, Granny! And now I've got them an all!'

Right, ah thinks. Ah may be an auld biddy, but ah can shout wi the best ae them. An now tae hear ma namesake grandbairn usin that fouty language like some shan dilly! Ah don't shout, though. No need fer me tae shout cause they aw shut their gobs when ah spik. No wan talks ower Auld Betsy. Ah can whisper an they listen!

'SHANESS! Shaness, the lot ae ye! You Duncan fer lettin yer ain daughter spik like that. Sit here, bairnies. Nobody tells ma family whit tae dae. Nae a hair on the heids ae these quines is tae be cut, ye hear? That's the last word.'

They're silent as the deid as ah fill a mug wi pannie at the tap an fetch the comb. Nae a peep oot ae them! Ha! Ha! Ho! Ah'll no hae the bairns' hair cut, though. Aw oor breed has these affae bonnie curls, an ye dinnae go takin that fer granted. It'd be years fer them tae grow back sae nice. The schoolhouse will still be there in a month or twa. So let it wait.

Ah mak a start on Rachel cause she'll no fuss an wammle aboot like Wee Betsy. Ah draw her locks through the comb in time wi the words ah mutter fae deep in ma chest.

'Whit do they think we are? Bloody sheep tae be shorn? The twa ae ye get oot ae here! Avree!' ah say tae Curly an Duncan. 'Oot ma road! Go oan, skedaddle! Ah've tae see the Batchie Woman later. Ah heard she had another wan ae her accursed visions, God hae mercy oan us. But ah'm nae missin that fer ony ae yous, nits or nae nits, ye hear? Let's jist hope she's got a good word tae tell me this time.'

Duncan goes aff doun the Lane an Curly goes up tae cook

106

some denner, shakin her heid. She thinks the Batchie Woman's an auld witch, that we should hae nowt tae dae wi her an her hocus pocus visions an dreams. But ah tell ye that Batchie Woman's been right afore.

'You're disgustin,' ah hear Wee Betsy say tae Rachel. Oh, me! Someone needs tae teach that kinchin! She's starin intae the pannie wi the wee black beasties floatin in.

'Now, you listen,' ah tell her. 'Ah wouldnae wint tae be you when ah'm done wi yer sister. Yer riddled wi knots an burrs as well as beasts, an if ye dinnae mind yer language in yer granny's hoose ah'll pull so hard ye'll forget yer ain name fer as mony days as there are hairs on yer heid. Ye got that?'

When it quietens doun, the ainly noises are Curly's footsteps, the fire cracklin, an the smooth strokin ae the comb's teeth ower Rachel's locks, gentle as Nancy's deep sleepin breath. The whole time the baby's nae opened her winklers. No even a crack. Ah pass the time tellin them an auld story ae ma daddy's. It's the tale ae a piper coull who fell in love wi the daughter ae a laird. Ach, some bits ah forget, but ah mak them up oan the spot. Onywye, the laird's nae happy, whit a surprise! Especially when he finds oot his daughter'll soon hae the piper's child.

'Owie!' Rachel goes when the comb gets stuck.

'Shhh, now. Listen,' ah go.

The laird ordered the piper coull tae be taken far awa on a ship, an though the piper chapped oan mony a door, aw the people turned their backs oan him. Ainly wan woman took pity, an auld grey-haired witch who lived in the middle ae a dark, thick wood.

'Did she give him gold, Granny?' Rachel asks.

No. It wasnae gold. She got him tae play a tune, an he wis so gifted a piper, his music put a smile oan her tarry auld face like a split doun a rotten apple. An then she gied him twa pears. That's aw it wis, twa pears fae the tree in her gairden, an they were hard as stanes. Oh, me, the poor manny!

But afore the piper wis forced ontae a ship, a hoard ae sailors returned fae a voyage. They saw his pipes an asked him tae play fer a dance, which he did, an by the end ae the evenin he'd got five coins in his pouch. He used the money tae send a message, an gifted wan ae the twa pears back tae his true love. An then he boarded a ship.

The dear dilly received the pear an put it tae her lips. But it couldnae be bitten open, nae even by her noble white teeth. As she did this the messenger whispered in her lug that the piper would return as soon as he'd made his fortune, an she smiled, fer she wis also in love. But that wasnae the end ae the message. The messenger turned the smilin dilly's cheek an whispered the last part ae the message intae her other lug. The piper's fortune would be made, an he'd be hame, afore the pear ripened. Now the dilly began tae greet great muckle tears, sure this wis a promise the piper couldnae keep. The pear would ripen too soon, or if not it would rot.

A month went by, an then another, an tae the dilly's great marvellin, still the pear hadnae turned. Her belly did grow ripe, though, an soon it wis roun wi the baby inside. There wis nae sign ae the piper, but nor did the pear turn, an nor wis the child born. There wisnae a soul had ony answers fer it, but they waited an waited an in the end they jist forgot aw aboot it. The poor dilly wis locked up fer five summers fearin her piper had fallen in love wi another woman.

'But that's when he came back!' Rachel says.

'Of course it wis, bairns. Things always happen when ye least expect them tae.'

The piper had suffered oan the seas. He'd battled wi storms an pirates, but the tunes had kept comin till wan day he sailed intae port a rich man. He walked right up tae the laird's door wi his ain pear still in his pocket. That same night Isabel had twins. The magic pears finally ripened too, an were eaten at the weddin feast.

Ah reach this point in the story an get oan ma tramplers. That's aw can be done wi the lice today. Ah throw oot the pannie an wash the comb, then set it up tae dry. Betsy an Rachel hae their gobs open at the end ae the story. 'But it's nae quite finished yet,' ah tell them.

'Descendents ae that family bide in the castle tae this day. Every wan ae them lives tae a hundred an twenty at least. An the auld grey-haired hag in the wood. Remember her, bairns?'

They nod, an ah dae a wee jig back ower the flair. The quines start laughin.

'Well, they say she's still dancin! Ho! Ha! Ha! Ha!'

Later, once the lassies are eatin, Curly helps me sweep their hair intae heidscarves. We couldnae get aw the beasties oot. That'll tak a month, wi the new ones hatchin on them. Fine fer noo, though. When we're done wrappin up the hair ah sit doun on the bed next tae Nancy, awake now, gurnin wi hunger.

Ah've speened aw the grandkinchins aff the breast milk mysel, jist like ma granny did fer me an ma mither did fer mine. Mind an tak yer teeth oot fer the speenin! That's whit ma mither used tae say, tuck em in yer pouch. Ah chew up lumps ae tattie an meat fer Nancy, an pass it intae her open mouie. Jist like a mammy an a babbie birdie. A spoonfy falls aff ma plate an ontae the flair afore ah can stall it. Dollop maks a thump.

'Waste not, want not, pick it up and eat it!' sings Rachel, soundin sae much like an auld wifey that ah get the belly laughs, an seein me laughin wi nae teeth in ma heid sets them all aff.

'Ho! Ha! Ha! Ha! Oh, mmme, bairns! Hmmmff! Oh, me! Would yous fffwwinish yer denner an let an auld woman get oot ae this damnmnmn hoose afooore she bursts? Ah've tae go an see thon Batchie Woman. Yer dear auld granny's work is nivver done! Nowt but stitchin an nittin an speenin aw the blessed day! Hmmmmff! But oh, mmme! Oh, me, whit a laughmf!'

Dawn

Dad had been back round and fixed the telephone with a few creaky turns of a screwdriver. His fingers weren't nimble as they'd once been, seizing with each twist. As soon as it was done he'd suggested a trip to the beach, as if what he needed was bracing sea air and a wide space to unfurl into. Dawn imagined him standing at the point of the lighthouse, the two long stretches of sand as his sleeves, arms open wide to wrap round the land he loved and called home.

Maeve had been easily persuaded.

Can I keep her with me today? he'd said. You could join us later, come for your tea.

She'd almost gone to the coast with them, but decided if she was going to visit the beach it was something she'd rather do alone. She put a clean towel and Maeve's wellies in the back of the car and stuffed a change of pants, socks and a pack of wipes into a welly leg. There was no need to worry, she told herself. Dad would be good to her.

Is Blue Scarfy coming? she'd asked, holding it out to Maeve through the open car window. Maeve reached for it but Dad laughed.

Whit's that old rag? You'll no still be needing a tuttie!

Maeve hesitated but took it and lifted it straight to her mouth.

If you're making sandwiches, she doesn't like egg or anything with pickle or mayonnaise, she told Dad. He nodded. Right-o!

Both of them waved as the maroon Escort coughed into action. Dawn lifted a hand, answering Maeve's tiny, pink palm and Dad's thick, speckled one. The sun had come out again, and where they were off to the bay would be sheltered, deceptively inviting.

Dad had taken Dawn to that same coast years ago, all the

different visits blurring into one cause she was so young, and each time they'd always done the same thing. They'd never built castles. Who wanted to lock themselves in a castle when there was all that sea to discover? Dad would set to work immediately, digging her a rowing boat. He always built up the sides so when it was finished she would have to be lifted in, just like a real boat. He even made the little benches. When they got hungry they would sit on them, eat their sandwiches and check for sharks. She would tell him 'Don't forget to row!', and Dad would heave-ho at the invisible oars and tell her stories.

Sometimes Mother came to the beach, but she never wanted to stay long. Wilma felt the cold. She would sit on a blanket shivering, looking sad, waving them goodbye as they set sail in the sandy boat. When Mother decided it was time to go the wee rowing boat had to be rescued. She would shout 'Ship ahoy!', and the game would be over. As they left the beach, scrambling up the dunes towards the road and the bus stop, Dawn always wondered how long it would take for the sea to burst through the walls of Dad's rowing boat, sinking it back into the sand.

That morning, Dad had peeped the horn as he and Maeve went round the corner in the maroon escort, and for a fleeting moment Dawn felt buoyed, that tight warmth of flesh and blood. The feeling almost had her running after them.

She hadn't had a whole day alone since before Maeve was born, and found herself out of practice. Her movements round the flat felt cumbersome, as though she didn't belong. A spaceman. It was as if she were on television and someone had put her on slow motion, the volume turned up full blast. Her own breath was blowing about her ears. Running the tap made her dizzy. The click-click-click of the ignition on the hob was a sickening crack of knuckles. Without Maeve in the flat she had the overwhelming feeling that someone else *was* there. Watching her. That was a stupid thing to think, she kept telling herself.

She wondered if a slowly supped cup of tea might calm her

nerves. But it didn't work. She heard the stroke of the teabag falling into the cup, the grind of sugar under the spoon, the liquid's lick and slop, the tick of the clock. She had to get out.

In fifteen minutes she was at the register in the Co-pie, feeling normal again and paying for cigarettes, matches and batteries for her Walkman. She picked up a local paper near the till, and read a few lines.

HAPPY BIRTHDAY MA BATCHIE! OLDEST RESIDENT
TURNS 121 Page 5

Dawn put the paper back on the stand, dropped the cigarettes and matches into the pockets of her black cardigan, ripped open the pack of batteries and fished in her bag for the Walkman.

She walked up High Street listening to the spools turn as she rewound a cassette. The miniature photo album from the cupboard was in her pocket. She put her hand round it and felt the bumpy design on the cover. It was stiff cardboard pretending to be crocodile and it was coated in some kind of shiny lacquer. The word 'Memories' was raised on the front in joined-up letters. Dawn traced her finger over the word. The letters were smooth strokes. They felt like the white seam on her index finger where the rough edge of a can had once opened her, slicing down to bone. Just her own carelessness.

The only clue about the pictures was still the name scribbled on the back of one of them. Lolly. It sounded American. The cassette rewinding in her ears came to a stop with a thunk and a click. She pressed 'play'. Lyle Lovett sung in a sleepy voice, but Dawn couldn't relax. Maybe that was her problem, the reason she couldn't be alone.

She looked through shop windows before going in, kept an eye on passers-by, checked left, right, round the corners and scanned the faces in cars. All of them were familiar in a way she

112

couldn't place. Near Plainstones she noticed a man who looked a bit like Warren.

If it really had been Warren, she'd have recognised his finely cut blue eyes, the daft smile with the perfect teeth. Not long before she left, his hair had begun to thin. He'd started wearing it very short. You could see then that his ears stuck out, just far enough that light glowed through the edges. An angelic sort of face and not a bad body, though he'd never made any special effort with it. Without ever trying she'd memorised him whole. On pictures she could point him out even if only a tiny part of him had made it into the frame: an elbow, a foot, an earlobe.

It meant nothing, though. She could trick herself into thinking a stranger was him. It used to happen all the time. Even in the city she'd seen him everywhere, a figure always turning a corner or disappearing at the top of an escalator.

Dawn found herself outside her grandfather's shop. It had a new owner now. Dad had never intended taking it on. Aunt Shirley used to pull her past the shop window, never stopping to say hello. She and Grandfather were on bad terms, she always said. Dawn would try and peek in as they hurried by, and inside he'd be serving a customer, wiping a knife down his apron. He was good businessman. He could get the customer talking and with a few smiles tempt them to buy the best cut.

Grandfather had never talked much at home, though. The only story he'd passed on was how he owed his life (and Dawn and Linda theirs) to his trade. If he hadn't already been an apprentice butcher he'd have fought on the front line in the Great War. Sure as a gun. But instead he'd won medals for feeding the troops and had come home in one piece to marry his fiancée.

Dawn had liked watching him carve a joint. He was deft with it, artistic. His work had been important to him, fascinating. The sharpening of knives and slicing of meat had demanded his full attention, and he'd performed these things with a seriousness like religious ceremony. He was a church-goer too: every Sunday morning till the day he died.

Dawn liked churches, even if she didn't believe in God. The best one she'd seen had been on a school trip, the only time she'd ever been abroad. They were meant to look at the paintings and admire the vaulted ceiling but Dawn didn't care about those things. Instead she'd found a corner where people had left messages on marble plaques, all offering thanks, and she hadn't moved from it till it was time to go. There were dates on the plaques, not just years but months and days. Some were a century old. She'd wondered if she would ever have a day so miraculous she'd want to cut it in stone.

Maeve loved sausages. She'd get some for her later in the week.

Dawn pulled her headphones round her neck so she could hear the people coming and going around her, and she turned into South Street. Up here was the bookies. A picture of a horse and jockey covered the entire shop front and cast a funny light inside, primary colours like a wendy house. She remembered the smell too, running shoes and cigarette smoke. There was a plastic floor that made squeaky noises as men shifted their weight and deliberated over bets.

She'd usually found Warren in here, but not today.

Their bad luck came all at once, that's how he would explain it. Somehow it leapt up on them, unexpected, like a strong racehorse clipping a high fence, losing its stride. And the final straw was the mark on the test, life announcing itself in a blurry burst, wishing for celebration. They'd waited so long for it. She had. She went through to him with the news on her lips and found him blinking sharp tears, his mouth a tight streak and a screwed bet in his fingers. He hurled the paper ball at the telly and looked like he wanted to spit after it. Ping! The bird's-egg ball bounced off the screen and rolled to a stop beside Dawn's foot. That was a moment she hated thinking about. That and the ones that came after.

She needed to sit for a minute. A haircut. She needed a haircut. If she was lucky someone would bring her a cup of strong coffee and she could smoke a cigarette. But they looked busy. She could see in the window of the salon from where she stood. There were already two women having their hair washed and another was sat in a chair with a tin-foil marigold for a head. There was nowhere else to go except Linda's shop, which was just at the end of the parade.

When the door opened a familiar bell tinkled a sugary sound over her head. The girl at the desk wore a coat like a scientist and the fabric looked unnaturally white next to her deep tan. Dawn wondered if the tan was painted on. They did that here.

Hiya, the girl said.

There were slatted blinds covering the whole shop front and Dawn had a good view of the street. If she waited long enough she'd probably see him. She kept looking everywhere she went. Maybe she even wanted to see him.

Is Linda in?

She's away for her lunch, the girl said. I'll tell her you came in, though. Are you wanting a sunbed? You're pale, eh?

The girl was giving the tatty black cardigan a funny look.

Aren't you boiling in that? She bit down on her Biro and reached for a clipboard.

Four's free, if you like?

Dawn looked round the shop. There was a yellowing tropical plant, a table with magazines on it and one chair with a hard back. The local paper had been folded open and left on the seat. There was a photo of the 121-year-old woman behind a huge cake covered in candles. Her face was an empty bag.

Can I just sit for a few minutes?

The girl nodded.

Dawn picked up the paper and sat. She looked again at the photograph of the ancient woman. She couldn't tell if the face behind the cake was really smiling. Ma Batchie's eyelids had drooped heavily, like leaves about to fall. Her hair still had life in it, though, a dandelion-soft fuzz that sprung out round her head.

121 years young, Ma Batchie — Elgin's longest ever resident and possibly the oldest person in the world — celebrated her birthday in style last Tuesday. Children from East End Primary School were invited to join her at Abbeyside Nursing Home where they asked questions about her life and Moray's past.

Ma Batchie was born in Findochty in 1877. As a young girl she worked for a fishmonger that had a premises in High Street, Elgin. She married Thomas Batchie, her childhood sweetheart, in 1898. Thomas passed away in 1935. Their only child, Margaret, died in childbirth ten years earlier. For most of her life Ma Batchie lived alone, but she kept animals and worked as a fortune-teller from her Elgin residence.

Ma Batchie says she always knew she'd live a long life. 'I read it in my tea-leaves,' she laughs.

Children of local families who attended the party were fascinated that Ma Batchie remembered their great-grandparents, and in one case even great-great-grandparents.

'She remembers everyone she's ever met,' a spokesperson at the nursing home commented. 'It's amazing!'

Dawn looked up from the paper.

Can I lie down in there? In those machines?

The girl nodded.

That seemed like a good idea.

You look dead scared! the girl laughed. Don't worry, it won't hurt.

Dawn stripped off in the cabin. There was a white plastic garden chair and she hung her clothes over the back of it and kicked her shoes underneath. She wondered if she should take her underwear off and stuff it into her pockets next to the matches and the photos. She didn't.

Her skin felt clammy and she had to wipe sweat from her thighs and forehead, from above her top lip. She thought of herself all white and sticky, that mini dough-man on the adverts. The shop girl was right about the cardigan. She'd worn too many layers. It was meant to be summer, for Christssake. No wonder she was pale, that's what Linda would say. Spend your life in a sack if you could!

Her chest was pounding fast and hollow now, like the music in cars that drove along with the windows down. She found an elastic band in her handbag and pulled her hair away from her face, then took the goggles the girl had given her, stretched the strap over her head and tried to wear them. They were useless. Light snuck in round the edges and the rims dug in. She snapped them onto her forehead. Christssake. She felt ridiculous. A cigarette would have been magic, but there was a 'no smoking' sticker on the door. She wondered if there was an alarm. How could Linda get through the day without a smoke?

The sunbed was a giant baguette with a split down the side, and as she lay down Dawn imagined herself becoming a sandwich filling. The thought made her laugh, and for the first time that day she felt pleased to have a moment to herself.

The machine whirred and flickered when the lights turned on inside and the whole cubicle jumped with ghostly electric blue and dull grey. It was like being back in the silvery dark of the disco, slow dancing, flashes of light, the outline of Warren's face imprinted behind her eyelids. That was 1974. Jesus. She'd known him all through school and they'd never said a word to each other and suddenly they were pressed up against each other. She went every week after that. 'Kung Fu Fighting' and 'Tiger Feet' and 'Waterloo'. It was a good year. She'd had pals and a good man and she was lucky. Everyone said so.

She still felt Warren's fist in her ribs. The blow stayed with her like a ball stuck in a fence.

Beneath her the plastic started to feel warm. She pulled the lid closed and the light intensified. Glacier blue. She closed her eyes. It would be easy to fall asleep here, inside the humming. She took deep breaths. That's what you were told to do when you needed to relax. Like during labour. Breathe and count. In and out. She was surprised how good it felt.

December 1977. They were in Aberdeen doing their Christmas shopping and he asked her to marry him right in the middle of a conversation about something else, as if the ring were just another item to tick off the list. Outside a choir was singing 'Silent Night', and inside the girl behind the counter polished the ring and pushed it into a velvety box. It came with a Free Gift! A silk neck scarf in emerald green that Dawn knew she'd tuck away as a keepsake but never wear. She wasn't a scarfy sort of person. The girl handed Dawn the bag while Warren stood aside shuffling his feet. He'd been too shy to say what the occasion was but he was happy, smiling down at his running shoes.

The woman wished them a merry Christmas.

✳ LEAD KINDLY LIGHT ✳

Wee Betsy, 1954

'It says so here,' Mammy says, pointing at leaflet she can't read.
'The light's good fer all sorts ae ailments.'

'Aye. Well?'

Daddy's setting his boots by the fire to melt the ice off them
and he pats me on the back and flips the cover of the book I'm
reading to see the picture on front.

'Well, whit, Duncan? Do ye nae think the kinchins have
missed enough school already? A month it's been! They're still
crawlin wi nits. Just get Jock up here tae read the rest ae this
leaflet tae us. Ah cannae make heid or tail ae it.'

Daddy crashes down onto a chair.

'Jingies! I'll hae my bloody tea first, that all right wi you?'

Today something really good happened. Miss Webster came
to the house! There was a knock and Mammy went down the
stairs saying, 'Who in the name ae the wee man can that be?' It
was her! There was a nurse with her too, and Mammy seemed a
bit worried when she followed the two of them back up the
stairs and into the room.

'So dark already, isn't it?' the nurse said. 'Can you get the
place warm enough?'

'Ach, we manage. Aye. Aye, we manage.'

Mammy looked at her feet. She had no shoes on, just stockings which were baggy and dusty round her toes like worms
that have been trodden on and have all dried up. She didn't
know what to do. Later she said she was sure me and Rachel
were going to be taken away right then and there.

There was a long silence, but eventually Mammy asked would they have some tea? I was really hoping Miss Webster would say yes, cause then maybe she'd still have been there when Jock came home all smart in his work suit. But the nurse and Miss Webster both said no and Mammy looked relieved. She didn't want to serve tea out of jam jars to country hantle. Daddy smashed all the mugs in a temper and we haven't got new ones yet.

The nurse held out a leaflet and Mammy said thank you. She took it and let it fall on the table behind her without even taking a look. But it had something to do with the sun.

'Mrs Whyte, I think your girls would really benefit from the treatment.'

When the nurse talked about 'the treatment', she smiled like it was the most wonderful treat in the world, a very special present. She had a kind voice, but she didn't say another word, just stood there like a smiling statue, all the way through another long silence, till Miss Webster cleared her throat and reached down into her tatty leather case, the one I usually see at the foot of her desk.

'I've brought some books for Betsy from the school library. I thought she might want new ones.'

A stack of books appeared from the mouth of the case, all with bright pictures on the covers, and Miss Webster brought them over to me. She's not even feart of getting the heid beasties, even though she knows I'm crawling with them.

'She reads that much we worry she'll get bad eyes,' Mammy was saying.

I've not moved from the cosy spot by the fire since the nurse and Miss Webster left, and I've nearly finished one of the books already. Mammy's been making the dinner and taking a peek at the leaflet on the table every time she walks past.

'Betsy, go and get them fae doun the dancers,' she goes. 'We're eatin.'

'COME ON, WE'RE GONNAE EAT!' I shout from the top of the stairs.

'GRANNY'S EATIN DOWNSTAIRS,' Rachel bellows.

Mammy rolls her eyes and we hear Rachel's footsteps coming.

'Come and sit yersels here and buckle that howlin. Yer like a pack ae wolves,' goes Mammy.

We all slurp our soup, not speaking, while the leaflet lies in the middle of the table, eyeing us. I get a good look now. The picture's of a naked baby, about the same age as Nancy. It's got its arse in the air, lying on a bed next to a wifey in swimming togs. Beside them a man in a white coat has a machine that's pouring out light, and written in the rays it says:

For sturdy body. For sound teeth. For strong bones. For straight limbs.

I don't know the last word, 'limbs', but I think it might be another word for hair. For straight hair. Granny wouldn't like that. She prefers curls. The strangest thing of all is that the three people in the picture are wearing flying goggles, just like you see in the war films. Daft grins are plastered on their faces and they've got gleaming gnashers, except the baby of course, and its wee gums are shiny in the glare of the light.

'Look like they're haein a good time, eh? Silly tatties!' Daddy says, prodding the leaflet with the end of his spoon.

When our bowls are clean Daddy picks the leaflet up. I bet he's looking at the wifey in her togs. Eventually he goes 'hmf', thumps it under his fist and goes to the top of the stairs. Mammy shakes her head as he roars, 'JOCKY, GIE US A HAUND WI SOMETHIN HERE, WOULD YE?'

'Duncan,' she mutters, 'it's you gies them that habit, shoutin doun the dancers like thon Tarzan ae the bloody jungle.'

Uncle Jock takes a seat at the head of the table and holds the leaflet up to read. Mammy stands on his left, Daddy on his right, and me and Rachel tuck our heads in over his shoulders. Uncle Jock's the cleverest man in the house, maybe in the whole of the Lane.

'Well? Mammy goes. Can ye read whit it says?'

Uncle Jock takes a deep breath. 'Well', he goes, `Ultra-violet radiation is recommended by the world's best medical men.'

'Whit the bloody jingie's that?' Daddy goes.

'Duncan, shhh! Gie him a chance tae read the thing, would ye?'

`Your local hospital can now offer your children tonic sun lamps. I've nae idea what that is, Curly. Shall I go on?'

'Aye,' says Mammy and gives him a nudge.

`A quarter of a century ago the remarkable benefits of true ultra-violet rays were discovered. By sun lamps, by exposure, by any means possible, we should obtain as much sunshine as we can. And here's why: in the rays of sun there exists a force, which acting upon the body produces that precious element: vitamin D. Sun lamps provide the necessary ultra-violet rays to help give children a good start. Are any ae you gettin this?'

'Whit, are you no?'

'How about askin Ma?'

'Are ye wise? Whit the jingies'll Ma ken about ultra-violent radio whitevertheyweres?' Daddy bellows.

'Ye've got a better idea, then?' says Jock.

'Fine, suit yersel, but she'll nae ken, ah'm tellin ye.'

Granny climbs the stairs slowly. You hear her skirts dragging along the narrow walls and she's got Nancy gargling in her arms.

'Whit's aw this aboot? Whit hae ye got me up here fer? Ah'm too auld fer thon bloody dancers. They're affae steep,' she goes.

Oh! Let me sit there, Jock. Aye, that's it, tak the weight aff ma tramplers. Good. Now, you lot, moociach roun aboot me.'

We huddle in beside Granny like a flock of sheep.

'Whit am ah meant tae dae wi this?' Granny goes, flapping the leaflet. 'Whit is it fer? A brown behouchie? Bare-arsed fighter pilots? Ho! Ha! Ha!'

'It's a treatment at the hospital, Ma,' Mammy says. 'Sun lamps. The kinchins can hae it fer nowt.'

'Laamps, did ye say? Whit? Sun lamps? At the hospital? O ho!'

Granny jiggles and holds her sides like they might split. Her wee eyes screw up tight, and every so often she opens them, points at the baby's bum, points at the wifey and the lamp, and creases up again. If she's not careful she'll rock back, her chair'll crash through the floor, and she'll end up hohoho-ing on the bed in Jock's room. I'm nae catching her.

Mammy looks at Daddy, and Daddy looks at Mammy, and then he looks at Jock, and Jock looks at the two of them, and Mammy looks at Jock and shrugs her shoulders. Granny keeps laughing.

'Oh, me! Sun lamps! Load ae nonsense! They stick ye in a hoose an tell ye tae come tae the hospital fer sun? O ho! Aye, that'd be right an aw. Ho! Ha! Ha! Haaa! Whit in Heaven's wrang wi runnin aboot kickin a baa outside, eh? Stead ae stickin the wee souls in a school aw day. Bloody daft! Oh, me! Sun lamps! Ho! Ha! Haaa!'

Granny laughs till tears roll down her cheeks.

'That's that, then,' Daddy says, 'whit did ah tell ye? Ma's right. The lassies should be oot, nae sittin there readin bloody books.'

'Aye, cause it's a fine day tae be oot! Snow on the wye.' Mammy starts clattering the dishes into the sink.

'Curly!' Daddy goes, waving a hand to me. 'That lassie'll go blind an turn all peely wally. End up like a bloody albino. Is that whit yer wantin, woman?'

123

'I'm nae peely wally, Daddy.'

But no one listens to me. I do my muntiest face, put on the sulks. Miss Webster thought the lamps were a good idea, otherwise she wouldn't have come over with that nurse. I love Miss Webster. I wanted to go up the hospital with her and sit with the goggles on and fly under the sunshine machine. Mammy would've let me if it wasn't for stupit Granny.

The next day I sleep late, but as soon as I'm awake I run to the window. There's no snow, just great splodges of rain. I lean my elbows on the ledge and stare at the terrace opposite, number five and number seven, where the Newlands stay. Their houses are just the same as our one. The slate roofs are wet and shiny and a fountain of water's spurting up out a broken pipe. You hear it splashing on the cobbles below. The wonky chimney stacks have smoke spiralling out already, and the crooked pots are like Granny's dirty teeth when she holds her pipe between them. My eyes follow the smoke to the sky. Thick and grey as week-old tattie soup. So much for going out in the sunshine, Granny. Not a bloody peep. The sun's up at the hospital, keeing out a lamp.

Pesky heid beasties. I wish I was going to see Miss Webster today to have roly poly pudding for lunch and go on a special trip to get the sun. I put my finger on the window pane, follow the trickles of rain from the top to the bottom; they sometimes go left and sometimes right, but most often they just follow the drop below.

Mammy's sweeping the floor and soon my feet are in the way. The broom skirts round my ankles.

'Why don't you go down tae your granny, like Rachel?' says Mammy. 'There's messages fer you tae fetch once the rain's off.'

'All right, then,' I yawn.

I don't go down right away, though. I stand on the landing at the top of the stairs, looking out to where Maggie McPhee lives. The McPhees stay in a sort of hut on the backside of ours.

They're even poorer than us, so their house is like a patchwork hutch, and the rain pummels down on the wavy metal roof. Wee burns run along each groove, and you can see a good few holes from up here. Maybe Maggie McPhee's drowned in her bed!

I ease open the window just a wee bit and stick my hand out, catch raindrops. My sleeve's drenched in seconds. The window frame's rotten, and I run my wet fingertip over it. Tiny specs of black wood rub off into the ridges of my skin. They're as tiny as the beasties in our hair. Occhh. Yeuchh. Scrichh. Thinking of them always makes me itch.

'Hey. Whit are ye up tae?' a voice shouts.

I look down. It's her, Maggie McPhee, poking her head out the door. She stares up at my window with one angry eye and follows the seagulls with the other. Maggie was born like that, eyes rolling all over the shop. She's clumsy and she's got a soor face, and she's useless at ball games so no one's friends with her. 'That quine couldnae even catch a cold,' my daddy says, but that's not true cause Maggie's always covered in snotters. She should be in the High School, but I don't think she ever went. Her mammy's dead, and her big brothers are daft eejits. 'There's somethin nae right wi those McPhee boys,' that's what my mammy says about Maggie's brothers. She tells me I'll stay away from them, if I've any sense.

'I ken ye're there, Wee Betsy. Whit are ye daein?' she goes.

'Nothing,' I shout, 'Go away, bad-luck McTootie.'

'McTootie' is what Granny calls the McPhees in the morning because it brings misfortune to say their real name before lunch. I don't believe Granny, but it makes me laugh to call Maggie a McTootie. 'Tootie-toot,' I shout, and slam the window shut.

Afterwards I sit on the stairs in the dark and feel a hole in my belly. It's not a hunger sort-of hole. I think about Maggie and how her mammy died, how Maggie's daddy likely killed her mammy cause McTooties are forever fighting and murdering their own. But the thing is, my granny's mammy was a

McTootie. She was called Georgina McPhee, which means Maggie and her brothers must be related to us.

I think Georgina's a nice name. I wish I was Wee Georgina instead of Wee Betsy. It would take longer to shout on me, or to say night-night.

I go into Granny's room to try and forget about the McTooties. There are visitors today. Rachel's sitting at the table with Granny and Big Ellen, and another old lady in black clothes. She's cuddling up to a lady I don't recognise, looking all pleased with herself. Their heads turn when I come in.

'Here she is, sleepy heid!' says Granny. 'This is oor Betsy.'

'Oh, would ye look at the bairnie!' whispers the old wifey.

'Dae ye ken Auld Jessie an yer Auntie Rachel?' Granny says. 'Ye've heard aboot yer Auntie Rachel, still oan the road?'

So this must be who Rachel's got her name after. I might've known there was a Big Rachel somewhere an all. She's beautiful, this auntie, with long red hair right down to her waist, burning bright, and thick skirts like blankets wrapped round her. She wears a woven cloak thrown over her shoulders, and Wee Rachel can't stop stroking it.

'Here, Wee Betsy,' she says, taking a paper bag out her pocket and holding it open.

I put my hand in, and out of the swarm of waxy twisted wrappers in the bottom I pull a square of dark toffee, not golden like the normal stuff. I put it on my tongue. It's wonderful! It begins to melt and run, all warm and creamy round my gums. Like chewy chocolate.

'Thank you!' I try and say without dribbling on my chin. I want the sweetie to last for ever.

The women laugh and go back to their conversation, all whispering, and Wee Rachel just stares and stares at Big Rachel's fiery hair.

'The poor gadgie!'

'He took a faa, ye say?'

'OH!'

'Oh, me!'

I'm only half listening cause the taste of that sweetie is like nothing I've ever eaten before. Brown sugar and salt and chocolate and buttercream, and something else, and all at the same time.

'An faraboots were they stalling?'

'At the well.'

'In the wood? OH!'

'Thon bosh wis the last place ma faither bided an aw.'

'Aye.'

'Oh, me! A terrible thing. Whit a curse.'

The sweetie starts trickling down my throat.

'Wee Betsy!' Granny says, 'standing there in a dwam! This is the Deil's news, nae fer bairns tae be hearin.'

She shuffles to the cupboard where she keeps her jar of pennies. 'Go get yer granny and her guests some broken biscuits, eh? And ah need milk. There ye go. Skit!'

We head off to the left at the bottom of the Lane, up the High Street and round the corner. I can still taste the sweetie even though I've already swallowed it. By the time we've fetched the milk, got a few biscuits, and looked in some shop windows, the sky's spitting again. It's going to rain all bloody day.

We're just going past the butcher shop when we bump into Uncle Jock. Rachel runs up and throws her arms round his waist and he jumps cause he didn't see us coming.

'Uncle Jock! What are you doing here?' I say.

'There's a hale flock ae sheep on the line,' he says. We cross the road together. 'I was in the signals this afternoon but they sent me away.'

Rachel starts whining. She doesn't like the rain and she wants to go to the pictures, but Uncle Jock says there's things he's got to do back at the house. He's mending some old bicycles. I tell Rachel to stop being a bubbly bairn. I'm looking after her and Uncle Jock has work to do.

Just then there's a gust of wind and a sheet of heavy rain that stings my cheeks. Jock takes our hands and starts running for shelter.

'Put your hood up, Rachel,' I tell her, cause that's what Mammy always says. But it's hard to shout through the rain, especially when I'm running to keep up with Uncle Jock. We run towards a close where we won't get soaked.

'Ow!' says Rachel from under her hood.

Woohoooo! Hailstones! From here we can watch the hail bouncing and rolling all over the road and down the hill to High Street without getting hit ourselves.

'We're being attacked by pandrops!' Jock laughs, lighting a cigarette, and then with a wink to me he says, 'If we wait long enough maybe we'll get cinnaminaminaminamon balls!'

A blue car's parked across the road and hail pings off the bonnet like inside the popcorn machine at the Playhouse. I'm just pointing this out to Rachel, and that's when my clever wee sister spots her: over the road, up the hill, and a wee bit round the corner. Miss Webster with a huge black brolly. She's pressed under the stripey awning of Yeaden's bookshop, which is also taking a beating. Pi-pi-ping-pi-pi-ping-ping-ping! Elsie and Shona from my class are there too, holding hands, and Bertie Topp's down on his hunkers in the gutter, picking up hail and chucking it at Frankie McAulay and Billy Murphy, who're holding their gobs open trying to catch. Miss Webster wags her finger at them.

I give Rachel a dunt with my elbow and whisper, 'All them are off to the hospital for the sun machine, I'll bet you. Dare you to go with them.'

'Granny said we're nae allowed.'

'I dared you, Rachel. That means you've got to.'

'No!'

'Do you dare me, then? I'll do it.'

She scowls and scrunches her hand round the bag of broken biscuits we've got for Granny, even more broken now, but never mind.

Then I get an idea. Miss Webster looks lovely today. If I point her out to my uncle, I'm sure he'll want me to introduce him. I pull on his hand till he leans down so I can whisper in his ear. I'm right! He takes hardly any persuading and stubs the rest of his cigarette against the wall.

'Well, I suppose so,' he says. 'I cannae see it doin any harm as long as your mother and father are none the wiser. Rachel, are you wantin tae come an all?'

But goodie-goodie pulls a face like a half chewed sweetie, about to greet. I push her further into the close, give her kisses on the cheeks, and tell her I'll bring her a treat if she promises not to tell. I don't know where I'm going to find a treat, but I'll work that out later.

Walking over to Miss Webster with Uncle Jock's hand in mine is like a slow motion scene from the pictures. Except for the stupid weather. But I don't care any more about the hail. It's turning back to rain, sugary clumps sticking in my hair. The only thing that matters is that Miss Webster's already seen us and she's watching us from under her big black brolly.

'That's your teacher?' Uncle Jock says halfway across, like he can hardly believe it. I'm sure it's cause she's so beautiful. I nod and feel Jock start to walk taller. He strides like a soldier. His uniform has shiny buttons, and his shoes are so polished when we get close I'm sure I can see Miss Webster's reflection in them, a big smile on her lips.

I've never been in Dr Grey's Hospital before, not even when I was born cause Mammy has us in the bed. It smells funny here. Not exactly like sick people. I know that smell well enough. It was horrible going into Granny's room when Granddad was ill before he died, and it smelt even worse when Wee May Townsley over the Lane's leg went black. After she came home from Dr Grey's she only had one leg left, and soon after Mammy told me I couldn't call on her any more cause she'd gone to Heaven.

The hospital smell's not like that. Mainly it's sharp, so strong it burns inside my nose and makes me thirsty. The only place I've smelt anything like it is in the hut at the back of the rag store, where Daddy and the other men tan rabbit skins and keep all sorts of tins and bottles I'm not allowed to touch. Maybe Granny's right about hospitals being bad places where evil happens, full of death she says.

We go in a crocodile down a long corridor that is painted green and white. The floor makes squeaky noises under our shoes and there are hundreds of doors with windows at the top but I can't jump up high enough to see. When I stop to try Miss Webster says, 'Come on, Betsy. You must keep up.' But she's in a good mood. I'm sure she liked Uncle Jock even though they didn't speak for long at all. He made her go all shy.

The boys go one way with a nurse and Miss Webster comes with us into a room where we meet a man in a white coat. I know right away this is Dr Grey cause he looks exactly like the man on the leaflet.

Soon we're all stripped down to our knickers, and Dr Grey is going along the line listening to our chests. My heart must be beating like the Elgin pipe band, but he doesn't seem to notice. The wee disc on the end of the thing he sticks in his lugs is freezing on my skin. He keeps it there a few seconds.

'Fine!' he says suddenly. 'Come and stand over here. That's it. Come on, it'll not hurt anyone.'

This isn't right! We don't even get to lie down. We're on our feet in front of big round metal lamps on long legs. The face of each one has a grill across like a dartboard, and inside it's all shiny. A bit at the back has tiny wee springs wrapped round, and in front are two black metal fingers pointing at each other like they're getting ready to touch. The whole thing's like a bowl of the strangest bits of scrap we've ever carted away.

'It looks like a flying saucer, miss,' Shona says, and speaking of flying, I remember.

'Where's our goggles, sir?'

'Goggles. No, only I wear goggles. You won't get those. No need for such a short treatment. I'll just ask you to keep your eyes closed. Right, are we ready?'

I frown at Dr Grey as he snaps his own set over his eyes, grinning like Biggles. I'm not giving him a smile like that stupit wifey in the picture if he's not going to give me goggles.

'Come on, now. Uncross your arms, please, and close your eyes.'

I look to one side. Shona's standing with her face tilted up, eyes closed already. She must've done this before. Elsie's on my other side, giggling but looking feart, standing way back.

Miss Webster's voice says, 'Come on, now, girls. Do as the doctor says, please. Quickly.'

I shut my eyes. When the lamp gets switched on, the colour behind my lids goes from black to brown to red. It's not painful, but I don't like it that much. I want to cover them with my hand but Dr Grey shouts to someone, 'Keep still, please!', and it might be me cause folk sometimes say I'm a fidget.

There's a heat off the lamp. That's the nice part. It really does feel like the sun on the hottest day of summer. Like the days when Jock takes us to the beach and we have a picnic on our favourite rock. He points out the birds as they fly past, telling us the names, and he chases planes through his binoculars. I rock a wee bit on my heels, thinking of the waves lapping in and out, in and out, whispering, the sun beating down. I imagine I'm there at the beach with Uncle Jock and Miss Webster.

CLICK. CLICK. CLICK.

'You can open your eyes now.'

I blink-blink. The room's all funny colours, bluish blotches floating over the walls in shapes like ink blots. My skin cools and it feels cold, and it's darker than normal, like it's about to thunder and lightning.

Elsie and Shona are rubbing their eyes and blinking too. The rain's battering against the window and blue blotches glide over the drips on the pane. They sail by, everywhere I look. Shivering, the three of us jump into our clothes before being led to a bench in the green corridor. Here the nurses are chased along by the blue blotches. What are they? I wonder if they're there all the time and you just need the lamp to see them. Maybe they're ghosts, like Granny says she sees, or maybe they're diseases. Whatever they are, though, I hope none touch me. As I'm thinking this, one of them slides over Shona's face. She doesn't notice.

Miss Webster waits with us while the boys have their shot on the lamps, and Shona and Elsie start quietly singing a hymn, one we do at school assembly.

'Do you have a boyfriend, Miss Webster?'

I want to tell her that if she doesn't, maybe Uncle Jock could take her to the pictures this weekend. I think he liked her. But Miss Webster doesn't answer. I look into her face and see I've made her go all red.

'That's a very personal question,' she says at last, sounding strict.

I stare at my knees and wonder how Miss Webster and my uncle are ever going to get together. I'll need a plan.

I've had enough of the hospital. I want to go home and listen to the wireless with Uncle Jock. To pass the time I play a game with myself. I see how many seconds I can stay totally still, without even breathing or blinking. I get to thirteen, but then spoil it by scratching an itch on my head.

'You were good girls, all of you,' Miss Webster says suddenly, and when I look up I see she's not blushing any more and my question's been forgotten. She catches my eye and smiles, and then takes a scrunched up bag out her pocket. Sweeties! I reach in quicker than any of the other girls and pull out a chocolate éclair, curl my fingers round it.

This one's for Wee Rachel.

Dawn

The door of the auction rooms was clasped with a chunky padlock and there was no notice of opening hours. Dawn walked all the way round the building and got on her knees to peer through a gap. The space inside was chilled with inky light, a ray of sun filtering through a crack in the roof. There was a hint of livestock in the air, a smell which must have clung for decades. The floor was a giant sand-pit, and somewhere inside was furniture waiting to be sold, cabinets and drawers all empty except for shadows. But she was lucky. Someone was scuffing their shoes in the dirt behind her, coming up the path.

It was Maggie Marbles. Dawn's memory of the woman had come back out of the blue, under the strange light of the sunbed. Maggie used to sit on the steps of the church at Plainstones, one eye keeking round the corner while the other was away up the road. That's how Shirley used to put it. And then Maggie had disappeared entirely one day. Folk assumed she'd died. She'd liked a drink, and there were often accidents with people like that.

But here was Maggie, back from the dead. It was her who'd begun all this, bringing back that ugly wee shoe. Maggie had become duck-like in her middle age, her belly rounded, shoulders slightly hunched, wearing that crown of matted hair and an oddly assembled winter wardrobe. The grey yeti jumper. Buttonless cardigans stretched round her middle, layers of lines and triangles in random colours.

Dawn had asked Linda when she'd arrived back in the shop, and Linda had sworn it was the same woman. Maggie had come back to town about three years ago, and Linda had first seen her slouching on a bench by the lake in Cooper Park. Maggie hadn't

133

announced herself. She'd just let herself be found as if she'd been there all along, like a lost sock.

Today Maggie had the same hairy, grey jumper tied in a pouch round her waist and she was carrying a box of mismatched crockery, one eye pinned on Dawn and the other on the auction-room door.

Dawn took the photos from her pocket and waited for some sign that Maggie remembered coming to see her. Maggie's eye rolled, but it did that all the time. Dawn didn't know what to say and suddenly it seemed like a stupid idea to have come looking. These were Shirley's affairs. But Maggie might be the only person who knew the people in the pictures, the girl, the boy, and the children with the slipper. Perhaps the pictures would mean something to those people. They looked like a happy family. At the very least, maybe someone would like them back. Eventually Maggie reached out and took picture.

Dawn desperately needed a cigarette. When she pulled out the pack Maggie looked up from the photo and grinned like a pumpkin. Dawn slid out two smokes and rummaged for matches.

Do I ken your name? Maggie said with a deep breath once she'd got her cigarette lit.

Dawn Dunn.

Maggie nodded then, smiling like she'd heard of her. Dawn Dunn, she said, two thick puffs of smoke.

Whit's aw this? Polis matters?

She leaned in for a closer look at the picture and laughed, a graveyard of dirty teeth.

Ha ha. Thon's the Whytes. Wha kens whit happened tae that lot! I thought someone would come asking sooner or later.

She took a long suck on her cigarette.

Why?

Maggie shrugged. Ask Big Ellen. If she'll talk tae the likes ae you! Bides near thon Halfway place.

Maggie had unlocked the auction door. She looked Dawn up and down and then gave her a last-minute bit of advice before slamming the door shut behind her.

Ca' canny!

The Halfway Café was a short drive away. It always looked deserted. Several times it had caught fire and made the papers, and Dawn had never been inside. It was a one-storey building and there was a new car park in front that didn't have a single tyre mark on it yet. The sign said 'Halfway Cafe! Pool table.'

She parked next to a Ford van and looked up and down the road. Halfway to nowhere. There weren't any houses or landmarks, no street lights, no road signs. There was no turn off either. As far as she could see it was just tree after tall tree, white dashes and cats' eyes that seemed to move even as she was standing still. A dizzying smell of fresh tarmac mingled with pine. It was making her head spin and her forehead sweat.

The pool table was near the door and you had to walk right round it to get to the bar. No one was playing. Three walls were boarded with bare slats and the fourth was tacked with Territorial Army posters, men's faces smeared green. There were pull-out shiny Christmas decorations strung along the ceiling which no one had bothered to take down, and a couple of fruit machines flickered bright colours in the corner. A group of men were propped at the bar and another two nursed pints at the nearest table. They stared. An Alsatian lay on the floor, tied to a table leg.

Dawn wished she had someone with her. She'd gone home for the car and Ally had waved to her from his front-room window. He'd have probably come with her if she'd asked. He seemed to like helping out.

All the conversations stopped and the Alsatian was panting. A lorry passed outside. She wouldn't be ordering a drink.

I'm lost.

They nodded.

Is there a turn-off near here?

The barman thought for a second, pulling down the corners of his mouth with a thumb and a finger. The others were leaning in, eyeballing. The nearest man put his hand on the bar and bent towards her for a word, so close his nose was almost parting her hair.

You needin a place tae stay?

He pointed over his shoulder to the group.

You can stay at his place, he said.

Laughter. Dawn watched the lights flashing up and down the slot machine. They climbed the buttons like rungs and then all the colours came on at once. Flash! Flash! Flash!

Forget it.

She let the door slam behind her, left the car and started walking. She found one path behind the trees. At the roadside there were two filthy trail bikes left leaning against a post. She was probably close to a house, and didn't really care, she just wanted to walk now. Higher up the path joined with a potholed dirt track which was as wide as a road, and still she followed it, stepping inside a groove that tyres had driven through the dust and stones.

Maeve and Dad would be on their way home now. They were probably abandoning a sandy boat and feeding leftovers to seagulls. Mother would be putting dinner in the oven for the four of them. She was a good cook.

The top of the hill came suddenly and Dawn was looking down at a caravan site. It was surrounded by a white fence, and inside it ten to twenty vans were moored round three porta-cabins. Near the entrance was a train wreck of vehicles and spare parts. The site was divided into smaller plots so each caravan had a kind of garden with a gate. Most areas were concreted over and broken with patches of stubby grass where dogs were tied and barking.

Dawn stopped. Maggie had told her to watch herself, and

perhaps the best thing would be to hang round the fence till she was noticed. The people would come out when they were ready. It was the advice given to birdwatchers, the softly-softly approach of bear trappers. It was what she told Maeve to do when going up to strangers' pets. 'Ca' canny!'

These places were like cobwebs, found in corners and along edges, hidden in the outskirts of cities and squashed onto verges of dual carriageways. Normally she'd be driving by and all she'd have time to see was a flash of colour in the trees, washing fluttering on a line. Passing a second time she might notice the hulks of metal, marooned, heavy with use like shipyard sheds. Another time she might catch a glimpse of a beach ball, a small bicycle, a rabbit hutch. The traffic was never slow enough to get a good look or make out any faces.

There was rattling. Movement. A boy in a red cap appeared by a van and Dawn tried her best to look harmless as she made her way down the path. When she got closer he took off his hat and a tuft of hair stuck up.

Hello. I'm looking for Ellen.

Oh, he said, standing straighter. I thought you were lost. People mostly come here by mistake.

Like Maggie, he had brown marks like wheat chaff on his teeth, a scuff on his cheek, but other than that he was nothing like her. He was a young boy with a nice face. His voice wasn't what she'd expected either. It was shy and polite with an accent from nowhere in particular. The boy was looking from her to the nearest van, where a rust-coloured dog was straining on its rope.

Quiet, Beanz! he shouted. He turned back to her. You know Big Ellen?

No. I don't think so.

I'm not sure she's here, he said. Are you from the council? The papers?

She shook her head.

We've had a lot of bother with the papers.

She was just about to make some excuse to leave when the boy started walking towards the far end of the site.

Come on.

They passed a tortoiseshell cat that was eating from a bowl, licking bones.

I'm not sure if my gran's in, he said. But we'll see.

He pointed at the cat. That one's been hanging round all summer, the boy said. She got dumped by someone. Take her, if you want. It's hard for us to keep her. You want a cat?

Not really, I can't.

He shrugged. Suit yourself.

A blue van slid past and the boy lifted his hand to the people inside, a couple with a child snuggled between them. The man and woman nodded, keeping their eyes on Dawn till they'd disappeared down the track. There was a smell of dust from the passing wheels but other than that there was only the fresh, warm air and food cooking in vans.

Another door swung open and a man came out. He lifted a hand to his mouth and shouted something. The boy put a thumb in the air and the man took a good look at Dawn before making a gesture and disappearing back inside.

It's okay, the boy said. My dad.

There were three fold-down steps. The boy went first. He didn't knock, and walked in without stopping to take off his work boots, which were cracked with pinkish dust from the track. Stepping in after him, Dawn had to duck so she didn't hit her forehead.

It took a second to adjust to the feel of tyres underneath them, not quite solid ground. There was a girl and a baby in the van, and it was quiet except for a small telly balanced on a shelf.

This is my wife, the boy said nodding to the girl. She was half lying on a U-shaped seat that would change into a double bed at night. The girl looked up quickly and then turned back to the baby, which was gurgling and jiggling in a bouncy chair.

That's Wee Jock. I'm Jock as well, and my father also.

It was a thing he was proud of.

And his father too? Dawn said, but the boy didn't reply.

The girl was fixing the baby's overalls, playing with the buttons.

Back in a minute, Jock said. I'll see if Gran's about. Do you want some tea? I can get water, if you do.

The girl moved to make room and Dawn took a seat. *Neighbours* was on the telly and the girl turned the sound up. Behind it they could hear the chainsaw-growl of trailbikes behind the trees, and every so often the girl would turn away from the telly, push the curtain aside and stare through the window to the top of the hill. Her expression was a tight knot, like she was expecting thunder. Dawn was relieved when Big Ellen appeared. The woman suited her name. She was tall and strong and her shoulders barely squeezed through the doorway.

Ye found us aw the way up here! she panted, the kind of welcome you'd expect after days of waiting.

Have some tea, if you want. My grandson'll put it on. Here he is. Let's see what ye have for me.

Jock was back with the water and he'd set it to boil. Big Ellen took a seat, her huge thigh pressing close to Dawn's. She took the album and flipped a few pages. Two men came up the steps while she looked, and they peered in to see what was going on. The van shifted under their weight, then rocked back into place. The revving trailbikes were getting louder, and Jock put the mugs down and leaned over the sink to check out of the window.

The bikes are coming back, the girl said. She took the baby from the chair and held him close.

What's wrong? Dawn said.

Big Ellen looked up from the photos. The men in the doorway were leaving.

Jock, you stay here, Big Ellen said.

Jock nodded but he went to the door all the same, opened it

and looked up in the direction of the noise. It seemed to be just outside now, the sound of the forest tearing in half.

Close that door! Big Ellen said.

She was still on the first picture, taking a while on it.

This lassie looks kind ae familiar, Big Ellen said eventually. But maybe not. I dinnae think I ken who this is.

It was the close up of the girl on the beach, her woollen scarf wrapped twice round her neck.

Big Ellen covered her mouth for a second with her hand and pulled the hand down over her chin. She gave Dawn a familiar look, one she used to get all the time. Folk would turn from Linda with a nod and a smile, but they would take their time over Dawn, shake heads, purse lips. Not able to see who she looked like. Mummy or Daddy.

This lassie looks a wee bit like you.

Big Ellen turned the page and looked at the next picture, the couple at the beach.

Now, he's a handsome one. They dinnae make them like that any mair, she said sadly with a bit of a smile.

The bikes suddenly stopped, the zip-zip-zip of their engines slowing to a low growl.

Gran, I'm going! Jock said, and he jumped outside off the top step. Big Ellen got up but she was too late to stop him. Outside an engine backfired, and some shocked birds overhead screeched Two! Two! Two!

What's happening? Dawn said.

You need to go.

Can I come back another time?

We've had a lot of trouble, tae be honest, Big Ellen said.

She had only looked at one picture, and now she was pushing the album into Dawn's hands and Dawn towards the door.

Well, maybe. But my memory's nae so good. Ye need someone who can remember way back. Sorry I couldnae be mair use.

Thanks anyway, Dawn said.

140

Outside the site was suddenly busy, people hurrying from one van to another or in through the gate. A teenage girl held the hands of two children and ran towards a car, and a man was crawling through the fence with a dog in each hand. The bikes were zipping round the site, looping around them.

Don't just stand there! someone shouted.

Dawn ran to the car.

Will you take me down the hill?

The girl nodded.

The car had a smell of the earth and of oil. As soon as the doors were shut the girl started the engine and they pulled away with a skid. Outside people were scattering into the woods, disappearing into the trees. Others stood guard in the doorways of their homes. One man had a walking stick and he was shouting at the bikes, but the words were lost.

✳ COO ✳

Auld Betsy, 1954

Oh, me! Anither birthday! Sixty-five years oan the go, an ah'm
puffin an blowin like a jenny whistle jist tae reach the top ae the
Lane. They gie ye cards fae Woolies nooadays, the grandbairns.
Birthday wishes to my Grandmother. Bonnie things aw fancied up
wi nice pictures an sparklies. Ah put them in ma tin tae keep.

They've aw gone tae bed doun at the hoose, but the louns are
in the store bailin the woollens afore the lorry comes in the
mornin. Jock's helpin an aw, lendin an extra pair ae haunds.
He's nae made fer the back-breakin work. The wools an some ae
the mendin, that's whit he does. Nae built fer heavin the scrap
aroun like Duncan. Jock wis a seekly bairnie, wouldnae stop
screamin aw the first winter after he wis born. George made me
a sunk tae carry him in, a stockin stuffed wi straw. Ah carted
Wee Jock roun ma waist in thon sunk aw day every day. The
minute ah put him doun he'd be muntin an howlin.

George had a hard time. His daft auld mither thought the
fairies had stole Jock awa fae us, left ahint ae them wan ae their
ain wicked craiturs! O ho! Ho! Ha! Ha! Oh, me! Ma Jock. Ma
youngest. He always wis the brains ae the brood! He'll be up the
top ae this hill wantin his tea an his paper.

When ah reach Hill Street ah hear voices comin fae the store.
Ah gie a knock afore goin in. It's aie toasty wi the wee stove goin,
even though it's nae much mair than a shed wi a warehoose
ahint it. They'll sit in there fer oors, oor men, hale lang evenins
bletherin, an we'll nae hear a peep doun in the hoose as lang as
they hae a flask brought up.

It's aw hustle an bustle the night, though. There's aw the rags tae sort afore the van arrives. A great pile ae claes is heaped in the warehoose, under the skins hangin aff the beams. Pile has tae be separated intae three: non-woollens, dark woollens an light woollens, then bailed up, ready tae go.

'Faraboots are ye wantin yer flask, sons?'

'Aye, the sill,' goes the Bissaker, busy tyin a bundle.

Jock's rubbin a scabbit cloth atween his wrists tae see if it has wool in it. Aye. That een's wool. Ah can tell jist tae look. He throws it tae the light pile. That's the best stuff. Ah did this aince an aw, sortin the rags, a fair few birthdays ago noo! Ho! Ha! Ha! The light stuff's whit yer wantin. The fowk'll come tae tak that awa, pay us a good price. They'll dae a wee bittie magic, turn it pink or yella or green, whitever they're wantin in London these days (could be blue wi orange dots fer aw ah ken). Then they mak it intae somethin else alltaegither. A braw suit, a blanket fer a bed, a bunnet fer an auld manny, a toy fer a bairn, anything. Could be some ae the wool in that dark pile went through ma ain fammels years ago. O! Ho! Ha! Ha! Weel, ye nivver ken!

Ah sigh an put the tea doun for them.

'Mind an drink it afore it gets cal,' ah say. 'Jock, ah've yer paper an aw.'

He gets on his tramplers an comes ower. 'That's grand, Ma,' he tells me, like always. He's a good boy.

'Yer a good boy, eh? Ma son. It'll soon be a nice dilly up wi yer tea,' ah go.

Oh, me! He doesnae like me talkin aboot his love life like that. Maks Duncan an the Bissaker laugh at him. O ho! Ha! Ha! Ha! Ah jist dae it fer a bit ae fun, though. Ho! Ha! Ha! Ha! He pours hisself a cup ae the tea, sits doun oan the bench an opens his paper.

'Whit's that ye've got? Local news, is it? Read it oot,' says the Bissaker.

'You can read it fine fer yersel,' Jock goes.

'Aye, well,' he goes. 'Ah'm oot ae practice. An can ye nae see ah'm busy here?'

'O ho! Ha! Ha!' ah go. 'Go oan, Jock, leave him be. The Bissaker's nae a learned man like yersel. He's a chiel ae the road, is that nae it, Wullie? Good man, ye are. A true chiel ae the road. Go oan, Jock. Hae a look in yer paper fer me, ah'm wantin tae ken if oor Eddie's Ebeneezer's in it. Curly wis tellt he got sentenced tae twenty days in the quad.'

'Twenty, is that right?' goes Duncan.

'Aye,' ah breathe, an stare doun at the paper wi its nonsense ae letters. 'Shaness!'

'Gie me a minute. Ah'm after the bill at the Playhouse first,' goes Jock. Ah see Duncan an the Bissaker throw wan another a look an share a wee nod. Jock'll nae be after some dilly? ah think tae massel. Oh, me! Ma Jock. Weel, ah hope she's a good lassie. No doubt she'll be country hantle, but ah need tae see ma sons aw married, maist ae aw the wee lad. Till that happens, ah cannae settle ma heid.

Ah still think aboot whit the Batchie Woman tellt me thon time. Her an her visions. Ah forgot it fer a wee while, till it turned oot she wis right aw alang aboot Auld Jessie. Poor Jessie went an dropped doun stane cal atween the gates ae the cemetery, jist like the Batchie Woman saw.

Oh, me! Afore Jock's married she tellt me. That's whit she went an said. She's a coarse auld bitch. Damn her an her visions! Ye should nivver dae that, nivver tell fowk the bad news. There's rules! Oh, me! Bad news is fer readin oot the paper after it's aw ower, nae aff ae fowk's palms. Ye keep it secret. Every wan ae us kens that. Oh, me! Ah've nae peace in this life. If ah wis wan ae the country hantle, there'd be fowk spittin at her like a witch fer sayin whit she did. *Afore ma boy's a married man.* Shaness!

Ah dinnae want tae scare him. Look at the loun! Nose glued intae his cinema pages! Ah stick ma auld fammels intae ma pouch an wind ma mither's rosary tight roun them, press doun oan the cross wi ma thumb. Nae a day goes by ah dinnae feel the words ae that woman in ma bones, scratchin, burnin like a curse, thon Batchie Woman. Oh, me!

Jock turns his page, laughs tae hisself at somethin.

'Whit's that?' Duncan asks.

'Somethin about neds in daft shapes.' He reads oot a few snippets.

Queer Potatoes. Mr Alexander Reid has on view in the window of his shop, 307 High Street Elgin, two remarkable potatoes grown in the Forres district. One curiously irregular, shaped almost like a frog, weighs no less than 5lb 5oz. It was grown on the farm of Newton of Struthers, tenanted by Mr Peterson. The other potato, which somewhat resembles a duck in appearance, was grown on Mr Mackessak's farm of Sanquar Mains and weighs 2lbs.

100 more houses for Elgin, non-traditional type.'

'Almost sunless month. Sunshine and rainfall were recorded at Gordon Castle Gardens, Fochabers. This month there were a total of ten completely sunless days, and ten days totalling 4.3 hours.

'The Forres Junior Farmers ploughing match took place at Cotfield House

Alves on Wednesday and was won by a Mr James McInnes.

Bishopmill Mutual Improvement Association are pleased to announce that the Saturday dance has now resumed in Bishopmill Hall. Come and enjoy a mixed programme of all your old favourite dances, modern and old tyme. Music by the ever popular Collegians. Admission 2s. 8 – 11:30pm.

'Does it nae say anything oan oor Ebby, no?'

'I cannae find anythin, Ma. Doesnae look like it. The bloody McPhees are in trouble again, though.'

'Wheesht, Jock! Dinnae talk ae oor folk like that. It's nae right. Shaness!'

'They gie us a bad name, Ma. Everyone kens we're related.' He looks up at the Bissaker. 'You ken if it wisnae for those eejit twins, I'd ae been able tae go away an dae National Service, like our Peter.'

Ah tell him nae tae talk bad ae oor kind, but ah ken it's true. The McPhee lot are aie in trouble. It wisnae always like that, though. Ma ain mither wis Ginger Frank McPhee's mither's sister. Or mebbies she wis his daddy's sister, or wis his mither mammy's cousin? Doesnae matter. But when ah wis young aw ae us shared camps wi McPhees. Half ae them ah cried Uncle or Aunt or Cousin. They were nae such a bad lot then. A good laugh. Three ae ma brothers an wan ae ma sisters married theirs an aw. An thon McPhees were great wi animals. That wis their gift. They could talk tae the horses, that's how it seemed. Ma daddy did a fair few deals wi them. Spit an shook, the auld wye. We got aw oor yokes fae the McPhees.

Maist ae that faimly went aff wi the show people after work oan the farms dried up. They ran awa wi the circus! O ho! Ha! Ha! We were quite a breed in oor day, but, afore we joined the clowns. There wis some real gangsters amang us! That's whit fowk'll tell ye! O ho! Ha! Ha! Ha!

Pity, whit the settlin's done. It maks fowk bitter. Ye dinnae see wan another. It sits fine wi some, an others tak tae the drink. It's nae a lie. That Ginger's aie in the whisky. He let his twin boys run roun like wild animals since they were jist wee lambs. It's nae wonder whit's happened tae them. Shaness! We hae tae deny where we come fae when we leave the hoose noo. It's the ainly wye tae keep oor heids up.

Ma Jock. He's the ainly wan carries oan aboot the travellin noo, him an his adventurin, seein the world. Rest ae us barely dream ae it these days. Barely dream. Shaness! Ye nivver mention oor past. The Bissaker an Duncan tak comfort in the drink, maistly when business is poor. Ah can keep ma een oan them.

Hawker's bad record. – In Court on Monday, Frank McPhee was sentenced to three months' imprisonment for theft. Baillie Wittet, who was on the bench, said that the charge was a very serious and could not be lightly dealt with. The accused had been at the court on two occasions this year already, under charges of assault and breach of the peace. On these occasions he was offered a fine. On Monday, McPhee pleaded guilty to the theft of a bicycle, the handlebars of which he had later painted green in an attempt to evade discovery. The court heard how on arrest, McPhee had appealed for immediate release, promising to give up drink. Mr McPhee is a character known locally for collecting and selling pine cones, and for appearing to consume a fair amount of drink with the proceeds.

'Poor Thomasina,' ah say. 'God rest her soul. Her family's aie the talk ae the toun wi her in her grave. Whit can ye dae, though, eh? Whit can ye dae? The tobies ken them too weel noo. O ho! Ye ken whit they tellt me?'

'Whit's that, Ma?'

'They're watched sae closely they get lifted if they dare tae sae much as fart! O! Ho! Ha! O ho!'

Ah get up tae go, shufflin ma hem ower the flair. At the door ah turn back, screw ma mou like a coo's arse an blow a 'pfrrrt' noise. 'Oh! There we go! They'll be comin tae arrest me! O ho!'

The boys laugh till Duncan gets the sneezes.

'Mind an get some fresh air soon, sons. Tak a wee stroll. Wullie, you send them oot!'

'Right ye are, Betsy,' goes the Bissaker.

'An aw yous stay awa fae those McPhee boys. Ah'm nae wantin oor name in the paper next week.'

It's dark as the Deil's den oot tonight. Nae a star in the sky. When ah get intae the hoose ah hear Big Ellen snorin. Ah light a candle an get ready fer ma bed quiet as a wee moosie. At the sink

148

ah've ma auld mirror. Ah look at massel in the light ae the wee flame while the pannie runs, pull ma hair roun like a length ae rope, untie it at the bottom, wind apart the twists. Ma hair's been slate grey fer years an ah've worn it this wye ever since ma weddin day. Almaist reaches doun tae far ma waist once wis! O ho! Ha! Ha!

George loved ma tresses when we met. Used tae be him untied them fer ma each night afore bed. He wis aie gentle. Jock taks after him. He's the ainly wan. Duncan's got somethin ae George's looks, but he has the quick temper ma ain father had, an Jugs is stubborn, affae set in his wyes. He learnt that fae me! There's a deep wrinkle atween ma eyes fae aw the frownin an sulkin ah've done! O ho! Ho! Ha! Wan look at ma face these days an fowk ken they've met their match. Ah dinnae get much bother. O ho! Ho! Ha! Ha!

Ah struggle oot ae ma lang black claes an pull oan ma night-dress afore blowin oot the candle an cooriein doun. In ma half sleep that article fae the *Courrant* goes roun an roun ma heid, an ah toss an turn.

There's Ginger Frank oan his bicycle wi the green handlebars, drunken cheeks, rosy-red like Coco the Cloun, jugglin wi his pine cones. An somehow in the dream the bicycle turns intae a big orange coo. Duncan's there, an Jugs. Ma Jock's in a plane flyin ower the big top, wi a lang ribbon oot the back that says *'Birthday wishes for my dear mother'*. But then it's nae a ribbon, it's ma ain hair, the colour ae a storm, aw loose an flowin oot, an nae a star in the sky.

The next day ah'm gettin the quines ready tae go oot fer cinders. A good bit ae exercise fer the lot ae us. We tak the pram tae fill. Rachel will ride wi Nancy oan the wye, Wee Betsy hangin aff the handlebar, an when the pram's full we'll walk hame, except Nancy, who'll sit oan top ae the cinders.

As we go oot the front door, Wee Betsy runs her haund alang the scuffs oan the wall.

'Whit did that, Granny? Wis it Jock wi the bikes?'

'No, quine,' ah tell her. 'That wis the coo. Ye ken aboot that.'

'The coo?' Rachel says.

'Aye. The routler. The coo.'

We bump intae Jock at the gate. He looks aw chuffed wi hissel an he's haudin a thing like a wee black lunch pail oan a strap.

'Wee Betsy,' he goes, pointin tae the auld wall. 'Go over there. You go an all, Rachel.'

'Photo!' Rachel shouts. Betsy starts askin how he got a camera, an the twa ae them get so excited ah hae tae tell them tae wheesht.

'A pal lent it. Stand there. Okay.'

Wee Betsy bends ower tae pull her kilt doun a bittie. It's gettin too wee fer her, an her daddy teases her fer her knobbly knees. Then she stands grinnin wi her chin up, an Jock maks the camera tak a photie. He turns roun.

'Ma! Say cheese.'

'O ho! Ho! Ha!' ah go. 'Whit's ye wantin a photie ae an auld wifey fer?' But Uncle Jock's already taken another.

'That's the photo shoot over,' he tells us, an he waves an runs awa up the Lane tae the store. Wi aw the excitement ah almost forget whit it wis me an the lassies were oot fer. The sight ae the pram reminds me. Poor Wee Nancy's still sittin there good as gold, waitin tae go fer the coal. We didnae even get a photie ae her.

'Tell us the coo story,' says Rachel aw ae a sudden.

'Again? No, bairns. Ah've tellt ye aboot thon daft coo a hunnerd times afore.'

'Sooo,' Wee Betsy's whinin. 'Ye tell us other stories a hundred times.'

An then ah remember the dream ah had, oor Ginger Frank in the circus an thon bicycle turnin intae a coo. Ah laugh at massel. O ho! Ha! Ha!

'Fair enough, bairnies,' ah go. 'Ah'll tell ye fer the last time.

An ainly cause it wis the wan time thon Uncle Frank McTootie ae yours haed his name put in the paper fer a good deed! The wan an ainly time.'

'Goodie!' goes Rachel. 'The coo!'

'Quiet, noo! When we first moved intae Hill Terrace we used tae jist bide the winter, me an yer grandfather George an oor bairns. It wis afore the twa ae yous were even thought ae. We still travelled every summer. Back then, the farmers used tae tak the coos tae the market alang the High Street. Right past the bottom ae oor Lane! Can ye imagine whit that wis like, bairns? O ho! Ho! Ha! ha! So wan day, this coo, great orange beast it wis, managed tae run awa fae the herd. An far did it go?'

'Up Lady Lane!' they both shout.

'The very same! Up oor Lane. An nae ainly that. It didnae stop there. This coo came right intae oor front door, which wis left wide open while yer daft daddy wis standin like a useless craitur at yer mammy's gate. He wis sae taken wi the lassie next door, he nivver even seen this beast walkin intae his ain hoose till it wis too late. The coo crossed the threshold.

'By the time Duncan got tae the door he found he couldnae get back inside. This coo's arse wis sae wide it filled the hale ae the hallway. O ho! Ho! Ha! Ha! Yer daddy wis nae very good wi cattle. He wis a wee bit feart an he didnae ken whit tae dae. But he gied this coo a wallop oan the haunches wi a stick, then a wee tug oan its tail. "Help!" he cried oot. "Daddy, come quick."'

Wee Betsy an Rachel are almost greetin fae laughter cause they ken whit's next. Ah go oan.

'George wis lightin the fire in the room on the bottom. O ho! Hearin Duncan's voice he popped his heid intae the hall. Jist then the coo let oot the maist angry MOOOOO! any human has ever heard. An yer granddaddy wis face tae face wi this monster. O ho! Ho! Well, George jumped back, an the coo, haein had enough ae the slaps Duncan wis giein it, bolted forward. Beast took itself right up the dancers! Right up tae yer room, quines,

151

where it nigh-on gied poor Auntie Jeannie a heart attack as it lay doun oan her newly laundered sheets an brought her hale beadstead tae the flair wi an almighty CLAP!'

Rachel claps her haunds. 'Did anyone tak a photie, Granny?'

'Aye, quines, they did. A manny fae the paper came, alang wi three or four farmers, a group ae tourists fae London, the hale ae the Lane an twa tobies'.

'What did they do?'

'Oh, me! They roared an shoved at thon coo. Brought handfuls ae the greenest grass tae tempt it. Tied tows roun it. Could they move the beast? Nae a chance. The thing wis as stubborn as yer auld granny! O ho! Ha! Ha! Ha! Nae a soul could mak it budge back doun those dancers. There wis three ae them mannys at its arse, an another twa ae them at the bottom ae the dancers haudin oantae a tow tied roun the coo's neck. Heavin an ho-in aw mornin. There wis sweat pourin aff these mannys. Ah wis feart they were gonnae shoot the poor beast. But they didnae have tae. Cause dae ye ken who saved the day?'

'Who?'

'It wis yer uncle Frank McTootie. Ginger Frank, the wan an ainly, tough as auld boots wi his flamin red hair. He wis the ainly manny wi the gaul tae stand beside the coo oan the dancers, orra-lookin beast that it wis. He stood jist wan step below it. An he took that coo in his bloody great arms an whispered sweet nothins in its lug. He stroked an smooth-talked the craitur doun, wan step at a time. Ah swear he looked intae that coo's een an it fell in love wi him. Weel seen it took him fer a bull! O ho! Ho! Ha! Ha!

'That Thursday next there wis a photie in the paper. It wis the coo, safely back ootside the door an giein thon Ginger Frank a smooch the likes ae whit ye'll ainly see oan the silver screen. Oh, me!'

We mak oor wye tae the gasworks. Ah allow a wee detour past the grocer's tae gie the quines a look at thon queer neds they put in the paper. Rachel says they're 'silly tatties,' an ah say, 'Aye, jist like us!' The pair ae them can go haukin the neds next year. They can tak the van tae the fields wi their mammy an she'll gie them each a wee bucket fae Woolworths tae fill aw on their ain. Then the farmer'll gie them some pocket money.

Nancy's happy in the pram, flappin her arms aboot. Rachel helps me tae push, an Wee Betsy goes oot in front. She scuffs her toes cause ah cannae go fast enough fer her wi the heavy pram an ma auld bones. Aye, weel, it's wan too mony birthdays has seen tae that!

Dawn

The park was exactly the same as she remembered it. There was a lake with an island for boats to circle, pedalos that rudely churned the water, and swans turning away their long necks. The only difference was the small painted booth that had once sold drinks and snacks. It looked empty now.

Dad and Maeve were feeding the ducks. The park was Dad's favourite place. He took a stroll through it every day to stretch his legs and get a bit of space. He'd started using a stick, but right now he was waving it to shoo the geese that frightened Maeve. It was strange, she thought, how small a thing could bring two people closer. How little it took.

Linda was with her on the bench.

Look at that! Linda said. He loves her.

It had been his idea, Sunday in the park and all his girls together.

Mother came back from the café with ice cream, coffee in polystyrene cups for Linda and Dawn, and two long packets of sugar. She handed an ice cream to Maeve and kept one for herself, a strawberry Cornetto. She took Dad's hand and they started to walk round the lake, Maeve following. They'd never been the holding-hands type but they seemed to lean on each other a wee bit now.

Dawn's best memory of living with them was of Sunday afternoons, a big lunch and flippy dreams on a full belly. She was always sent upstairs for a nap, and in the front room Dad played his accordion, tapping his foot in time. When Mother closed Dawn's bedroom door she rolled over and looked at the wall. The paper was patterned with green leaves, and she'd stare at it through half-shut eyes, listening to Dad's accordion floating up the stairs. Ooom pa pa, ooom pa pa.

154

The wallpaper was magic. The leafy pattern shuffled itself up and turned into pictures. There were wee men with top hats walking their dogs. On fine days they doffed their hats and the dogs wagged their tails, and in bad weather the ladies carried brollies to keep the wet off. They wore bell-shaped skirts like Mary Poppins in the film. Everyone danced to Dad's waltz. Ooom pa pa, ooom pa pa. The leafy shoes tip-tapped her to sleep.

The day she went to live with Shirley, she sat on the bed watching her mother folding vests, rolling socks into balls and flinging them at the suitcase like peeled tatties into a pan. Dad was in the doorway.

Can I take the wallpaper? she'd said. Dad laughed and Mother got cross with him.

They were across the other side of the lake now.

Imagine being with someone that long, Linda said.

Dawn shrugged. She wanted to drink her coffee but it was too hot, so instead she fiddled with the finger shape packet of sugar. It had Italian writing on it. *Zucchero*.

You seen Warren yet?

Dawn shook her head and they sat in silence for a while.

I've seen him, Linda said. Quite a bit. He's with someone.

Is he?

Linda offered a cigarette.

I thought I should let you know. So you're prepared.

No wonder he hadn't shown his face. Dawn felt a bulge in her throat like the packet of sugar she was nipping at both ends. A young couple was walking round the lake arm in arm. They looked happy. The girl was tall and thin with a strangely large head, a short skirt with knee-high boots and a white knitted hat that made her look like a cotton bud. They stopped for a second and the girl put her cheek near to the boy's as if she was asking a question, thinking about kissing. Dawn noticed a wee hole in the girl's black tights, just behind the right knee, a hole the size of a cigarette end with a white circle underneath. When the couple walked away the wee hole behind the girl's knee winked back at Dawn, disappearing and reappearing with each step. 'Bye-bye!' it seemed to say, its numb 'blink-blink' becoming Dawn's for the rest of the day.

She put the lid on her coffee. It was still too hot. Shall we get going?

Suppose so.

Dawn imagined the boy with the girl later on, stroking his fingertip through the hole in her tights. Warren would do a thing like that. He could be gentle in small ways.

What's she like? Dawn said.

Who?

His new woman.

But Linda said she'd never seen them together.

Dawn hated the name she'd ended up with. Double 'D'. A letter that always stood for horrible things. She should have stuck to Hendry. Someone had made a joke of the new name for the wedding speeches.

Hasn't it Dawn Dunn ye yet?

Ha ha ha.

What about you? Linda said.

What do you mean?

Anyone on the scene?

Dawn laughed, but she was thinking of Ally.

No gossip here, she said. Sorry.

Dad and Mother were coming back round the water. Each held one of Maeve's hands and they were swinging her between them. They were chanting together, making her swing higher each time.

A-one-and-a-two-and-a-one-and-a-two!

They set her back on her feet and she kept saying it. A-one-and-a-two-and-a-one-and-a-two!

You could get a job in that café there, Dad said.

Don't think so, Dad.

Why not? You've had a job before, haven't you?

She'd done loads of jobs, temping in offices (she'd enjoyed the feel of warm photocopies on her lap and the taste of envelopes), delivering leaflets (sneaking a look in people's front windows), stocking supermarket shelves (the sound of the wee machine that stuck price labels on), cleaning (as long as the house was empty and she didn't have to make small talk), and walking dogs (they didn't answer back).

She'd never thought of what to do next.

Later, after tea, Dad read the paper and Mother did her knitting. Maeve had fallen asleep between them on the sofa.

You seen this, Dawn, eh?

Dad held up the article in the local paper about the old woman. Dawn nodded.

They say she's maybe the auldest person in the world. Fancy that, eh? She's been auld for seventy years.

Poor lady, Mother said. They should leave her alone.

Dawn wanted to be alone herself, so she went up to have a look at the room she used to sleep in. It looked no different. The wallpaper had never changed and even the furniture was much the same. Linda had got her own place years ago so they just used the room for storage now. Dad's uniform was in there, retired on a hanger. She stroked her hand over the black suit. It was still perfectly pressed. The silver insignia on the shoulders were gleaming bright as the day they were minted. She'd never asked him what the numbers and symbols meant. The tall black hat, the bit he'd always let her play with, was nowhere to be seen. Probably in a box somewhere. She remembered him coming home from the station and letting her wear it even though it was way too big. She used to make him laugh like the song, fooling round with the hat pulled over her nose. The laughing policeman. Her Dad.

The accordion was by the door.

Are you making a mess up there? Wilma shouted at the bottom of the stairs.

Dawn jumped. Down in a sec.

There were some old books piled in a corner. She sat on the floor, pulled a book from the pile and flipped back the cover. Notes were pencilled on the blank pages and there was a school certificate pasted in the front.

Shirley Hendry, Senior Prize for English, Elgin Academy 1953.

She flicked a few pages. More pencil notes in the margins. Doodles. Shirley had never done doodles. Dawn was just about to throw it back in the cupboard when a scribble caught her eye. Two names.

Lolly and Jock.

Dawn's mouth went dry. She swallowed, closed the book and got to her feet, stepping over the accordion. She lifted it by the straps, felt the weight of it, like a child, and piggy-backed it over her shoulders. As she left the room she stopped to look at her reflection in the mirror by the door. She tidied her hair, pressed her lips together. She was sure there was something she was meant to see.

Downstairs she manhandled the accordion off her shoulders and onto Dad's lap. Give it a squeeze. I've not heard you play in ten years. I'll be in the garden.

She breathed in the cold evening air. Dad was getting ready to play in the house. It's like riding a bicycle, he shouted. He started with a long chord, a great sigh on the bellows, breathing life back into the old thing. And then came a tune she remembered from a long time ago. Ooom pa pa, ooom pa pa.

She could still taste the dust from that book.

Dawn looked into the trees. The wind blew and some leaves fluttered to the ground, dancing to the music. Dad had taught Maeve a song that day he took her to the beach, and she'd been singing it over and over ever since, a silly old number about lollipops. Shirley used to hum it sometimes, 'On the Good Ship Lollipop'. No, that was something else. It was starting to get on her nerves.

She pictured the girl in the photos, the long hair and glossy smile. Lolly and Jock. Jock and Lolly. She lit a cigarette, and as she smoked she tried to blow that song out of her head, but it didn't work. What she needed was the oldest fortune-teller in the world.

✳ LINES ✳

Jock, 1954

I wait for her at the bus station, opposite the hydro-electric and the wee shop, leaning on the rough wall, pressing the heel ae my shoe against it. I tilt my head back, blow smoke intae the sky. Today there's the first hint ae sun we've had in a month, nae that it'll last. But as long as it doesnae start pouring down like Ma promised when she saw me getting my coat on, I'll no complain. What was it that health leaflet said about the sun's rays? Something about super-vitamins, turn you intae a superhero? Well, anyway, I left them tae it, Saturday in the Lane, my brothers all lazing about the yard, the kinchins being fussed over by Curly, the wireless on, a kettle boiling. 'Are ye nae after a cup ae tea afore yer awa?' Ma shouted. I was already out the door and halfway down the Lane, my mind set on Lolly.

I wish I had that cup ae tea in my hands now. It might be sunny, but there fairly is a nip in the air. Here she is, though. Hair tied up. She's in a brown skirt, same one she had on the first time I clapped eyes on her. Folds ae it dance below the bottom ae her blue coat, the hem stroking her stockings as she runs. I pretend I've nae seen her till she's across the road, and when she reaches me she puts her arms round my waist, looks up, kisses me. Just a peck on the lips and a wee smile.

'Told them I was at the library,' she whispers. She pinches my cigarette out my fingers, takes a quick puff, and sticks it in my mouth. I take a long sook on it and put my arm round her, pulling her close tae warm me up. The old trout beside us tut-tuts. You'd think she'd just seen Burt Lancaster and Deborah

161

Kerr canoodling half naked in the waves in thon picture. Lolly furrows her brow like the old woman and gives me one ae her smiles that says they can shush and tut all they like, she's no listening tae them.

The Lossie bus pulls up by the wooden shelter and we form a line with the other passengers, ready with change for the tickets. When I go tae the beach with the family we walk there and take the bus hame, but I made sure I kept back enough of the week's wages tae get the bus in both directions today. We dinnae say anything. Naebody ever says a word in the bus queue. It's like the ticket queue at the station.

I've never been on a train before. Working in a station and the closest I've been is the edge ae the platform! I'd like tae. I suppose if I had been on a train I'd have been too excited tae think ae much else, so maybe that's where it comes from, this nae talking business.

Flying would be ten times better, though. If I was going in a plane I wouldnae be able tae breathe or eat for days just thinking about it, let alone talk about the weather with folk.

I gie Lolly the eye as she squeezes past me in the narrow aisle ae the bus. I want tae grab her. 'What a dish!' I think, and laugh, watching her cheeks go hot cause she kens what's on my mind. My Lolo's a peach! I take the bag with the sand-wiches and the blanket, and follow her up tae the top floor, where usually you can hae it tae yourself cause the auld wifeys willnae climb the dancers. She turns round at the top and smiles back at me over the rail. There's a group ae kids climbing up behind me with pokes ae chips. They'll go tae the back seat, they aie do.

'Nah,' I go tae Lolly. 'Other way. Let's sit up front.'

Lolly's been on loads ae trains. That's where we met, at the station, even though we never spoke tae each other there. But I saw her keeking at me over her ma's shoulder. When I saw her at the Two Red Shoes that time, I just went straight up and asked her tae dance. It was easy and she said yes. After, she told me she'd liked me for ages.

Once the driver gets the engine going, folk start tae feel more at ease. I put my arm round Lolly's shoulder and she puts her hand on my knee. We sit touching. It'll be a half hour or so till we get tae the beach, and the best bit ae the journey's when we go past the base with the big aircraft hangars. You get a good view from the bus.

'I ken all the planes, Lolly. I can tell them apart just tae hear them.' She doesnae say anything so I go on. 'I could fly planes one day. What do you think? Would you nae fancy me in thon uniform?'

She laughs. 'You've been watching too many films, Jock Terns. Anyway, my da hates the planes flying overhead. He preferred the beach before, you ken, when it was all peaceful.'

'I suppose,' I go. I'm disappointed she's nae more keen on the idea ae me bein a pilot. I love the sound ae that word. Pilot. I thought even Lolly's father could be proud ae a job like that. Lolly doesnae take me seriously, though. 'Must be a great view from up there,' I add, 'the sea and the beach and the hills. Do you nae think?'

'Aye, till you crash. My uncle was shot down in the war. Did I nae tell you about that? You're lucky you've nae got your letter yet.'

My letter. The lie I told her, them forgetting tae call me up for National Service, rises in my throat. It was a stupid thing tae make up, cause of course Lolly believed me. Now she keeps mentioning it, aie worried the damn thing's in the next post. I dinnae want tae tell her there'll no be a letter. I'd have to say I failed the medical cause ae my feet, but anyone can see my feet are nae gammy. Nothing wrong with my tramplers! And even if there was, you dinnae need feet tae fly a plane.

It was my bloody cousins' fault I couldnae go, the twins, Benny and Isaac McPhee. They turned up drunk and started a

163

fight outside the office, made it look like I was one ae the gang, one ae The Desperates. The whole town cries them that cause each ae them looks like Desperate Dan, big, hairy and stupid. I dinnae want Lolly thinking I'm one ae that lot. Anyway, all three ae us were exempted, me for my feet, them for what they said was 'educational failure'. I suppose the services just dinnae want tae deal with too many from our background, never mind that we fought in the war like everyone else. My uncles were pipers. They were brave.

I wonder if Lolly's dad went, but I dinnae ask. My father was too old, but the Bissaker went the second time round. He was under-age. We've photies ae him back home in a wee cherry-shape hat with painted squares round it, standing all important-looking next tae a big, bonnie horse. It's Jugs that paints all our photies. He learnt it off an Italian prisoner ae war he was escorting up tae Orkney where they built thon famous red and white church inside a Nissen hut. Jugs has aie been good at painting. When I look at our photies, sometimes I wonder what happened tae the Italian who taught him. Maybe he stayed and opened an ice cream shop, or maybe he had a sweetheart back in Italy who he missed too much. Who knows.

I cannae think what tae say about Lolly's uncle who died, so I just tell her nae tae worry cause I'll be safe, willnae crash or get myself shot down. She stays quiet a wee bit too long after that, and I wonder if I've upset her.

'Hey, what's that you've got?' she goes all ae a sudden. 'It's digging intae me.'

I was going tae wait for a nicer time tae gie it tae her, but I'm just glad we can get off the subject ae planes crashing out the sky. It's the slipper the Bissaker gave me. I remembered tae take it today. I'd put it in the chest by my bed and forgot all about it till now.

'Oh, that,' I go, feeling a bit embarrassed. 'Aye. Well, it's for you. Just thought you'd like it.' The button on my pocket's a bit stiff and I have tae lift myself off my seat a bit, wriggle round till it comes free. Then I lean over sideways tae slide out the slipper. It's nae wrapped or anything, and I notice now there's a wee hole on the front, just a tiny hole where the pink lining shows through. I should've mended that.

Lolly's really pleased anyhow. She brushes her fingertips over the velvet and fur, then turns it over tae look at the heel. It's the sole she seems most interested in. She traces her finger over the wear, the scratches and indents that would ae been put there a hundred years ago by its owner.

'Aye,' I go. 'I might ae waited till yer birthday or something, but Wee Betsy's had her mitts on it already. I thought it best tae gie it tae you now, before it vanished for good.'

Lolly laughs at this cause I'm aie telling her stories about my nieces. She says Betsy sounds like a wee so-an-so, and I tell her she's right.

'I can probably mend that for you there, if you prefer it neat,' I mumble, pointing at the wee hole in the slipper. But Lolly likes it fine how it is. She says she doesnae mind the tufty bits.

'That's right. You like them a wee bit scruffy!' I laugh, and gie her a wink.

For a second she looks like she's going tae slap me, but then she puts the slipper gently intae her bag and holds my hand instead. Further down the road she lays her head on my shoulder. Her hair smells good. One ae the kids behind whistles and I wonder if it's cause ae us. Lolly ignores them and she tells me I smell good too. That'll be all the scrubbing with the soap this morning behind Rachel's ears, her screaming like a piglet while I held her by the collar. You could have grown tatties on her, she was that clarted with muck. But I'll nae tell Lolly about that. We go the rest ae the journey sitting quietly and watching the fields go past.

The tide's out, as if the beach was waiting for us, dragged back like a wide open door. It's hundreds ae lines. Nae just three strips, earth, water and air, like in the pictures Wee Betsy and Rachel paint. At the shore the sand is flat and smooth, covered with water, still, shallow as skin. The water reflects the sky, brush-stroke clouds, gies them a gold outline. It pools round the odd shell, darker there, like freckle stains on my old shaving mirror. Gentle breakers stroke, in, out, frothy like lace. Wee pebbles flip, laupin like fishes as waves surge back. They make ripples in the sand. Tracks have been left by folk dragging their feet along the shore, heads down, combing for cowries or staring out tae sea. Where the sand's hard and wet, a scattering ae stones, black in this light, has been tossed out ae the ocean by the night-time's crashing waves. They lie like seeds sown along a border. There's a row ae casings left by the lug worms, piles ae wet sand coiled like broken bootlaces, and higher up, a bank ae rotting seaweed, a line ae dark dashes along the beach, alive with tiny flies and the wee creatures the birds feed from. The coarser sand is at the top, strewn with dry seaweed, rocks and driftwood.

Lolly's taking off her shoes, rolling down her stockings, getting ready tae run. Her feet are beautiful, pink with the cold. Behind us is the long path with the odd bench keeking over a wall ae dunes and grasses, and the path finally meets the water at the Covesea lighthouse in the distance. This is where all the lines end, as if the whole world's being drawn intae that one point, waves and ships, sand and seaweed, sky and clouds, birds and all the wee beasties.

At the other side ae the lighthouse I imagine another beach, the lines spilling out again like sand through an hourglass. Everything here's reflected there. The same, but different.

Lolly throws her bag tae her feet and tells me I look all pensive standing there. I'm nae sure what 'pensive' means, but I do like watching her, skirt hitched up, bare legs skipping. It reminds me ae that picture again, *From Here tae Eternity*, that scene on the beach. I imagine me and Lolly doing something like that. I have tae push the idea tae the back ae my head.

Her hair flies out behind her. I follow. Our bodies make long shadows, ghosts in the wet surface. Our footprints draw new lines in the sand, striking through all the others. We pick up pebbles. Lolly finds a small round one that glitters with mica in the sunlight. She asks if I want tae skim it, cause she's no good. It'll be a waste if she uses it. I take the pebble but dinnae throw it away. Instead I put it in my pocket. Later I'll make a wee hole so I can wear it round my neck on a cord.

'My mother was born near the lighthouse,' I tell Lolly when we sit down for our sandwiches. In my pocket I'm playing with the pebble.

Ma was born in one ae the caves. It's where the family aie used tae stay in winter. Ma's full ae stories about it. She swears it was a smugglers' cove once, and that her great-grandfather was the middle man, selling stuff on land and keeping a fee for the family. It was a good system. The ships barely had tae drop anchor.

That was over long before Ma was born, though. She says once they were moved intae a cave, they never left it empty till spring. They'd tae fight tae keep the spot tae theirselves, so there was aie someone on guard. One man would bide in the cave while the others went tae work.

These days it's just a big, empty hole in the cliff, but there's still the old marks scratched in the walls, if you ken where tae look.

I dinnae tell Lolly about all that. I will take her tae the caves, though, later on. It's a lovely spot, and we can be alone there, nae that there's many folk out on the beach, a day like today.

'What was it like when you were a wee boy?' she asks.

I stare at the water, spilling and splashing about the Skerries rocks, and wonder if I should tell her about the summer trips we used tae take here. I've got good memories. Near the cave there was a rock shaped like a crocodile's back. Birds would land on it, and we saw dolphins swimming round it sometimes.

There was fresh water from a spring, and you could collect it in a can. The spring's dried up now, though. First thing I'd wake up tae the gulls and the waves crashing and go and get some water. If it was a warm day there'd be the smell ae the broom bushes mixed with the salty sea air. We were surrounded by yellow flowering broom. What a lovely smell that stuff has in the morning sun, like coconut. Even if I did slip on the rocks and fall intae those wicked prickles a hundred times, it was worth it for the smell, just like when you win a coconut off the shy at the showies and you first crack it open with a hammer and chisel.

I got my nickname at Covesea when I was a bairn. Father had taught me the names ae all the different birds, gulls, oyster catchers, sand martins, herons, kestrels, all ae them. But terns were my favourites, Heaven kens why. I must ae carried on about terns the way Wee Betsy does about her teacher, the good-looking one, Miss Webster. Anyway, I loved going tae Covesea cause there were so many terns there. So 'Jock Terns' it was. I dreamed ae the flying even then.

There's another family story from Covesea. The day Ma and Father met, Father saw a fishing boat go down at the caves after it hit some rocks just hidden under the water. You can see waves breaking over them in low tide. Now the rocks are known as the Nellie and Jane, after that boat, and Father said if I'd been born a girl I'd have been called Nellie Jane too, if Ma had allowed it. But Ma believes too much in the old ways tae name a bairnie after a shipwreck! They fought over it, though, before I was born and the matter was settled in a glance. Ma says I came intae this world laughing at the pair ae them.

I dinnae ken what tae say tae Lolly about those days, so I take a sip ae my drink and look down, studying the bottle. It's a Moray Cup, sweet and fizzy, turns yer tongue red. The glass has a seam down it like a stocking on a dilly's leg, and the label has a picture ae a wee coloured boy: '*Ask for Sangs MORAY CUP – The one and only*'.

'Years ago,' I point tae the label tae show Lolly the picture ae the boy, 'I was feart tae drink Moray Cups cause my big brothers tellt me they would make me turn black!'

It's no true, that story, but I heard Rachel and Wee Betsy arguing about it the other day. It made me laugh. Maybe Sangs didnae exist back when I was their age. I cannae remember it. The only coloured person I knew was the landlord, Darkie Smith, and even that wasnae till I was ten and we moved intae Lady Lane.

Lolly stares out tae the Skerries. I ken she wants tae hear more about the family really, how we lived, nae daft stories about Moray Cup. Suddenly she turns and asks, 'Is it true what they say about your ma being a seer?'

I look back tae the lighthouse, away from her, take another sip ae drink and gie a wee sniff. Bubbles up ma nose. 'A seer, you say? I dinnae really believe in all that stuff. But, aye, she'll do palms sometimes, if she's in the right mood. With the other old wifeys.'

I dinnae tell Lolly the story about Curly. Nae long after moving intae the Lane, Duncan was marring with a neighbour over the hall. He was a labourer, nae one ae us, and his wife was pregnant. The man took against Curly and said he'd nae stand any noise up and down the dancers once his child was born. All Curly said back was, 'Better nae count yer eggs before they hatch.' His wife died giein birth, the child too, poor manny. I only ken that story cause Curly was full with the drink one night and she began greeting about it. Ach, but it's all rubbish. I told her nae tae feel so bad, but I ken she still feels responsible.

When I turn back tae Lolly she's staring intae her hand tae examine her lifeline, or her loveline, or whatever it is they call them. I wonder if she kens about the Batchie Woman. All our women go tae visit the Batchie Woman, but it's rare that they trust her so much, cause she's nae one ae us. She was born in the town. Ma says she's a fisherman's daugher. One time the Batchie Woman told Jeannie she'd got visions ae Duncan and

169

Curly in the Lane with a monkey! Well, we all thought she wasnae wise, except Ma of course, who believed her. Till one night Ma was out in the garden and we heard her shouting.

'Come and hae a look. I tellt ye!'

It was a bloody monkey made ae sacking. It had velvet ears, glass eyes, a woollen smile and a purple waistcoat. Even from a distance we could see the long tail between the legs, arms stretched out like a wee child. Hauding a velvety hand each, swinging this thing to and fro, were Curly and Duncan. It was a favourite toy for Wee Betsy, came off ae the cart. 'Monkey! Monkey!' Wee Betsy learnt tae say, cause she was just a baby then. So 'Monkey' was its name, and that was what the Batchie Woman had seen.

'Show me your palm!' Lolly goes, and takes my hand. 'You'll live tae a hundred, Jock Terns. That's what I see.'

'Well, that's a relief!' I go. 'Ma's nae in agreement with you there, though. Apparently your poor wee Jock here's cursed.' And actually, the Batchie Woman agrees, but I try nae tae think bad thoughts like that.

'Then it's definitely a load ae nonsense!' says Lolly, but she looks worried, just for a second. I kiss her tae take the frown off her face.

'Stop it, Loll! She's nae a seer. All Ma's ever predicted was floods. She kens when the river will be high, and you dinnae need the gift tae predict that in this part ae the world! It's just old wifeys having a laugh with us, and other folk with imaginations running away, getting themselves all feart. There, now.'

I take a long swig ae my Moray Cup. 'Come here,' I go, and we kiss again, for longer this time. I feel all the tiny sweet bubbles ae the drink on the smooth insides ae my lips and it mixes with the salt, the fine sand on my face, the taste ae my Lolo.

'Hey,' I go, reaching intae my bag. 'I've got your da's camera.' She takes it and holds it up to take a snap.

'Aw, I come out all gawky in photies. Dinnae.'

'Wheesht, Jock Terns. What rot! Say cheese.'

I turn my head as she takes her snap. 'Can I no get one ae you, beautiful?'

'We should do one together. Let's find someone tae ask.'

'Come on,' I go, standing up and pulling Lolly tae her feet, 'I want tae take a look at the caves. There'll be someone on the path can take a photie.'

Once we get tae the top, past the quarry, there's a wee track down tae the beaches and our cave. The broom's thick on both sides, and it can be slippy an all. Lolly takes fearty steps all the way down and I have tae tell her tae look up, cause the cliff's beautiful, golden, orange, brown and bronze in the sun, sandstone in all different colour layers. I want her tae see it.

At the mouth ae the cave, and inside it, it's black with soot. I take a wander in and have a kick round while Lolly waits for me tae call her. There's some signs ae fires near the entrance, and what's left ae the wall halfway in. I guess that was built years back by one ae us lot. Everything's just how it was when I was wee, except for a few more initials and dates scratched or painted at the back, near where it gets deep, the bit we cried the Monster's Gulp.

'Come on!' I shout. 'Come in! It's like being swallied by a whale.'

Lolly looks a wee bit nervous. 'Coooooo-weeee,' she goes, intae the Gulp.

'Oo-weeeeeee,' groans the monster.

'I hope there's no forky gollachs in here!' she whispers, 'or I'll scream.' I tell her I'm the only beastie in this cave.

'Your horns aren't the kind I mean,' she laughs.

We spread the blanket near the wall. Loll takes a key out her bag and says let's put our names on the rock, just here, near the ground. I wonder if she's gonnae put a heart round it or something like that, but you've tae scratch quite hard, and neither ae us has the patience. I touch the rock with my palm. It comes

171

away damp and cold, itchy with grains ae sand. That's what's holding this cave up, wet sand all pressed together. I wipe the hand on my trouser leg.

'Are you cal?' I ask, cause I feel a shiver go down her.

She doesnae answer. She rolls over tae face me and I touch her nose with the tip ae my tongue, which aie makes her smile. Our voices echo off the walls, hers high like a bird, mine deep in my throat, like two different creatures crouching in dark corners. We start kissing. Grains ae sand tickle my scalp and I can still smell Moray Cup on her lips. Soon it's nae enough tae be holding her, trapped beneath woollens and buttons and stitching, six layers ae material keeping us apart. I'm bursting tae touch her again, and I tug at her coat toggles, the loops ae her scarf. I have a bit ae trouble with the sleeves, shunting round like a rowing boat with a standing passenger. She tries tae giggle and I kiss her roughly. I want tae feel again how smooth she is, her thighs, the softness ae her belly against the wool, her breasts in my hands, her nipples going hard and cold. Kittens' noses. At last the coat's off. I slip my hand ontae her skin. One feel, freezing and sandy, gies her instant goose bumps, has me catching my breath and her reaching down tae touch me. I almost lose it when she undoes the buttons. I have tae pull away. I want tae taste her this time, nae like our quick fumbles in the dark at the Deil's hole, where abody could catch us at it. I open her blouse and kiss her belly, push up her vest, feel greedy at the sight ae her bare skin, all shivering and shiny from my tongue. I trace my fingers gently up her stockings, find her slip. She's warm. Her slips are aie silky smooth. I shut my eyes tight and stroke my thumb over it, pushing forward. Her breath gets warm against my neck, and lower down my skin prickles with the cold as I wriggle off my breeks. Our breath feels smaller in the cave. And maybe it's nae a bad thing, the fact that the cal wind is jeeling my arse, cause it stops me concentrating too hard on Lolly's nakedness, the look on her face, all toot-mou'd, her skin on my skin, hands down my back, legs round my waist, the silky slip brushing against me. Her name goes through my head, and maybe I'm whispering it onto her lips.

There's nae a sound I love more than what wakes us up. The whirring purr ae a jet engine. That'll be me one day! I'm gonnae find a way tae get up there, medical or no, flying wherever I want, cutting through all the lines, both sides ae the lighthouse, dipping my wings and riding the currents like a bird, like the terns. I'll fly a Sea Fury, a Vampire, a Venom, a Shackleton, maybe a Skyraider. I'll dive through the spray in my baby, sweep along the beach, shoot over the waves on a tail wind, my engine so loud it'll stop folk's hearts down below. If you go fast enough you can swirl up the sand, I've watched them dae it. Aye, that'll be me one day, soaring past, thundering by, disappearing intae the clouds. Catch me if you can! I'll be the best pilot in the skies. I'll be faster than Flash Gordon, even with my twa left feet. 'Watch this, ladies and gentlemen,' they'll shout from the dunes, 'Jock Terns loops the loop!' HOOOOOOOOOOOEEEEEE!

'Well? What's that one, then?' Lolly whispers intae my ear as the plane flies over us. I hold her tight against me.

'Sea Hawk, chicky. That's a Hawker Sea Hawk.'

Dawn

She'd expected a smell of instant mash and surgical sock bandages. But this place was different. It smelt of antique furniture and creamy porridge. There was a shiny piano, an ornate hearth with a real fire, deep-pile rugs, velvet armchairs on brass castors, and a great oak staircase, the walls hung with antlers. None of the elderly residents wore dressing gowns and slippers. Visitors were offered tea with rich fruit-cake, scones with cream and jam, and sandwiches in triangles filled with salmon, egg mayonnaise and cucumber. It felt Christmassy. Dawn wondered what it cost. A fortune, surely.

But fortunes had always been Ma Batchie's business. She was in a wheelchair. A nurse in a sky blue uniform pushed her into the lounge, positioning her so she could look into the fire.

She might fall asleep on you. You never know when they get to this stage, said the nurse.

Ma Batchie didn't seem to have noticed Dawn and Maeve. She was staring at the opalescent glaze on the fireplace tiles. The flames made them gleam darkly.

Oh, it's fine, said the nurse. She can't hear you less you shout.

Ma Batchie was motionless beneath a tartan blanket that was tucked in round her bony frame. With every few breaths her eyes would close completely, rest awhile, but always open. Eventually she turned to face them.

Maeve held Dawn's hand tighter as the ancient mouth opened, wide as a fish rising to swallow a midge. Ma Batchie had one tooth in the middle of her face.

Ye've come tae ask about yer mam and dad, she said, her voice catching and slipping, a scratchy 78.

What was that? Dawn asked.

The nurse gave them an uncomfortable smile.

Oh, pay no notice. She says things like that to everyone.

The nurse took the old woman's head in her hands, one palm under the chin, the other on the crown. She tilted the head sideways and leant close to Ma Batchie's ear. It looked like a primitive telephone call.

THE LADY IS RELATED TO SOMEONE YOU KNEW.

Dawn stiffened. The other visitors in the lounge were interrupted, mid-sentence or mid-sandwich. They turned to look. There were lots of raised voices here, like in any retirement home, but this was shouting at top volume, the kind of voice you'd use to a dog.

The nurse looked into Ma Batchie's face to see if she'd understood.

Yesed somethin?

THIS LADY IS RELATED TO SOMEONE YOU KNEW.

That was a lie, of course. Dawn was embarrassed, about the lying and the shouting, and at herself. She'd believed the paper. The article said Ma Batchie was in good health, or at least that's how it sounded. But the old woman looked in no fit state for a birthday party. It had probably all been a publicity stunt for the retirement place.

The nurse stood upright and straightened her uniform. Everyone in the room was watching, but she must have been used to the staring and shouting.

Ye've come about yer mam and dad, Ma Batchie said again.

Dawn was holding the photo of Lolly and Jock.

Yes, Ma Batchie said. Them in yer haund. She nodded to it.

Dawn shook her head. No, they're just . . .

The nurse apologised. Some days it's all a load ae nonsense. Don't be offended by it.

Ma Batchie flashed her one tooth and leaned forward. Her limbs were stiff as ice, but her flesh was liquid, skin dripping from fossils. One hundred and twenty one years was two lives.

It was superhuman. It should never really happen, but when it did, this was what it looked like – hard to look at. Distorted and not quite of this earth, like an octopus or a palid deep-sea giant, but with human features. A line of pink make-up had been half licked from her lips.

She spotted Maeve.

Wee Betsy! Is that you, Wee Betsy? Ken where I'm going tonight?

Maeve's eyes were wide.

Dancing! Ho ho! Magic pears!

Ma Batchie laughed, if anyone could call it a laugh. It was more like a tussle going on inside, and Maeve ran behind the armchair where Dawn was sitting.

Oh, don't worry, pet, the nurse said. She's just very old. She's one hundred and twenty one!

Huh. Whatyessay?

Ma Batchie glared till the nurse grabbed her head again.

I SAID YOU'RE ONE HUNDRED AND TWENTY ONE.

The old woman grunted and rubbed her lips together, moistening them and mopping up what was left of the pink lipstick.

One! Two! One! the old woman said. And next year it'll be one-two-two. One-two-two, buckle my shoe! she cackled. Dae ye hear that, lassie? ONE TWO ONE!

Maeve crept out from behind the armchair, with a smile on her face. One-two-one. Her angels.

A bell rang and the nurse said she'd have to leave them to it. She reminded them to shout, because otherwise Ma Batchie would get frustrated, and then she went. There were three other residents left in the lounge. A fat lady was knitting in a chair in the corner, and beside her a man in a hat had fallen asleep with his mouth open. There was also a feeble gentleman with a couple, perhaps his son and daughter. The couple were eating sandwiches and scones in silence, while the old man watched.

Come!

Maeve was taking jelly-tot steps and Ma Batchie's eyes were twinkling.

Come on! Ma Batchie said. Ah've got cinaminaminamin baws in ma pocket fer ye!

Maeve giggled. She reached the wheelchair and, quite confident now, spread Blue Scarfy onto Ma Batchie's lap. Maeve put her little hand into the ancient one that was held out, and their fingers intertwined.

Ahhh! Said the old woman with a one-tooth smile. Her eyes closed. She took a deep breath, settled her bones, and let her head fall back against the rest of the wheelchair.

They waited. Dawn felt conscious of the feeble man, sorry that his two visitors whispered so he couldn't hear them. They ordered more scones, and soon their knives tinkled again round the wee pots of butter and jam. In the corner the fat woman's knitting needles ticked, and the sleeping man beside her had started to snore.

Ma Batchie still hadn't let go of Maeve's hand. Maeve tapped her on the shoulder with her free arm, but Ma Batchie still didn't make a sound or move a muscle. Her eyes stayed closed. Maeve looked at Dawn, who shrugged, and the woman knitting must have dropped a stitch. The rhythm of the needles stopped dead and she tutted.

Ma Batchie still didn't open her eyes. Maeve tried to pull her hand away but the old woman's fingers were locked tight. Maeve looked worried.

Mummy, is she dead?

No! Dawn said. I'm sure she's just sleeping.

Hello! Maeve said as loud as she dared. She pulled at the old woman's sleeve.

One-two-one!

Dawn got up from her chair. She would have to shush Maeve so the old lady could sleep a bit. But what if Ma Batchie *was* dead? The knitter had put her work down. Even the feeble old man and his visitors were aware of the scene now. They turned in their chairs, gulped down scone, and waited. Everyone began to look round the room, hoping to see a nurse on the way. Was she finally?

Dawn looked at the others. Um? Maybe we should get –

AAAAAAAAAAAAAAAAAAHHHHHHH! Ma Batchie cried out. Got yis!

Maeve and Ma Batchie's fingers were still woven together in her lap, and the two of them laughed. Ma Batchie shook till her wheelchair creaked.

I knew she was alive, Mummy! Maeve said. She winked and you never saw. I was only pretending!

Ma Batchie's laugh turned into a cough. It was a cough like Dawn had never heard before, like a tree trunk snapping in a storm. And it snapped over, and over.

ARE YOU ALL RIGHT, MA BATCHIE?

Ma Batchie was losing the pink from her cheeks. The colour was sliding off her face.

Let go of her, Maeve! Dawn said.

Maeve tried to pull her hand free from the old lady's.

Mummy, I can't!

Ma Batchie was gripping it tight. Too tight. Tears were pricking Maeve's eyes. The old woman's fingers were still strong. Her nails needed clipping and they were digging in.

She coughed.

She coughed.

Ach, here we go, said the fat lady, who had recovered the lost stitch in her knitting and was now unwinding more wool. One Tooth has a performance on the way. Just wait. She haughs them up like hairballs.

Get somebody! a quiet voice said. Go on! It was the sleeping man. He'd been woken by Ma Batchie's coughing.

He's right, Dawn thought. Someone should get help. But the

couple visiting the old man were already on their feet, one headed for the reception, the other up the grand oak staircase.

Ma Batchie coughed and coughed.

She's having you on! the woman with the knitting said. Always playing up!

And then the coughing stopped.

I told you, did I not? said the lady. She tutted again and went back to her stitches. Knit one. Purl one.

Just like that it was quiet, like nothing had ever been wrong. Was Ma Batchie tricking again? She was still gripping Maeve's hand, and Maeve was crying. But Ma Batchie didn't seem to notice. She wheezed.

Just wait. Here it comes, said the lady. She ticked her needles louder as if her knitting could muffle whatever was coming next.

The one-hundred-and-twenty-one-year-old woman was reaching for the mantelpiece. The tartan rug slipped off her lap and down round her ankles, and with her free hand she was pulling the whole length of her splintery body from the chair. Dawn was amazed. Could everyone see what she saw? Ma Batchie had started spitting sparks, real sparks of light, as though something deep in her throat were about to ignite.

AHHHHHHHH! AH CAN FUCK! FIGHT! AND HAUD A CANDLE TAE ANY MAN!

There was a sharp suck.

Nurse! the old man tried to shout. The fat lady roughly bundled her knitting and padded away down the corridor as quickly as she could, averting her eyes from the ugly business. The other old man was still waiting for his visitors to return. He'd turned to watch, and now he threw his head back and laughed, his false teeth rattling loose.

Maeve pulled at Ma Batchie's arm with all her weight, but she still couldn't free herself. The old woman was in a sort of trance. At first, words were spat like orange pips from a mush of nonsense, but then she seemed to get into a groove. They began to drum from deep inside her. Sentences took her over, resonating from deep inside like a reel bewitching a fiddle.

Anitherbirthdayshixty-five yearsoan the goanah'm. Ah'm ah'm ah'm ah'm puffin an blowin. Pufffffin like a jenny whistle. Ishatchoo, Rachel? Pairweethingyeare. Ah'll sing ye a song: ken awthe planes, Lolly. LOLLEELOLLLLL. HO! HO! Ha Ha Ha! Look at me. I'm a filthy cat! *I LOVE plooms. Plooplooploopllooooo-PLOOMS!* 'Any old rags?' And I meeeeaaaaooow! Sea. Hawk, Chick. Awkerseawk. Hawkrseashawk.
AND THEY SAY SHE'S STILL DANCIN! HO HO HA HA!
Ah've been swallied byawhale. A WHALE! 'Waste not, want not, pick it up and eat it!' DDdddDevil stop meeeeeee an aw yousstayawafae those MCPHEEEESS. Lolly. Lolly. Mr Alexander Reid had on view in the window of his shop, 307 High Street Elgin, two re-mar-ka-ble potatoes. Lolly. Lolly maks yea lollipop. *Jourrrrneyeeey intaeeeeSpace! Ma dilly ma dilly ma dilly's a secret ma dilly ma dilly's a secret.* 'Any old rags?' Put this inyer pipan smokit. Jock Terns loooooooops the looooooop! HOOOOOOOOOOOEEEEEE! Tat cooooo. Tat coos een. Cousin. Coo's een. He fellinlove wee it. Weel seen it took him fer a bull! Shoutin doun the dancers like thon Tarzan ae the bloody jungle. **Whit did ah tell ye? The Batchie Woman's nae a circus act, right enough, an Auld Betsy's nae a bloody fool!** Desperate Dan, big stupppid Dantheman. O ho! There'll be bluebirds sssoverrr. *Hello hello again, SH-BOOM! SH-BOOM!* There wis some real gangsters amang us. *Ultra-violet radiation is recommended by the world's best medical men. Shalalalalalalalalala!* It wis easy tae see ah'd been swept aff ma tramplers! BITCH NURSE ae a burker's daughter! 'Any old rags?' An de ye ken whit he said? Ye damn tinky who'll not get a penny oot'a my pocket. Oh, me! Whit a temper he'd get oan him when the winds started tae blow. O ho! Ha! Ha! O ho! Ho!

Ha! Tears runninuninunininiuninuninunin down her cheeks, while that stupid number went on turnin. The trap goes SNAP! Almost cuts the mousey in two. **'Any old rags?'** The rest ae the eveninsablurblurblur. Aye, well. Damn us bloody Whytes! *Dat-dat-dat-dat-dat-duh.* We're all tink*sss*. RohwlEE pohwlEE pudding, is it? **ONE!** He sinks his foot intae my kidneys. *To my darling Martha from your ever-loving Duncan.* Look! Thon's Duncan yer Daddy. Daddy Daddy daddydadddydaddydd-dadddddy. Dadda. O shaness, Wee Betsy! Whit-a-shame! **And TWO!** This is how ah feel, Curly. Look. DEEK! **Fond kisssssssssss.** Beasts crawlin in her hair, Granny, and a toe-cap skims ma ribs. Spoonfuls aesugar anamargarine. Goggles, sir? Widopen space. Oh, me! We had good times in the camps. Ma Mary. Mamaery mammary. Mamery. Memmery. Mermaidy. Ma mairy's in toun next week. *She*'s nae courtin, ye ken? FffffFammelssssssffffffffat as sausages. **Hello, Lunar 142. Landing Control, please.** Yon manny fae Forres. 'Any old rags?' Shut yer fff or ah'll fuckin murder you! A hundred thousand faces. Nivver speak ae those days. Nae wonder ye stare. Shaness! Whit in heaven's wrang wi runnin aboot kickin a baaaaaaaaaaaaaaaa? CAUSE YER A BLOODY USELESS PACK AE DESPERATES! **CRACK.** Same sound as the heidie's belt on Bertie Topp's palm. Ye've aie been a saftie wi her. *Oh, what a panic's in thy breastie!* Namesake grandbairn usin that fouty language like some shan dilly! **Bad-luck McTootie.** Toot. Tooootie tooootootootie. Thick as thieves, the pair ae ye. A place that smells like the beachnd tastesae peatanberries anpokesae chips. *That precious element: vitamin D.* Keep right on to the end of the road! Ma jingies! THE HALE BLOODY WORLD CAN PUT THEIR LIP IN MY STUMMEL! The pear ripened, so it did! My lipsaretweaking my lugs. **We're being attacked by pandrops!** Some sair gift's turned wicked. Spoiled spotty, pot-belly pigs right enough. Eat your mother'sssshit! The sun's up at the hospital. 'Any old rags?' And God, his shoes! The shoes were a size big. It kept fallin aff him.

An ah'm, agone. Gone. Dawn, he never saw you! But Big Ellen knows. Bigellenahsaid.

Ma Batchie screamed like an animal and looked, suddenly, like she would fall into the fire. She took one last gasp.

GONE IN A BLINK!

A world
>> so small
>>>> it would slip
>>>>>> through a buttonhole.

There was a whine and Ma Batchie's body was suddenly released from whatever power had held her up. She let go of Maeve's hand and she fell back into her chair, a scarecrow cut down.

Dawn grabbed Maeve into her arms. She looked from the old woman and down at her daughter, whose tears were soaking her face. Maeve's forehead was feverish, and she could feel her child's heart and her own, beating fast against each other.

Three nurses ran into the silence and saw they were too late. Two went to Ma Batchie and began trying to revive her, stroking her arm, her hair, feeling for a pulse. The other came to Dawn.

The ambulance will be here soon.

I'm sorry, Dawn said. She just . . .

The nurse told her not to worry and turned to go, but Dawn stopped her.

Wait! The old woman said things just now, the names of some people I was going to ask about. But I hadn't got round to asking yet. And there were sparks. I'm sure I saw them.

The nurse stuck her hands in her pockets and gave the unconscious old woman a sharp look. When she turned back to Dawn her face was sour.

Please don't ask me about that kind of thing, she said. Tinkers and curses and black magic. I go to church. I don't believe in such things.

The nurse took herself away, clicking her heels on the parquet floor with a new kind of vigour. Ma Batchie just smiled a peaceful smile.

✻ SECRETS ✻

Wee Betsy, 1955

The fatter Big Ellen gets the more people round here are talking about the baby. If it's a boy it's going to be Duncan like my daddy, and if it's a girl we're going to have another bloody Betsy. That means I'll start being called Big Betsy, cause I'll be bigger than the bairn. So I've got my fingers crossed tight for a boy.

I keep thinking of the story Granny told us about the piper and the lord's daughter. How is it that the lord's daughter was having Fearghas's baby when they weren't married yet? The thing is, I thought you had to be married first, even if your man has gone away to sea like Big Ellen's. I'm just having a scratch of my napper and wondering about this when Mammy comes in. She nags me to stop my fleching, cause I'll get the beasties from my hair under my nails. Rachel's out playing, so I think now's a good time to ask about the story.

Mammy explains. It was all down to music! Music and dancing can make people do things they normally wouldn't, she says, a bit like Daddy when he's on the drink.

Music. It makes sense somehow. That'll be why this family keeps growing, with Granny always hammering away on her organ and puffing at that whiney old chanter downstairs. I don't want more sisters, and I definitely don't want a brother, so I hope Granny keeps it down from now on. Otherwise she can give the new babies to the fairies she's always going on about.

'Away and play with Rachel for a wee whiley,' Mammy says.

I hate to leave my nice seat by the fire, but I go to the top of the stairs and put my boots on slow as I can, thinking whether I should tell Rachel what I've learnt.

'Oh, Betsy, can ye nae tie those pints any faster?' Mammy complains.

By the time I've done double knots in my laces, I've decided to let Rachel in on the secret, but only if she promises to hand over her quarter of the Mars Bar we get on Saturday, and I get to choose what flavour drink we get off the Hays van.

Uncle Jock comes out his room at the bottom of the stairs. He's holding up part of his station uniform.

'I've lost a button,' he says to Mammy, waving the waistcoat in his hand.

'I can dae that for you, Jock, bring it here. Need it in the morning, do ye? Have ye kept the button?'

'Aye,' he says, and he fumbles in his pocket and starts to climb the stairs as I run past him shouting, 'Bye, Uncle Jock!' Maybe one day he'll have a baby with Miss Webster and they'll call her Betsy after me. I wouldn't mind that.

Rachel's at the drying green, standing right in the middle of the claes tows with everybody's white sheets flapping round and around her. We like to stand in the centre and turn till we're dizzy. It's like being inside a huge white rose.

'Can I play?'

'Aye! Come on!' Rachel says, her voice a sing-song, spinning up and up even though she's stopped moving. She holds her hands out to the sides and waits for me to join her, my back against her back, arms stretched out together, touching all the way to the tips. She leans back, and where our heads meet it feels strange, like we're being pulled together by magnets. We are melting into one. This is probably how I got the heid beasts off her, but I'm not minding about that now. Rachel giggles in my lug as I call out.

'Ready, steady, GO!'

We do the spinning game for a while, and then we do a clapping game.

'Skidamarink – adink – a dink
Skidamarink – a doo!
Skidamarink – adink – a dink
I love you!'

When we're bored of Skinny Malinky we separate and fly through the sheets, pretending to be seagulls soaring through the clouds. All I can hear is laughing, Rachel's and mine, our boots pummelling the earth, stamping down the weeds, the sheets billowing. They beat and fill out like a heart, Granny thumping dust from the rug. Most of the game all I see is whiteness swirling past, waltzing ghosts. For a second my head spins and I feel lost. The sheets are alive! Twisting and trapping and tying knots. I flip round till I catch a glimpse of Rachel's face. Phew! There she is! She's got two teeth missing on her top row. It makes her say 'ethith' instead of 'esses', and when she smiles it looks pink through the gap, same as Nancy's mouth.

Rachel falls to the floor panting and holding her belly, and I sit on my knees beside her. I stroke the soft fringe on her kilt between my fingers. I wore that kilt once, till it got too small. The pin catches the sun as my wee sister rolls about like a jolly joker, and her lovely black curls snake over the grass. I want to tell her about the music and the babies right now, and decide I don't mind about getting her quarter of the Mars Bar. She must've come from Granny playing a really pretty tune.

We sit with the circles of giant white petals all around and above us, and I get Rachel to be serious and listen. She tries, but Rachel doesn't seem to understand what I'm on about, or if she does she doesn't find babies all that interesting. I wouldn't have gotten her bit of Mars Bar for it anyway. She rolls onto her back and starts being stupid again. I give up, call her a silly nickum.

Lady Hill's at the top of the Lane behind an old wall. I think it's haunted and it's like a mountain to climb. I watch the toes of my boots dunting into the grass like a donkey's hooves. On the steep bits I throw back my head and stare at the statue on the pillar at the top. I think there should be a lady on the top of Lady Hill, but it's not a statue of a lady at all. It's a boring manny who was the Fifth Duke of Gordon. Looking up at him's like staring at the headmaster in assembly, and the feeling's like toppling on the edge of a cliff. All you can hear is the wind and the seagulls crying, except for the crashing coming from the scrap yard. But I hear voices today as well. Sounds like the Newlands clan are already up there. I pull Rachel behind me till we're almost running.

'Hurry up, you warridrag!'

The view's nice on a clear day. You see all the way to the hills. Ben Rinnes is the biggest. I'd love to go there. Down below you can see most of Elgin, the big church at Plainstones with the thing on top that's shaped like a vase of flowers, the ruined towers of the cathedral, a bit of Cooper Park and the boating lake, but no boats now cause they take them away in the winter. Nearer by there's the River Lossie, the green dome of Dr Grey's Hospital, and the rag store and the yard where Daddy is right now. He's making a racket clanking bits of metal. Beside the yard is the drying green with the white sheets flapping, where we were just a minute ago! Granny told me they used to hang people there, so the green must really be haunted. Maybe from up here we'll spot the ghosts. But there's no time to waste getting all dreamy.

We come here to fight! It's lassies only today. Boys and girls never fight together, and it's always one on one. We take turns. Us Plugs against the McPhees, Maclarens or McMillans. The Williamsons usually fight the Camerons, the Lesleys, and the Newlands.

'RIGHT!' shouts Robina Williamson. She's the oldest, the

tapster, so she decides whose shot it is. 'Betsy Whyte and Jenny Maclaren.'

The Maclarens are fearsome. Granny says they're the only breed could ever scare the burkers who dug bodies out of graves. But Jenny and me are about the same size, so she's usually who I fight. The others climb up onto the ruins of the old fort to watch us go at each other. Granny might not want our hair cut off, but I'd say a fair bit of it gets torn out in each other's fists. No rules. Ripping hair and scratching and biting's all part of it.

To start off we ram each other shoulder to shoulder like two billy goats. After a bit of digging my nails in and pulling, I get Jenny under me on the grass, face down. I yank hard as I can on her pigtail, but it slips through my hand, like guddling a fish. She's got shiny soft hair, not like most of us tinks. Mine's always full of tangles. If Jenny was tall enough she could get her fingers in, lift me right off the flair and hang me off a branch.

I keep my belly tight, barely breathing. When I fight my body hardens all over, sort of turns to stone and aches with it, stiff and strong. Jenny slips her hand under my shirt and scratches me in a line down my ribs. I squash her cheek into the grass, try to get her loose arm under my knee to hold her down. If I manage it, I'll have won! It works like in the boxing matches Jock and Daddy go to.

I can hardly hear the bigger girls over me and Jenny's panting, our breath coming out in bursts, 'Oof, oof, oof.' I know what they're shouting, though. 'She's going tae kill yous, Plug! Bite her! Aye, on the leg! Tear her fuckin lugs aff!' Stuff like that anyway.

I'm about to win. Robina's started the count, and when she reaches ten, instead of ten she'll shout 'PLUGS ARE CHAMPIONS!' But Jenny Maclaren's a cheat. Her sister has their Dotty the Dog up the hill, a crazy wee bitch. The thing terrorises the entire Lane, scrabbling over the cobbles on its stumpy legs, baring its teeth and nipping your ankles. Uncle Jock says Dotty's the She-Hornie herself, straight out of Hell. Unless you're a Maclaren, of course, she loves all the Maclarens. Robina's reached the count of eight when that devil of a creature comes running straight at my face.

'GET YER STUPID WEE SHITE AE A THING OFF ME!'

I have to lift an arm to protect myself. Jenny grabs her chance and tips me over and over, like she's rolling a carpet. It's not all good news for her, though. The wee bitch is so excited she can't work out who's who in the tussle, and Jenny takes a few nips on the bum.

Down in the dirt, there's a good smell filling my nose, warmth and cut grass, a taste of earth in my mouth, but my cheek's grazed and stinging and the mutt's skipping over our bodies and yapping and clawing and nipping. I get Jenny's hair again and scramble to my feet. Jenny screams. She tugs my head to one side and I peer over to the rock where the others are. Just for a second I see them clearly. Teeth and eyes.

A gulping jolt goes through my chest as I fall again. And I'm lucky, cause right where I land I find just what I need! A big round stone. It's nearly as big as my hand, smooth and cold as a cannonball. They're rare up here on the hill. I send it flying over my shoulder without a second thought, without even aiming for anything in particular. No time for that.

'SHOT!' Robina shouts from the rock, and at the same time there's a yelp. Dotty is off like a bullet with her tail between her legs. That ends the fight. Jenny starts greetin and blubbering that she'll tell her ma I did it on purpose. But wee Dotty's okay, she'll live, and Jenny willnae tell. She's just a bubbly-bairnie. I stomp off, and Rachel comes running after me.

'Go away, Rachel. I'm going for a wee wander.' Just in case that stupit Jenny does go and snitch, I think to myself. 'I'll be back before supper.'

It gets dark fast. I know I should really head home. But I love being out by myself, away from everybody's noise, nobody telling me what to do. The time passes too soon. I dare myself to do things. Tonight I decide to run past the falling down cathedral, where crumbly gravestones loom out of shadows, damp with moss, and topsy-turvy in the ground. Above, the Cathedral's ruined circle window watches me like an eye, a huge hole filled with gloomy indigo and grey sky. It's a hoop for the witches to fly through on their broomsticks, into the world of the dead and back into ours. Just the thought sends shivers down my spine!

The air feels thicker here, harder to run through. It's like something really wants to drag you away. Don't look behind you! By the time I reach the bishop's house my heart pounds like hooves in a horse race. I imagine Rachel or Granny's warnings in my head, their words about the Devil, and I can't decide if it makes me happy to ignore their voices, or if I'd rather they just left me alone.

But I am alone. No one's here but me.

My feet take me down by the Lossie, right round to the hole in the river where it's murky in the water. It does feel spooky here, and I think of what Granny says again, 'The Deil bides there and plucks folk right aff the path! Oh, me! Dinnae yous go playin doun by thon Deil's hole, quines!'

I know why Granny thinks that. Before I was born one of my uncles went swimming in the hole and he died not long after. That was my uncle Francis, who's a ghost now. Daddy told me. Maybe Uncle Francis lives in the hole too.

I sit on a boulder by the bridge, staring into the river, disobeying Granny. But I've not been there long when real voices start humming from somewhere. My first thought is that they've got to be my daddy and mammy out looking for me, and maybe they're angry. I decide to hide. I'll let them walk right over the top of the bridge, and when they're just past I'll lowp up and frighten them out their wits. They'll think I'm Granny's Devil come to get them!

191

I wonder if I've made a mistake when I crawl round the boulders and slip my head under the walkway. There's a damp smell and it's even blacker in here. I don't want spiders crawling on me when I can't see. But the voices have gone silent, and somehow that makes me afraid and glad to be hidden. It's just footsteps. If it's Mammy and Daddy, why aren't they calling for me?

I don't like to crawl too far under cause it's so dark, but as the footsteps get close I edge in, far as I dare. The boulders are freezing and they scratch my thighs. I don't want to smear myself with slime, and I look behind me, trying to find a flatter, drier place to sit. It takes a second or two for my eyes to see right. My head feels funny, and greenish colours swirl in front of me like a spell wafting from a witch's cauldron. There's a few splashes of red too. Devil red. My heart starts to race.

And suddenly he's there, right in front of me! I nearly hit my head on the bridge. I'm looking right into a pair of eyes! Is it really him? Satan? Uncle Francis?

'Would ye shhhhh!'

Jesus Christ! I nearly went and wet myself and it's only fuckin stupid marble-eyes, Maggie McTootie.

'You stupit hoor! What are you doing here? I thought you were the fuckin Devil himself.'

'Dinnae you speak tae me like that. I'm hiding fae ma brothers. Did I gie you a fright?'

'Don't be daft!' I tell her.

'Well, keep yer fuckin wee trap shut, then!' she goes.

I pull a mou at her. Stupid McTootie. I'm still trying to slow down my breathing so she won't hear what a fright I really got. I pretend Maggie's not there as the footsteps get closer. So close I can hear wee bits of grit crunching under the soles of the shoes. There's two people. But it doesn't sound like my mammy and daddy at all now. Mammy's heels don't clop on the cobbles that way. And it's nae Maggie McPhee's brothers either, cause they'd be stomping and haukin up spitballs.

I put a hand over my mouth and swallow. Right above me the four feet come to a stop. Who are they? How aren't they saying anything at all? There's a bit of shuffling up there. Sounds like a girl crying into a pillow. Then I hear the voice again. A voice I know really well.

'Why are you greetin? Will ye nae tell me what's wrong?'

I can hear him kissing! Lots of little kisses like Mammy puts on Nancy. They go tick-tock onto her, but for some reason she cries even more and tells him to stop. Granny was right, though: Jock's got a girlfriend! That stupit Maggie starts sniggering into her sleeve and nudging me with her elbow. I wish it was just me here. They might catch us if she doesn't shut up. She'll ruin everything.

Who's the girl? Could it be Miss Webster? I pray it's not our Big Mary that Granny's always talking about. It doesn't sound like Big Mary, though. Not that the girl's saying much. All I can hear is Jock asking her why she's being like that tonight, and her snivelling, sniffing into a hanky. But she does it all daintily. If it was Big Mary up there she'd be blowing and howling like a bloody elephant.

This goes on for ages, her greetin, him asking what's the matter, saying please tell him. My shins start to go numb. Maggie's so annoying, making sucky kisses on her hand and nudging me. I ignore her. I'm scared she's going to start whingeing about the cold on her legs and refuse to stay. But if we spring up now Uncle Jock'll be angry with us, he'll think we were there on purpose to spy on him and his dreepy, weepy dilly. I don't think my teacher would do that, so it must be someone else.

I close my eyes and wish they'd just go away. And then, sudden as a coal jumping out the fire, Jock shouts something, angry, and she chokes back a few words.

I can't believe my ears! I think maybe I've heard her wrong cause she gulps, sort of swallowing the secret she's just told him. Above me I hear them stumble for a second, and a big lump rises in my throat as the feet, just hers this time, clatter back onto the path by the river.

It's quiet on the bridge for a second, but then he calls out like a maddie. I watch her leaving. She doesn't turn back. She has a blue coat and long blonde hair, like Cinderella, and in a few seconds she'll be gone into the night. I know who she is! Everyone knows her, even Maggie who's peering all cock-eyed over my knees. She's the girl who sells tickets at the pictures. The men say she's that beautiful, one day she'll be on the big screen herself. She walks like she knows it too, like a movie star. So *she's* Jock's girlfriend! And I know her secret: A really big one! Oh, me! Someone's fairly got an awful lot to answer for this time.

It's been quiet for so long on the bridge that by now Jock must've crept away, but I still hold my breath as I crawl out from my hidey-hole and brush my clothes down. My heart's pounding like a drum, and not cause of the Deil or the dark. Because of the secret! My uncle's nowhere to be seen.

'Jock Terns is dead!' Maggie goes and slices her finger over her throat.

'Don't fuckin tell or I'll murder you!' I scream at her.

'Shut up, shite-face,' she laughs, and starts to walk away.

I watch her disappear into the dark. Who knows where she's going. It's not fair. No one cares if Maggie's late for her supper. She can do whatever she wants, ugly gobstopper eyes. But I couldn't give a fiddler's about being late. Not even if I've to bing to my bed early every night for a week. I'm carrying a secret they'd give their eye-teeth for!

As I'm heading home I wonder how will I be able to eat my tea when I've to keep a story like this inside? Minute I open my gob I'm scared it'll come screaming out. How can I stop myself blurting it in my sleep? Not that anyone would believe me. 'Him and thon bit of skirt? Jock Terns can fairly dream!' That's what they'd say. But Uncle Jock would never forgive me if I told.

I nearly trip over him in the dark. He's folded up against a wall, near where the river meets the bottom of the Lane, and he's down on his hunkers in the dirt. Rascal's lying at his side, ears low and tail still, like he's just been given a telling-off.

'Jesus!' I cry out, and then I see the look on Uncle Jock's face. He's staring at the water like he wishes it'll surge up and wash him away, which makes me embarrassed for the word I've just said. Uncle Jock does nothing. He's dead still, and my voice seems to wait above me, a leaf trying to fall.

I've only seen my uncle like this once before. It was the day they said he couldn't fly planes. Secretly I was pleased he wouldn't be leaving us any more. But it's scary to watch him looking that same way now. I don't know what to do; if I should say anything or touch him, or just run and get my daddy. I stand there and feel like a dummy.

'Uncle Jock?' I go eventually, and my voice sounds silly so I try again. 'Uncle Jock?'

He pretends I'm not there at all for a bit longer, and I wonder if he's going to greet. His eyes start to shine like the stale water in the Devil's hole. And then he seems to do several things all at once. He drops his face in his hands and makes a strange noise, and then looks up again, rubbing his splayed fingers tight over his scalp. For a second he looks like a monster with wide eyes and spikey hair.

'YOU-SHOULD-BE-IN-YER-BED!'

His words come out all at once, like he's been waiting for years to shout them. At the same time I'm sure he starts to greet.

My feet sink into the muddy path, and whatever I was going to say, I don't even remember what it was, I swallow it and it slips down like a slimey river rock.

'Go home!' he says.

But I can't move till he stops looking and puts his face back in his hands. I run past him then, dizzy like I might fall in the water. When I get round the corner I slow down, and by now

I've got knots inside me and I'm ready to greet. He'll never marry Miss Webster now.

I reach the back end of our Lane and stop running. I know when I get in they'll be sitting at the table, faces all angry and the supper eaten. A tear tickles my nose so I wipe it away with my sleeve. Daddy'll be horn-mad, and Mammy too. They'll shout and scare Rachel and Nancy, who'll both scream, and then Granny'll hiss at me like an old cat.

And then I start to wonder what it would be like if I didn't go home at all. What if I went back on the road?

I could dare myself.

Dawn

There were cuts on Maeve's palm from the old lady's fingers, but she said they didn't hurt her. Only Dawn could feel a sort of pain, a digging in.

She imagined Ma Batchie felt that too, hands grasping, clutching at her loose skin and deeply buried bone, lifting her from the chair to her bed, from her bed to the chair, from the chair into the ambulance. They passed it on the way home. The ambulance was speeding up Maisondieu Road, calling on chaos with its sirens.

Heelabalow! Maeve said from the back seat. She was suddenly full of energy.

Dawn gave her a funny look. Maeve didn't normally make up words. Do you mean hullabaloo?

Maeve shook her head and put a thumb in her mouth. Dawn was worried about her. It wasn't nice for a child to see a thing like that. Ma Batchie's turn had been pretty violent, and she'd looked pale and wrung out when it was over, even if she was smiling.

Will she make it? Dawn had asked a nurse quietly.

Who's to say? said the nurse. She's been that way before, if that's what you mean. Usually she gets worse afterwards, poor thing, but she's always made it.

Ally came out the front when she pulled up. Dawn straightened in her car seat and lifted a hand to him, expecting him to wave back. He didn't. Instead he waited, shuffling his feet the same way Warren used to do. It made her nervous. The feeling of him standing there went right up her spine, strummed her ribs like guitar strings. When was the last time she'd felt that? Maeve had fallen asleep in the back and Dawn was hoping to get her into

197

the house gently, without making a sound, but with Ally there she felt clumsy and bound to wake her.

She got out.

Nice afternoon, he said.

She nodded and looked up at the sky as though she hadn't noticed before. It was unbroken blue.

You okay? he said. He moved a step closer.

She wondered if she could tell him about Ma Batchie.

Yes. Well, no. Something strange just happened.

Ally lifted a hand and let his palm scuff her shoulder.

Do you want to come in? I'm alone. We can have a drink. You look like you need one.

His other hand took hers now and she felt him squeeze her fingers, once, twice. It felt like a code. Once for no, twice for yes.

She took a breath.

I've got to get Maeve in.

Right, that's okay.

He watched while she opened the back of the car and leant down to unbuckle Maeve.

She's sound asleep, Dawn whispered, standing up.

He smiled and gently put a hand on her. It felt good and she let him keep it there while she just breathed. She reached behind him and put a hand on his shoulder, leaned a bit into his side. Her palm was flat against the fabric of his T-shirt and her fingers touched his skin at the neckline.

The wind was coming in from the sea and she could smell the salt, the cleanness of it. The smell reminded her of summer bonfires on the beach, and that phrase, warming the cockles. What were cockles? Some kind of shell? They were something cold and in need of heat and she liked the sound of them. This was the feeling she got from Ally, something essential seeping in, like walking with bare feet on warm stone.

Shall I carry her in for you?

No. She smiled. I can manage.

Another time, then?

Dawn nodded. Maybe she would see him another time and she would tell him about Ma Batchie; get it off her chest. He took her hand again and squeezed her fingers.

Once. Twice.

But she knew already she would never say yes.

The flat was stuffy and quiet. Dawn opened the windows and went to the fridge for a drink. Maeve had woken on the way in from the car. She came through to the kitchen, rubbing her hand where Ma Batchie had clawed her.

Is it hurting? Do you want special cream?

No.

What do you feel like for tea, sleepyhead? Dawn asked.

Cloodie tumpling.

Dawn laughed. Where did you learn about cloutie dumpling?

Maeve gave her a guilty look.

The old lady, she said.

Are you all right? Did Ma Batchie hurt you? Dawn said.

No.

Maeve pulled Blue Scarfy from her belt loop and swept it through her fingers like a magician.

She told me a story.

What sort of story? Dawn said.

Maeve just yawned.

Dawn made pasta. Maeve liked the unusual shapes, the ones that were hard to find. Wheels were the best. Dawn used to send Maeve to a daycare centre in the city, and she'd come home one day with a picture made of pasta shapes. It had bows and twists and spaghetti all glued onto sugar paper, and the pasta pieces had made the shape of a train, a dozen wheels clacking and rolling along the bottom. Dawn had put it up on the wall in their old kitchen. She'd kept it there till the pasta started falling on the floor and leaving tacky bits behind on the paper.

Maeve didn't eat much.

Are you not hungry? Isn't it good?

Maeve shook her head.

We can see Grandpa tomorrow, if you like?

Normally that would do the trick, brighten her up a little. Dad always spoiled her. But Maeve shook her head again.

We could go for a picnic.

NO! NO! NO! Maeve huffed, kicking her legs backwards and forwards under the table and catching Dawn on the shin with her heel.

Ow!

Dawn decided to put Maeve to bed early. She'd been acting funny since the visit to Ma Batchie, probably the shock of it. A good night's sleep and she'd be right.

Later, she ran herself a bath and switched on the radio. They were reporting a drowning. Old news. It had happened some time the week before, but Dawn hadn't paid much attention. A woman had been found floating face down, eyes clouded, the lapping waves dunting her against the hull of a small sailing boat. Thud, thud, thud.

The man on the radio insisted it was nothing suspicious. Drunks often toppled like skittles over the edge of the harbour, attracted by the moon on the water, like moths. A fatality was nothing unusual, especially given the season. The sun was up late and folk tended to drink more. The water was still icy cold.

Dawn put her feet by the taps and tipped her head back to wet her hair. She opened her mouth to feel the water on her tongue, ran her fingers over her wet lips. They felt soft, swollen as if from kissing. As if. She remembered hearing how water caused a dead body to swell. Tenderise. It was a word her grandfather had used with his customers at the butcher's.

She couldn't sleep that night. Maeve's mood had unsettled her. That and the way she'd taken a shine to Ma Batchie. Dawn wasn't sure about the old fortune-teller. It was the way she'd laughed with her one tooth, and when she'd moved, that sound like sticks snapping somewhere inside.

Normally when she couldn't get tired, Dawn would sit up and read something, but tonight she didn't do that. She wondered if she could fit everything together if she thought about it really hard: the photograph, the things Ma Batchie had said, Jock and Lolly, splinters of other stories. The old woman must have known them well once. She must have seen the photo and gotten confused. That was the only explanation. There was no such thing as fortune-telling. That was the answer – something simple. Dawn tried to push Ma Batchie to the back of her mind, and instead she wondered if Ally was awake. He'd said he was alone. It was only just gone ten.

Dawn's last nights with Warren had been sleepless. He'd begun going to bed in his clothes, too drunk to take them off. He splayed out on the bed, never even bothered taking his boots off, great dirty boots that looked way out of proportion. Him and his stupid big feet. Him and his daft smile. Dawn had often thought of tying his laces together, just for a laugh. But he'd have killed her in the morning. Not that anyone believed it other than Shirley. Dawn and all her nonsense.

She'd always taken his boots off herself, hated putting her hands on him, his trousers that reeked of smoke and sweat. Clammy socks, always one with a hole in. A big toe would poke through, prune-like and pasty, a fleshy pad. The nails were always too long. It made her feel sick. That one pinkish bit of him sticking up in the air. His tongue lolled like a sloppy butcher's cut when he tried to speak.

Dawn thought about kissing Ally. She wondered what it would have been like, if it would have felt good like his hand on her waist. But she couldn't remember anyone's kiss except Warren's.

It's the strongest muscle in the body, the tongue. She'd heard that somewhere. And it can do the most damage.

Eh, hen? Gie's a cuddle.

Warren's hand would crawl over like a crab, creeping from round her back, fingers reaching her breast. And the reek of him! Stale beer and hot, dank breath. His woollen jacket sleeves itched her bare skin, but her disgust at him was quiet; anger muffled under the duvet. Even when he'd drunk too much to get hard, something of him was still up there, on top of her. It was in the stench hanging. His voice. The weight of that arm.

Somehow the wee things could press down the hardest.

If she thought too much about those times, she'd end up wanting to wake Maeve just to hold her. She turned away from her sleeping daughter and watched the digital clock flicking through the minutes, the tiny green broken lines that configured the numbers.

22:21 became 22:22.

One. Two. Buckle my shoe. Maeve and Ma Batchie's numbers. She couldn't get the old crone out of her head.

✷ WOLF ✷

Wee Betsy, 1955

Nothing good happens to wee girls in stories who go off in the dark on their own. For a minute I'm stuck on the corner of the Lane wondering which way to go. I scuff my toes into the dust and stones, and a breathful of wind sends some dry curly leaves rolling and crackling towards me. Some of them settle round my feet. I think of Hansel and Gretel, and look to see if there are any white stones nearby so I could make a trail, but most of the stones are the same pale grey.

I walk a few steps towards the Lane, remembering Uncle Jock's angry voice. I have to swallow hard. Then I walk back to the spot I was in before and take a few steps along the river, away from home and into the dark. My heart leaps like a salmon at the dare. I'm feeling brave.

Soon my eyes are dry and I've sniffed till I can breathe properly again. I cross the river at the next bridge and turn back towards the cathedral on the other side, darting from tree to tree just in case Uncle Jock is still slouched there against the wall and sees me. The shadows of the branches are a bit scary. They reach out like charred fingers with long witches' nails and I stamp hard on every one. I imagine them pulling back, suddenly feart of me. 'I'm a tinker! All the paths are mine!' I shout at them inside my head. I'm careful never to peer back over my shoulder, just in case.

It's much easier being on the road again when I reach the park. The lights are still on in Peter's Café, and from the patch of grass where I choose to sit I can see the waitress pushing in the chairs and wiping down the tables. I sit cross legs to pull my knees under my coat, and stuff my hands in my gloves to try and keep warm, but I'm already freezing. I rip up handfuls of grass from all round me, making a circle and telling myself it will keep me safe. I make a heap of cuttings on my skirt. I wish I could light some sticks and have a campfire all to myself. I remember the night when the showies came and Granny lit a fire outside. She started singing and clapping in a funny way which made the bairns dance and the grown-ups all hush. Everyone's faces glowed orange from the flames.

Elgin Cathedral's just a shadow across the park, jagged like a tooth. Most of it got destroyed when the Wolf of Badenoch came in the dead of night and burned it. That was a very long time ago in history, further back than Granny or anyone else remembers. I imagine the Wolf of Badenoch like the wolf in Red Riding Hood, but bigger. He walked on his hind legs, tall as the McPhee twins, and he had thick black hair. He stood in the woods and howled with laughter while the sky lit up from the cathedral's flames.

Once I hid Rachel's teddy in the coal hole and told her the Wolf of Badenoch had taken him. Granny said that was a sin, and not to be silly, that the Wolf of Badenoch was just a nickname for Alexander Stewart, who was an earl or a lord, or something boring like that.

We were told the story of Elgin Cathedral at Sunday School, how the Wolf of Badenoch torched it and stole all the treasures inside, which definitely *was* a sin. I asked Father O'Brien if the Wolf of Badenoch was like the Black Dog in the story Granny told me, the one where the dog is the Hornie in disguise. Father O'Brien didn't know the story, so I told him how the Black Dog steals into churches when there's a thunder storm and mauls everyone inside to death. The end of the story is that if you look close on church doors, you can see the dog's bloody claw scratches in the wood. The Black Dog would be much more frightening than Dotty, the wee bitch over the Lane.

Up until that day I'd thought the Black Dog was a story from the Bible, but Father O'Brien was raging at me when I told him. He said I was a pagan and gave me a clip round the ear, and ever since then I've gone to the Baptists for Sunday School instead.

I've ripped up a good bit of grass by now, so I stuff the cuttings up my jumper and lie back pretending to be pregnant. I put my hands over the bump just like I've seen Big Ellen do, and then stroke them up and down. The grass tickles my skin through my blouse, and I pretend it's the feeling of the baby moving inside. I wonder when Uncle Jock will marry the girl from the bridge, and if they'll fit into our wee house. Maybe we'll all have to live in tents again. Can you have a wireless in a tent?

When Granny's in the right mood, she tells me what it was like when she was on the road. Other times she just laughs when I ask her, and says, 'The past is the past,' or sends me out to play. When she does tell stories, I don't know what's real and what's made up, especially the bits about the horse deals and magic, and murders and shipwrecks, which sound like the fairy tales we read at school.

Granny remembers so many people you never know who's who in her stories of the old days. There were hundreds of lassies called Betsy or Maggie, and boys called Jock and Georgie and Willie. They all moved about together, one big family living in the woods or up in the mountains, or huddled in the caves by the beach. Sometimes I imagine them swinging in the trees, especially the McPhees, and I don't know if that's real, or a story, or something I just dreamed up. When they stayed in the caves there would always be a fire at the entrance, so if you went out for a pee at night, you could always find the path back.

I realise I'm needing myself, so I get up, holding onto my belly of grass and groaning like Big Ellen. I look for a bush to go behind, but there are none nearby, so I head in the direction of the cathedral. When I find a spot, I take my knickers off. I don't want to wet them by mistake. I squat down, turning my back to the cathedral and checking the shadows cause the Wolf of Badenoch must be prowling about somewhere. The pee is just starting to splash between my feet when a strong beam of light flashes over me. I nearly soak my shoes with fright. The Wolf!

A huge fanged beast lurches into the beam. I fall backwards as a long, coughing bark fires from between its jaws. Every bone in my body and every skeleton in the cathedral graveyard trembles. Even the stones of the cathedral shiver. I taste the grass from up my jumper going into my mouth. It's gone everywhere. I'm trapped between the hedge and the beast, watching a glistening string of slether swinging from its gums as it lunges forward again and again, in and out of the beam of light. Even though I know I'll be clawed to death against the cathedral door, I still feel embarassed at the warm dribbles running over my knee. I didn't really have time to finish what I was doing.

'Down! Enough!' a voice shouts.

The Black Dog suddenly disappears, the beam of light steadies on my face, and my eyes adjust to the light. I scramble to my feet and I don't know which way to go. I can still hear the monster panting somewere very close, licking its lips.

'It's all right, girl. Polisss!' The man's voice comes again, a whistle.

I'm not sure if I'm more or less feart, or whether I should run. I try not to greet as sweaty handfuls of grass tumble out the bottom of my jumper, loot tipped from a robber's sack. It tickles my shins on its way to the ground. The tobies tell you off if you pick the grass.

The beam of light slides from my face, down over my damp legs, onto the pile of grass cuttings at my feet, then across the ground to where I've left my underwear. The dog barks again, and for a second it springs back into the beam. I scream and press myself into the hedge.

The toby hauls the dog away and asks my name. He asks me in an angry voice if I have been tampered with, but I don't know what that means. I say no, just in case it's a crime I might've done, and I start to greet because he might throw me in the quad with the McPhees.

'I'll need to have a wee chat with your father, won't I? You been picking the grassss?' he says, looking at the green clippings stuck on my face, down my kilt and all over my socks. His dog appears back in the beam, growling and snapping, and this time the toby doesn't pull it away so fast cause he's waiting for some answers.

The Black Dog pins me against the hedge. It's hard to breathe with his fangs so close, and somehow, something I don't mean to say turns into words. In between the breaths I feel them slipping out my mouth like torn-out stuffing, and in a few gulps I've told the toby the really big secret. He gets it out of me like water from a tap. Straight away I know I've made a mistake. I want him to forget about it so I also tell him about me going back on the road, and about my teacher Miss Webster, how Jock was going to marry her one day. I keep explaining, but in the end I'm greetin too much for the words to find a way out. I want the toby to take me home and not lock me in the quad. He hasn't said a word all this time.

'Sorry for picking grass,' I say, when I can get a breath.

He points to my underwear. 'Sssort yoursssself out and we'll get a move on,' he says, turning his back and lighting a cigarette while I put my knickers back on and brush off my clothes. I stay as far from the dog as I can, and try to see the man's face, but it's too dark. All I can make out is his grey hair, which glows in the moonlight, and the red circle at the end of his cigarette. The dog is quieter now.

'I thought it was the Wolf of Badenoch,' I sniff. This makes him laugh, and I think then about taking his hand, but before I can he puts it into a pocket.

'Where do you live?' he says.

'Lady Lane,' I tell him.

He takes a suck on the cigarette. 'Lay-dee-Lane,' he hums. He yanks the dog hard on its lead and marches off at a pace, whistling back over his shoulder that I'd better *ssss*kip and keep up.

Dawn

Dawn had found a small magnifying mirror. She was standing in the light of the window by the door, using the mirror to get a better look at the photo Ma Batchie had pointed to. She was sure she'd come up with the only explanation, that the old woman had somehow seen the picture in Dawn's hand, and made an assumption. But the old woman's eyesight would have had to be perfect.

It would be easier to examine the photo with a proper eye-glass, the kind stamp collectors used, but the mirror did the trick once she held it steady and got the distance right. The focus was soft, but Dawn could still see what she was looking for. A beauty spot on the girl's left cheek, her right cheek in the mirror image. Shirley's chocolate chip, proof that she had once been Lolly. There could never be two people more different than the girl in the picture and Dawn's aunt. But there was no doubt. Dawn swallowed a lump.

In Shirley's bedroom, the clothes were still hanging, arthritic ghosts in the overstuffed wardrobe. Heavy wool and stiff cottons fought against Dawn as she heaved them along the rail. The familiar smell was here too, the same scent of talc and dry-cleaned tweed that had been in the bag from the morgue. Underlying it was the musty walnut of the wardrobe.

The blue coat was at the back. Shirley had kept it. Dawn recognised the unusual round collar, the darker velvet trim making a 'U' shape over the bust. It was the same one that Lolly was wearing in the photographs taken at the beach. She'd kept it all that time.

Dawn remembered years ago, she'd snuck in one day on tiptoes, wondering where her aunt was. She'd found Shirley sitting on the bed, smoothing her hands over some piece of clothing. Was it the coat? She was crying, and Dawn tiptoed out again without being noticed.

Outside the weather had got up again. Branches of the tree were stroking the bedroom window, cold bones. Dawn put the blue coat over a chair. In the bedroom mirror she found herself staring at her reflection, studying it again, the bridge of her nose, the curve of her upper lip and the soft pastilles of her ear lobes, which she could peer at out the corner of her eyes. She lay down on the bed. Maeve had been dropped off at Dad and Mother's house, and the flat felt too still. Dawn pushed her face into the bedcover. She wanted to sleep.

The phone rang.

Warren?

The first thing she thought, even now. But that was silly. When the phone rang it was always Dad. Dawn dragged herself up and cleared her throat.

Hello?

Dawn, that you?

It wasn't Dad. It was Mother. There was a quickness to her voice, like in the old days.

You'd better fetch Maeve away, the voice said. I don't know what you've been telling the child but she's upset him . . . Yes, really! She's said terrible things. I never heard anything like it. He's left to take a drive and I want her gone before he gets home. I want her gone.

Mother began to cry.

I'll come now, Dawn said. I'm on my way. But Mother had already hung up and the line was ticking. Dawn put down the phone. She felt dizzy. For a few seconds she stood there wondering what she needed; her keys, her shoes, her coat. She suddenly couldn't remember where she'd left them or which way to go first. Then she saw the keys, lying right by the phone. Her shoes were on her feet already. Dawn walked into the bedroom. She grabbed Shirley's blue coat and threw it over her shoulders.

Dad couldn't have gone far because he was back by the time Dawn arrived. He was in the sitting room smoking, something Dawn hadn't seen him do in years. Maeve had been sent into the garden like a naughty pet. They'd put her into her coat and shoes, ready to go, and her shoes were muddy so she wasn't allowed back in the house. Dawn could see her playing through the back window, piling armfuls of fallen leaves by the trunk of the tree.

Dad wouldn't look at Dawn, but he nodded to the garden.

The bairn's out playing.

What happened? Dawn asked.

She got some funny ideas in her head, he said.

Dad stood up and began beating the cushions on the sofa with one hand, raising the dust. There was a smell of tobacco and digestive biscuits. He sat down again.

Mother was in the kitchen, shouting through to Dawn.

I've lined her toys up here for you.

She appeared in the doorway and stopped dead.

What on earth's that you're wearing?

Dad looked at Dawn in the blue coat and he started to say something.

Was that nae . . . ?

We ken fine whose it was, Gordon! Mother snapped.

Dawn smoothed her hands over the blue coat. She fiddled with one of the buttons that was coming loose. Mother leaned towards her and sniffed. She looked like she would be sick. It did have a faint smell, old waxy make-up and wet wool.

You look just like she used to in that, Mother said eventually. Apart from the hair. It's creepy.

Dad was watching them and slowly finishing his cigarette.

Will someone tell me what happened? Dawn said.

211

Mother turned to Dad. She pursed her lips and when she spoke she was on the verge of tears again.

She'll not call him her granddad any longer.

Ach! Dad said. It's nae matter.

But Dawn knew when he'd had his feelings hurt.

Oh, Dad, she said, Maeve doesn't know what she's saying! I'm sorry, but she's only four. You mustn't take it that way.

But that's not the half of it! Mother shouted. She said some awful things. And it wasn't like that. She's been acting strange all day.

Wilma! Dad said. Leave it!

I'll talk to her, Dawn said. She had a shock yesterday. I told you about the old woman, didn't I?

Mother sat herself down beside Dad.

That poor old lady died. Did you nae hear the news? Mother said. We saw it this morning. It made the national round-up.

Aye, it did, said Dad.

They were quiet now, and for a few moments Dawn could hear Maeve singing to herself outside, a song she'd never heard before. She felt a strange kind of relief to hear that the old woman was no longer alive. She tried to remember Ma Batchie's last words. Gone in a blink. Something like that. To think a hundred and twenty-one years could go so fast.

Did you tell Maeve? Dawn said.

Mother blew her nose.

No, of course not, Dad said. No one's said a thing.

Mother sniffed, balled up her tissue and stuffed it under the cuff of her sleeve. She patted Dad on the leg and the conversation seemed to be over.

Dawn said she'd go and get Maeve.

Half an hour later they were climbing the hill to the caravan site, Maeve in front and Dawn following. Maeve liked the woods and they didn't rush. The trees seemed to lean together to whisper about them as they passed, and the rain had left a rich smell of earth and moss. But Dawn had too many thoughts in her head to relax. She wondered what she was doing, being led by Maeve's insistance, and by the ravings of the oldest woman in the world, who had died yesterday.

Maeve had still been heaping up leaves in Mother and Dad's garden when Dawn had gone outside. She'd also been babbling in a funny voice, as if she had a mouse or a kitten in her hands.

Dawn had asked her what she was building, was it a nest?

Maeve had shaken her head.

What is it?

It's a house.

Well, isn't a nest a sort of house?

Maeve nodded.

We're going to go now, Dawn had told her. Do you want to say sorry to Granny and Grandpa?

Maeve had shown Dawn the back of her head, a messy pigtail, and stared up the trunk of the tree.

It's all right, Dawn had told her. You don't have to see them any more today, if you don't want.

Slowly Maeve had turned round.

Who's Big Ellen?

When they reached the top of the hill and looked down at the caravan site, Dawn felt sure she'd made a mistake bringing Maeve. The site looked eerie and deserted. Most of the vans were gone. She'd warned Maeve about the dogs, not to creep up on them, but now there weren't any there. Without the barking it was oddly quiet.

Come on! Maeve said, pulling her hand.

Dawn couldn't remember which van had belonged to Big Ellen, but she went up to one and knocked.

Stand back! a familiar voice shouted from inside.

Dawn was relieved. The round handle spun ninety degrees and the door burst open.

By faith! Dinnae be standin there, ye'll catch a death.

Big Ellen put her arms round Dawn, almost enveloping her as she dragged her inside. When she saw Maeve, Big Ellen beamed, her cheeks like two sponge cakes rising. She crouched down as far as her great belly would allow, a circus elephant on its knees, and kissed the top of Maeve's head.

What a bonnie wee thing ye are. Dae ye like beasts? We've cats, dogs, rabbits . . . what else? There's a horse an all!

Maeve grinned.

Oh, ye'll be fine here! Big Ellen said, clapping her hands together.

Maeve pulled her own pet, Blue Scarfy, from her pocket to show Big Ellen.

Benny? Big Ellen shouted.

A man appeared in the cold open doorway. He climbed the steps, walked in, and took his pipe from a ledge. He nodded to them. It was the same man that had collected the furniture from Shirley's flat when Dawn sent it to auction. She recognised the coarse red hair in his nose, a tuft from each nostril. He looked at her differently now. Benny gave them a smile and his eyes twinkled like a toymaker's. Maeve took his hand, and once the two of them were down the steps, Benny lifted Maeve onto his strong shoulders.

The electric heater in the middle of the van gave off a roasting, chemical smell and the orange bars across it were hypnotic. They seared Dawn's eyes when she looked too long. She was sweating buckets. It must have been on full blast. Big Ellen was already setting water on to make tea, and before it had boiled Dawn could hear Maeve and some other children playing together with the animals.

What was it brought ye back up here? Big Ellen asked when she'd sat back down and taken a sip of tea.

Sweat prickled Dawn's neck and forehead. She loosened Shirley's blue coat. It was a bit too small so she had to tug to get her arms out.

It was Maeve who asked to come. She's been strange since we went to see Ma Batchie.

Big Ellen chuckled to herself. You met the old woman. Is that so?

Have some people left? Dawn said. The place looks a bit empty.

Big Ellen nodded through the window to the hill, and Dawn remembered the bikers.

Some local folk were causing too much trouble, Big Ellen said. Trying tae force us tae shift. It's thon place on the road that's the problem – the café. The young lads go there. The army boys and the scouts use it. They dinnae like our sort. My grandson, Jocky, had a run in wi them.

He's all right?

Aye, Big Ellen said. She was still looking out the window, gazing at the view as though she could ink it into her mind.

They set five vans alight and put Benny in the hospital, but. We're all shifting now, in the next few days.

Big Ellen pointed out the window to the plot next to hers. The ground where the caravan had been was branded black, burnt pan loaf.

They go up quick, she said.

I'm sorry.

Ach, Big Ellen shrugged. She looked as though she might say something else but didn't bother.

I hope you don't mind me coming back, Dawn said.

I'm glad!

Big Ellen breathed deeply. She motioned again to the charred patch of earth out the window.

There's something I decided nae tae talk about before. I thought the past is the past. But this here changed my mind.

215

Dawn could feel a question on her tongue now. She could almost taste it, dry like rice paper stuck to the roof of her mouth.

You knew Shirley?

Big Ellen shrugged. Well, now, that I couldnae say, if ah had or if ah hadnae. She didnae work in the cinema?

Yes! Dawn said. Her first job was there. She sold the tickets.

She did, ye say? Big Ellen scratched her chin. Well, maybe ah remember. Maybe.

Dawn had heard all about Shirley working at the pictures. That was before she went to Aberdeen and became a nurse. She'd always said how much she'd loved it, sitting in the booth with the rolls of coloured tickets all wound up like ribbons in the haberdasher's.

But I wanted tae tell you about another person, Big Ellen said eventually.

Big Ellen had found a loose thread on a cushion and was pulling it free, winding it slowly, finger-painting swirls. She seemed nervous, as if she were waiting till the thread snapped before she could start.

Dawn was thinking about her aunt, and about Shirley's secret. She'd been wondering for a while now. When Shirley said 'her Dawn', had she really meant '*her* Dawn', that Dawn had been *hers* all along?

Since meeting Ma Batchie, Dawn had studied the tiny picture of Jock and Lolly till her eyes were sore with it. More and more she stood herself in front of the mirror and compared. The long, straight nose, her full upper lip, earlobes, eyes, Jock's shiny black hair. Sometimes she had a sense there was something there, but the picture was too small. Sometimes it felt like a tall tale, the kind they would all expect her to come up with, Linda and Dad and Mother.

Dawn wasn't particularly shocked by it. In some ways the thought had always been there. Maybe it was a film or a story-book that had first suggested it. You heard stories like it all the time. They were probably as old as history. So maybe Shirley's secret was much bigger than she'd ever imagined. Or perhaps she should say it was exactly as big as she had *always* imagined. She couldn't decide any more.

Ye ken about the Batchie Woman, dae ye? Big Ellen said suddenly. Shame, she whispered. A terrible shame.

Dawn nodded and looked away. On the window ledge behind them was a line of cassettes. Dawn read along the row of titles. There were names she recognised, all country singers. She had them in her collection too; albums she hadn't listened to in ages. She laughed to herself. She and Big Ellen liked the same music.

I can read your palm, if you want, Big Ellen said out of nowhere, as if she wanted to change the subject.

But Dawn didn't believe in all that hocus-pocus. She pushed her hands deeper into the seat cushion, keeping her scarred wrists hidden.

Big Ellen looked at her for a long time. Ye've got sense! she laughed. When is it ye were born? Fifty-five, was it?

Dawn nodded and Big Ellen's lips tightened slowly, as if she were reading Dawn's fortune in her face and finding something there to hide.

Your aunt knew our Jock.. That was him beside her in the photo. I think they were going together, ken? It's lucky ye came up here when ye did. She took a deep breath. We'll be gone in a week.

Big Ellen stood up and pulled a drawer from under the seats. She reached in and took out an old doctor's bag with a broken brass clasp. The mouth of the bag sagged open and the leather was dry and beaten, covered in scratches and grazes. It held a heavy mess of envelopes and papers, other bits and pieces, and at the top was a tin with a picture of a castle on the lid. The weight of all this had disfigured the bag. It was full of lumps, like a badly stuffed bear.

217

This is the only thing that survived the fire next door, Big Ellen said. It was Maggie's van. Ye ken Maggie?

Big Ellen patted the bag and did crossed eyes. Maggie Marbles. Dawn nodded.

It doesnae mean much tae me, and when I saw it lying in the middle of all that flames I thought there had tae be a reason it didnae go up wi the rest. I spoke tae Benny, and we decided it belongs with you.

Big Ellen started pulling things from the bag, covering the floor.

Ah'm after something in particular. Here, have a look in that tin there.

Big Ellen handed her the old shortbread tin that had a castle picture on the lid and red tartan painted round the rim.

That was Auld Betsy's tin. The auld woman in yer photie. Ah'll check on the bairns in a minute, let ye get a look through in peace.

The tin was packed so full it made no noise when Dawn gave it a shake. She eased off the lid. On top was a photo Dawn didn't recognise. Five teenage girls round a boy perched on a bicycle.

Big Ellen leaned over.

That's Auld Betsy's grandbairns. Your Jock's nieces – Wee Betsy, Rachel, Nancy, Elsie, and Wee Helen, who's named after me. They never had boys. The laddie's Jimmy Starbuck. He used tae drive the mobile library.

Are they still here?

Ach, no. Wee Betsy and Jimmy Starbuck got married right after she finished university in Edinburgh. She was a clever clogs. Folk says they moved tae Canada. Heaven kens what happened tae the rest. Ah heard Nancy was in London, workin fer the BBC! That's what someone says tae me! Helen and Elsie, they were in Glasgow and Edinburgh, last ah heard, but doing what ah couldnae say. And Rachel, well, ah've nae idea where life took her.

Big Ellen left to check on the kids while Dawn kept looking through the tin. She tipped the contents out to sort through them faster. There was a rosary with shiny red beads, a tiny carving of a plane, some old threads in different colours wound into finger-sized circles, and a framed picture of Maggie Marbles as a little girl, unmistakable with her crooked eyes.

Dawn found what she wanted at the bottom. It was a portrait photo of Jock, taken in a studio with his hair neat, wearing his best clothes. The picture was printed on a hard piece of card and had been given an old-fashioned pastel wash. The artist had put some colour in Jock's cheeks and lips, and given him greeny-blue eyes.

A newspaper article was wrapped round the photo, roughly cut out with a shaky hand and folded in three. The paper was brittle and stained, but not torn. It had been carefully put away, as if whoever put it there knew it would be important one day. The article was printed in an old typeface and the paper was yellow with age. There was a strong smell on it, like library books. Dawn rubbed it between her fingers. It felt too thin, too ancient to be part of her story. The cold sun outside was blinding white and outside it was noisy. As Dawn read, she lost her place a couple of times. She could hear the children playing, and one voice she knew was Maeve's. She could hear it even across a playground. A mother–daughter frequency only she could hear.

There was nothing in that moment to mark what she was reading. Jock was gone. It had happened at the police station, the old place where Dad had once worked. Dad might even have been there. Would she ever know? The old station was gone now. It had been pulled down a long time ago and the shopping centre put up in its place. The exact spot where the truth should have been, balancing just under the surface, would now be one of the fast-food counters on the ground floor. It would be wiped clean every day.

Ye've found what ye were after, then? Big Ellen said, coming back and seeing the article in her fingers. Her voice was clipped.

He wasnae like that, that's what the papers never tell abody. Your Jock was clever. He was grand. I named my first child after Jock. Normally you wouldnae do that so soon after, but there was something special about him and no one wanted tae let go. You met our grandson, and the wee boy. They've all taken his name.

Big Ellen came back to the seats and reached down, smudged a thumb briefly onto the photo. She pressed it over Jock's chest where the buttons down his suit had been given a bluish colour by the painter. Dawn held the photo for a while, running her fingertips along its soft, worn edges, and then she put it back in the tin and put the lid back on, feeling the pressure of it closing like hands round her throat.

Big Ellen showed her more photographs, trying to shift the mood.

These were Auld Betsy's an all. Here! This is what ah was after.

It was an old photo of a lady in a wooden wheelchair. A bright red tartan rug was draped over her legs and she was surrounded by a garden. It was full of orange and yellow flowers. Auld Betsy's body was flimsy and pale like a doll, but her sage-green eyes looked right at the camera and there was a hint of laughter about her rosy lips.

Ha! she seemed to say. Ah made it intae colour!

She was ninety-two or thereaboots when she died, Big Ellen said. God love her. I'll tell ye a story ae Auld Betsy's. It's a good een.

There was this tinker who lived in a hoose, she says. And he didnae ken who he was, ye see? Oh, he was confused. He didnae ken who in the name ae God he was! So she says he tied a tin pot tae his ankle one night. She says, if this tinker woke in the morning wi the pot still tied tae him, she says he'd ken he was the same manny he was the night before. So he goes tae sleep.

There was a loud bang outside and Big Ellen lost her concentration. What the Devil was that? Are those bairns all right?

But Dawn could hear Maeve. Maeve was fine and there was laughter outside.

What are those bairns at? Where was I? Oh, aye. Now, next tae the tinker in the bed was his wife. And this was a clever woman, the daughter ae a sea captain. So she says, in the middle ae the night when the tinker was sleeping, she says this wife untied the tin pot, and instead attached it tae her ain ankle.

The morning came and the tinker woke up, and oh me! she says, oh me! What a confusion he was in. Cause, she says, he looks at the wife wi the tin pot tied tae her ankle and he cries, but in the name ae God, wife! If ah've no got a tinker's pot tied tae my ankle, and you have, then you are me! So who in God's name am I? Who am I wi nothin tied tae me? Oh, me!

They both laughed, and Dawn looked at the picture of Auld Betsy, wishing there were more stories.

Big Ellen helped Dawn put some papers back in the bag.

Is this everything of the old woman's that you've kept?

Aye. Almost everything of hers got burned when she died. Even the wooden organ. She says we were to smash the bonnie thing tae pieces and burn it after she went, she says. It was the auld way of doing things. It's a belief, ken? That it's nae clean otherwise. Folk say a person has tae go tae the next life, nae hang around here caught up in the million wee bitties they collect.

A fat envelope had fallen on the floor beside the leather bag and Dawn reached down for it. There was a label on the front, letters punched out by an old typewriter: 'John Whyte – Personal Effects'.

The mouth of the envelope was curled open, and Dawn's fingers sank into the contents as they slid onto her knees. It was a woollen rag, rough, threadbare in places. It smelt of the envelope it had been kept in, the paper so old it was soft as cotton. Some of the paper fibres had wiped onto her fingers and into the wool. She began unfolding, smoothing out the rag.

It was a blue scarf. Dawn felt the stains before she saw them, and she knew it would be blood. Hard and dry like burnt paper. She didn't throw it from her. She drew the rusty stains through her hands, wanting to touch them, watching as they appeared from the folds. It was a girl's scarf. Shirley must have given it to Jock, the same one she'd worn in the photographs taken at the beach. There was a snowflake pattern on it. Dawn imagined Jock's neck against the wool, his skin and soft, black hair. She pressed the scarf against her cheeks, closed her eyes and breathed in the smell. Paper and damp. A strand of wool was unravelling.

Big Ellen took Dawn round the site and showed her where the other vans had been. No one had called for the fire engines and no one had brought water. There wasn't enough water anyway, just what came from the two taps in the prefab at the site. There was no way to stop a van from going up, Big Ellen told her. They disappeared in a few minutes. Dawn imagined the flames, the billowing black smoke, and then the wind blowing it away, nothing left but rectangles of crumbs.

One more question, Dawn said.

Big Ellen had come to the gate with them, and Dawn was wearing Maeve across her shoulders, sleepy and happy again.

Did Jock and Shirley have a child?

Big Ellen clicked her tongue. Wee Betsy, one ae his nieces, she heard a story about that. But, well. Wee Betsy was a bairn. She told lots of stories! And even if it was true there was nothing tae be done. Folk could dae what they wanted with their families back then. Sometimes it was better that way and sometimes it was not.

Big Ellen pushed the old bag into Dawn's hands and waved

222

them goodbye. Inside the bag was the tin, the scarf, and the inquest on the death, which Dawn hadn't read yet.

When you read that, remember they didnae ken him like we did, Big Ellen said. But I'm glad you have it. Now we can all move on.

✳ SONG ✳

Jock, 1955

I want tae look my best. I do my hair at the sink, flick it over at the front, smooth it down with my fingertips. Brylcreem keeps it in place, more or less. I use a bit extra today, and shine my shoes with stuff out ae another pot which doesnae look much different from the Bryl. I managed tae get a wee hole on my best shirt, near the shoulder, a pity, but it hardly shows. I could cover it up with a waistcoat, only the best one I've got is my uniform. Loll might recognise it. I go for a thick jumper instead. It's bloody cal outside, and the waistcoat needs a mend anyway.

A button came off today while I was working. It only happened cause Lolly's father came intae the station. I get the jitters round him, need something for ma fingers tae do. He queued at my ticket booth. I could hardly breathe cause I kent I'd have tae speak with him. It's stupid, but I was wondering if he'd cottoned on tae me. He'd a look on his face, concentrated, like when he's hacking the meat in his shop. I lost my heid, had tae ask the passenger in front ae him three times where she was going ('Was that Rothes or Forres ye wanted again?'). I forgot if she was after a single or a return. Bloody useless. I didnae ken where tae look. He got tae the front.

'Single to Aberdeen, leaving tomorrow.'

The man wouldnae look me in the eye, which was fine by me. But then things got much worse. Lolly's da was just turning away from the booth when Munro arrived tae buy his fags from the stand. They're nae right, that whole toby family, and this one, the father, he's the worst. He struts round in his bobby's hat picking fights with folk cause he kens everyone laughs at him. He talks like a jenny whistle on the boil, whistling through his teeth.

Duncan went for one ae Munro's sons a couple ae months back when he wouldnae pay him for a job. It was daft, but he didnae hurt the man. Still, he was lucky he didnae get a sentence for it. If you get on the wrong side ae that family you've nae a hope in God's earth, and we're aie in the bad books.

Anyway, just my bloody luck, they ken each other, Lolly's father and Munro. Normally people sit in the waiting rooms if they're just having a chat, but Lolly's father stood there till Munro'd bought his fags and then he called him over. He led him ontae the empty platform and started asking questions. I could see them talking through the windae and it didnae look like ordinary small talk either. I tried nae tae stare, nae tae look guilty. I tried tae tell myself maybe it was a bet on the horses, or a police matter.

Anyway, I started fiddling with my waistcoat button and it came loose. It fell intae the wee brass bowl in the counter that's there tae take the pennies off the customers. The auld lady I was serving pointed down and said tae put the button in my pocket, take it home safe so my ma could sew it back on. So that's what I did.

Ye cannae go tae work with a button missin or ye'd get in trouble with the station master. The other lads complain about him and his rules, and call him the Sergeant Major behind his back. He checks our shoes are clean and ties are straight every time he walks past, a sergeant on parade. I kid on with the rest ae the lads, and pretend tae salute when he turns round, but really I get a kick out ae wearin ma uniform. Naebody else round here has togs like it, so tae look at me you'd never guess I'm from Lady Lane.

The station's a great building, the kind ae place ye'd feel small if ye werenae scrubbed up. It's the grandest building I've ever seen. The ceiling in the ticket hall's high as three ae ma hooses one on top ae the other, and it's all decorated at the top. There's a patterned wood floor, more like a ballroom than a station. Arriving here by train, folk would think Elgin was paved with gold.

I spend most ae the time in the ticket booths, behind a glass windae with holes in it so I can hear the passengers. They wait at a rail till it's their turn, and all the dillys make eyes. I've seen them! Sometimes the older ladies do it an all. I've had an offer or two off the auld wifeys, monied types with fur coats and silk gloves, jewels strung round their necks, dripping off their ears! Most ae them are married. I get a glimpse ae the wedding rings when they jingle their pennies intae the bowl.

I thought about an offer I got, just once. Well, more than once, if I'm honest, but just one time in particular. An American woman with red lips like in the pictures. I'd been working out on the platform and she tottered up in her heels, asked me tae escort her tae her automobile, carry her cases cause her feet were sore. We've wee louns tae dae that job, but she wouldnae take no for an answer. Anyway, she didnae waste any time telling me where she'd be staying and how lonely she'd be. Aye, you get the picture.

Later that night I took a stroll, caught a look at her hoose. It was a bloody castle. I stood a while at the gate, but she never came tae a window, and some jumbo jingies I'd ae needed tae strut up the driveway and ring the bell.

Of course, this was before I met Lolly. Maybe we'll go tae the pictures tonight. She loves the pictures. I go tae my paper and turn tae the entertainment pages tae hae a look at what's playin. Joan Crawford, Sterling Hayden and Scott Brady in *Johnny Guitar* is on with *The Case ae Soho Red*. Might be all right. I'll ask what she thinks. We're meeting at Peter's Café for a cup ae tea first anyway. As soon as I've got this button sorted.

I'm on my way over the hall tae Ma, but I catch sight ae Curly with Wee Betsy at the top ae the dancers.

'I've lost a button.'

I hold up the waistcoat tae show her where. Curly loves me in my smart clothes, so I ken she'll mend it for me, and the truth is, she's better at stitching than my ma. Ma's eyesight still keen, but half the time she's in a dwam these days. Sure enough, Curly smiles.

'Oh, I can dae that for you, bring it here. Need it in the morning, dae ye? Have ye kept the button?'

I fumble in the pocket ae my waistcoat. For a second I feel like I did at the station, remembering that look Munro gave me. I swallow, ken the button's in here somewhere. I'm just up a few steps, nae lookin where I'm going, and my wee niece nearly knocks me over, rushing past on her way out tae play. She looks back with a grin plastered across her face.

'Bye, Uncle Jock!'

'What's got intae you?' I want tae ask, but she doesnae gie me the time. I sometimes wonder what planet that bairn's fae. God love her.

'Dinnae slam . . . ' shouts Curly.

The door slams and Curly sucks in her words. She shakes her heid from side tae side.

Lolly's waiting for me in the café. She doesnae turn round when I open the door and the bell tinkles. Smoke twists up over her shoulder. She must've been here a while cause there's an empty teacup pushed tae the side ae her. I'm nae late, but.

I decide tae put a song on the jukebox, one she'll like. My coin drops intae the slot and I watch the arm fetch the record. The Crew Cuts start singing.

Hey nonny ding dong, alang, alang, alang.

'Loll!' I say, puttin my hand on her back. I kiss her cheek and then scoot round tae sit in the chair opposite. That's when I see

228

she's been greeting quietly, staring out the window and letting the tears roll down her cheeks. Her eyes are red and there's a balled-up hankie in her fingers. In a hurry she dabs at her face, and for a second she pretends everything's dandy and as usual. She stabs her ciggie a bit rougher than she needs tae.

Oh life could be a dream, sh-boom,
If only all my precious plans would come true . . .

I'm nae very good when dillys start greeting, tae be honest. I get embarrassed. My stomach turns over as the waitress comes asking what I'll have. A tea, I tell her. Two more teas, please.

'Lolo?' I feel like half my breath's being stolen. I'm dreading what the matter might be, and she doesnae even bloody answer. I swallow.

'Yer da?' I say.

He's my worst fear, her bloody da. She stares outside, willnae look me in the eye. I clear my throat.

'Yer da was at the station today.'

Sh-boom sh-boom Ya-da da Da-da da Da-da da Da.

I wish I hadnae wasted my money on that stupid song now.

Lolly makes a funny noise and puts the hankie up tae her lips. I think how much she looks like a wee dilly, like Rachel thon time, greeting in the corner for an hour cause she'd saved up her sweeties for months, thinking she would hae a feast, and then found them all rotten at the bottom ae the tin, poor craitur.

Ba-doh, ba-doo, ba-doodle-ay
Life could be a dream

The waitress arrives with two cups and a wee pot ae tea. She keeps her eyes lowered but I notice her glance up at Lolly as she pushes one ae the saucers across the table. It makes a scraping sound. She probably think's I'm the reason Loll's upset, and I feel guilty even though I ken it's nae my fault, whatever it is.

'Cheers,' I say, maybe too quiet for anyone tae hear. The waitress is embarrassed for us. She whips round and scurries back behind the counter, where I ken she'll sit listening fae behind the coffee machine. The song finishes and I hear the record being slotted back in place. It's so silent I hear myself breathe out. Thank Heaven we're the only customers.

Nae a word passes between us. The tea sloshes, bubbles roun my belly, and it's nae till halfway through the cup I realise I've forgotten tae put sugar in. I aie take two lumps. As I stir them intae what's left ae the tea, the thought going round my heid is that thon film's starting in half an hour. We'd be there if things were different. There's no point in mentioning it, but I just cannae get the thought tae go away.

When she's finally stopped greeting she starts tae talk, quiet, nearly a whisper. I look up. She's wiping her nose with the hanky, still starin out at the park.

'I cannae see you any more. They're sending me away, to Aberdeen.'

My arms are stretched out on the table, reaching for her, but she doesnae touch my hands. I look down intae my empty cup, and she starts greeting again.

'Your da was at the station today,' I say again, cause I cannae think what else tae tell her, and I'm sure he's the reason. She doesnae say anything for ages, and it's me lookin out the windae now. There's a bird on the lake, ruffling its feathers against the chill.

'Maybe I could have a word,' I say. I ken it's a desperate idea already, the way he was looking at me in the station, like I wasnae fit tae sell him a ticket. Lolly doesnae even bother answering. Her face crumples and I decide we have tae get outside. I make a neat pile ae coins on the tabletop and screech back in my chair, hands in my pooches. 'Come on,' I say. 'I need some air.'

When we're out the café, we walk side by side tae the edge ae the lake. There's a film ae ice on the surface.

'Might snow later,' I go, as if everything was fine.

'I should go home. I cannae stay,' she says, and she turns away. I stop her, hoping that's what she wants.

'Loll!' I cannae think how to make her change her mind so I just ask anything. 'Did you like the photos I took?'

'Aye, they were nice,' she says.

This is useless. Before it's too late, I pull her towards me and wrap my arms round her, hold on tight. She's stiff as a post, pushing at me tae leave her alone, but she's shivering with cold an all. When the warmth grows between us she loosens up a wee bit. I feel her start tae calm herself, and I whisper till she rests her cheek on my shoulder. The song off the jukebox is still going round my heid.

I dinnae ken what I tell her next, whatever I can think of tae make her stay. Some ae the things I blurt out make her greet even more, but this time I dinnae mind. She holds me tighter and it seems tae be working, so I keep at it.

If you would let me spend my whole life lovin' you
Life could be a dream, sweetheart.

We start walking again. We head down by the river towards the Devil's Hole, the way we've gone so many times before. I start shivering and she gies me her scarf. Keep it, she tells me, and I cannae speak for a few minutes cause I ken I'll greet if I do.

Somewhere along the path we hear barking and Rascal tears down the bank from the top ae Hill Street. I'm more glad than ever to see him. He follows for a while, his tail wagging as he winds through the trees.

Soon we're standing on the bridge in the gloaming, lookin

intae the hole in the river. I try kissing her on her cheeks but she pushes me off and that makes me angry. All she says again and again is no, and no, stubborn as a bloody coo. She makes me feel like a stupid wee boy. I ken I'm making an idiot ae myself but I put my arm round her. It's my last move, and I ken already it's useless, but it's better than kissing her goodbye. She'll meet some other lad at the dances, one who could marry her next week. Her father willnae be ashamed ae him.

Lolly wriggles away from my touch. I pull my hand back and clamp it round the rail ae the bridge. My knuckles go white. Maybe they've met already then, her and the new dreamboat. I ask her what's wrong. It's a stupid thing tae say cause it's fairly obvious what's up, the way she's carrying on. Maybe her father has found out. Maybe he is sending her away. But she could still be with someone else already. What if he lives in Aberdeen? I clench my jaw.

If you would tell me I'm the only one that you love
Life could be a dream, sweetheart.

I snap, wanting tae ken who he is, and Lolly gets a shock. I've never raised my voice like that before with her. I'm sorry already.

She starts crying.

'I'm having your baby,' she says. 'Father's sending me to Aberdeen, and when it's born they said they'll give it away.'

The look ae her hits me like a smack. They're giein it away! That's the bit she greets over, like the words were biting her tongue. And then she reels away from me like she's draggin in a net, a secret she was meant to keep. She starts buttoning her coat furiously. And before I can say anything – We were careful! – Nae careful enough, though, eh? – she's running away down the path.

I try and go after her, but it's dark and I cannae see where she's gone. I close my eyes, let her go. Rascal finds me again later, slumped against a wall like a deid man. He whines in my ear till I run my fingers through tufts ae his fur.

I ken what'll happen. It's nae like it is with us. We look after our babies and help each other, no matter what, like Granny did taking in Big Ellen. We used tae care for other people's bairns an all, the unwanted ones. Some country folk would do anything tae get rid ae the poor wee souls that came before marriage. They'd swaddle them and put them on the cart with the scrap, and we'd have tae drive them round till they found a new family. That's how the Bissaker and Jeannie's Peter came along. Jugs remembers it all from when he was wee. Ma and Father took one or two unwanted babbies themselves. Ma let Jugs hold them in the cart. If the babies were lucky, they'd find a couple that couldnae have bairns, people who hadnae had a son, or a wifey with six boys and wanting a lassie more than anything. But more often than not it was a dour-faced farmer and his wife that needed an extra pair ae hands in the fields. Poor craiturs. But no one puts bairnies on the cart these days. They're sending Lolly away, ashamed ae her.

I wonder about asking Ma for help. She'll tell me tae bring the baby intae the family. She couldnae care less if me and Lolly are unmarried. She and Father never married in a church themselves. If you were together you were together, and kinchins were God's blessing enough – that's how they saw it. But Lolly's father wouldnae agree. His daughter living with the likes ae us? No chance. Even if I got us a council house, he'd disown her for ever.

Wee Betsy comes along the river as I'm sitting there. She's out late in the dark and it's after teatime. She nearly trips over me. Any other night I'd see her in safe, but I cannae face goin back home. I shout at her and make her cry, and she runs off on her own. When she's gone I get to my feet and I start greeting too. It stings, bloody great tears rolling down my cheeks as I walk. I'm headed up the street. I try tae hide behind the scarf Lolly gave me. It smells sweet like her. I wrap it over my nose, pushing my fingers under my oxters and bending forward intae the wind. The scratchy wool on my face makes the stinging worse, but I dinnae mind that. I think ae Lolly so hard it hurts.

Nae much folk out tonight. It's too cal. But I'll not go back tae the Lane. I cannae face the chance that Ma or Jeannie'll still be awake, and the Bissaker and Duncan could be late in the yard, wanting me tae help. Sod that. I'll go for a drink somewhere, keep warm. Maybe some ae the lads will be in the pub, or maybe the station boys. I've still got the money that would ae been for the pictures, and quite a bit on top from my wages. The folk in the pictures will be coming out soon. I wonder if that film was any good.

I get tae the City Hotel around half past eight. I have tae stop twice on the way when first one shoe, then the other, falls off. It's the ones Duncan got me after Wee Betsy and Rachel dropped my boots in the fire. I've nae got thick enough socks tae keep the new ones on.

I get to the hotel eventually. Tommy the Barra, an old pal, he drinks here when he's in town. I heard he'd come round these parts again lately, biding at the Bogs ae Mayne. I let the door slam behind me and peer round the bar for him. Rascal sees him first, and I follow where he's headed. Sure enough, there's the Barra, sat in his favourite seat by the leaded window. His face brightens, all cheery, and he motions at me tae join him. I order us a Double Century each and find myself swallowing all mention ae my troubles with the first few sips.

'Why the lang face?' the Barra says. 'Isn't every day payday for Jocky Terns? Father tells me ye've a job at the station.'

The Barra gies me a wallop on the back and asks me what I'll drink next. I shake my head but he says he'll line up a double for me and goes off tae the bar.

It's grand tae see the Barra again. I swallow doun a good

measure and get a rush ae hot blood through me. It's a feeling I need tae keep hold of tonight, for as long as I can anyway. I slam my empty glass on the table and the Barra lifts his finger tae the barman for more of the same, his face cracked with laughter.

'Jocky Terns, auld pal. Terns, eh? Remember how we aie called ye that?

My evenin with Lolly's already fadin away, drowning in the waves of laughter that lap through the bar.

❋ STITCHES ❋

Auld Betsy, 1955

Night fell an hour ago an ah've nae left ma chair tae light the lamp. Nae even tae sort the fire. Ah'm sittin in the dark, sair awa wi it, sookin oan ma pipe. It's a song an dance, death. Been near enough five days. Five sunrises. Five sunsets. The in-atween time afore his soul can go free. But time's as stubborn as an auld yoke. Ah've been oan this earth lang enough tae ken that. Ye want whit's gone, an ye dinnae like tae imagine whit comes next, sae yer mind rocks atween the twa, like me in ma chair, this wye, that wye. If ah could dae magic, ah'd rock back an bide in the past fer ever mair. But this is ma lot, time keeps shuntin along an taks me wi it, like sittin in a rusty wheelbarra, that's whit ah told Duncan! Dear me, it's a funny thing, God's will.

Affae lot ae practice ah've haed at this. Nae difference, though, each time ah mourn it's like the first time. Each time it's worse cause ah mourn the lot ae them aw at once. He's beside me, at least, hame safe wi me now. 'Yer ma's here tae tak care ae ye,' ah whisper. Whit a haundsome loun ye are in thon uniform ae yours. Light ae the candle oan yer face. Even now. Yer dreamin. Sleepin deep. Oh, me! Is that a wee smile oan yer lips? Why would ye be smilin? Curly's makin a cloutie dumplin. Can ye smell it, ah wonder? If ainly ye could. She's comfortin her bairnies, like ah comfort you. Cloutie dumplin. Stuff tae melt the belly ae a snowman! O ho! Ha! Ha! Here, ma Jock, let's pull thon blanket up roun yer lugs, keep the chill awa. But oh! Yer cheeks are stane cauld! Ah almost didnae mind. Ah hae tae sit back doun an bite hard oan ma pipe. Ah'd tell ye a story but ah cannae think ae any. Aw ah can think ae is the questions goin roun ma heid.

The weather that night wouldae put frost oan the canvas. Ah'll nivver be able tae forget it. Hellish date. Wis the kind ae night when ye were wee ye'd cuddle doun beside me, afore it wis even dark, wi Daddy an yer brothers an sisters. Aw ae us thegither. How mony times had ah tellt ye, Jock Terns? Ye cannae gang ootby wi nae coat. Ye'll catch a death! The bairnies cooried in cosy when it wis bad oot. Is that whit did it son, the cauld? They're sayin it wis yer hert, and that ye must've got intae a fight. But that disnae seem right at aw.

We were in the hoose wiout ye. Aw in oor beds, even Wee Betsy after her night-time wanderin adventures that scared her mammy half tae death. Ainly your bed wis empty, an outside it wis jeelin. Ah couldnae sleep. A bad feelin. Whit were ye thinkin? Abroad in the toun aw alane. Worse than Duncan wi the drink is whit we hear. Ah cannae understaund it. You styterin foo in the gutter? Shaness! Nae like you, ma Jock! Ah thought ye wis a good boy. Wan wi the brain, eh? An noo? . . . *oh.*

Ah let ma pipe drop fae ma mou, place it oan the side ae the coffin, an ah stamp across the boards tae the windae. Cannae look at ye lyin there aw peaceful an silent ony mair. Ma hair's swept back, but the loose bits at the front are aw wet fae greetin, stuck tae ma face. They feel cool in the draft fae the windae. Ah tug whit there is ae the curtains ower the pane but they're nae big enough tae keep oot the light fae the gas lamp in the street.

Room's aw sunk in the darkness when ah turn roun so ah light another candle. Ma shadow falls tae the flair. The ootline ae ma high collar an the bun in ma hair's creepin like ivy ontae the cupboard door. An there's the perfect shadow ae ma Jock's face oan the wall. Him sleepin, sound as stone, a saint oan a tomb. Ah go back ower tae him.

Ye are ma good boy, aie will be. Look at ye. If ye could feel me stroke yer cheek. Still rosy. They'll nivver get wrinkles like mine. Thon cheeks. Break herts, that's whit we said ye'd dae wi them.

Break herts!

Fer a second ah cannae catch a breath. Feels like ma ain auld chest is giein up the ghost fer good. 'Enough!' ah want tae shout. The pain's like ah've been pierced through. But part ae me welcomes this, start ae the end, cause at the tail ae it there'll be ma George. Ah'll see aw ma bairnies whase wee bodies ah carried an then had tae kiss goodbye, gie back tae God. Ma Francis, poor Francis. Wee Georgina an Wee Peter. An ma Jock'll be there noo. Ma Jock. Shaness! Shaness! He should nivver hae gone afore me. It's oonnaitral.

Ah'm breathin again, deeply intae yer black hair which smells ae dust. The prison flair. Nivver broke a single hert, did ye? Nae till thon night. Whit did ah tell ye? Ah said it'd be the death ae me if thon wicked manishee wis right. Thon cursed Batchie Woman. Shaness! Curse the night her evil mither gied birth. Ah tak ma rosary in ma fammels an pull at thon beads till they might snap. Ah could choke wi the anger against her. Devil tak her tae a frozen grave! Or yer auld mither'll murder her.

Ah drop the beads back in ma pouch. Ma fammels are shakin as ah pick up ma pipe an tak a lang sook. Ma throat's raw an the smoke scaulds. Ah mustnae think evil things. Jock needs peace. Hush, wicked thoughts!

Ah've been watchin ower ye aw the time, ma Jock. Daein the sittin up. Keepin ye safe fae harm's wye, haudin yer haund, smoothin yer hair. But ah hae tae rest a wee bit. Ah'll hae tae keep mysel breathin a while yet cause somethin's wrang here. Ah ken it in ma bones. Sure as ever, somethin's sair aff.

There's words restin oan yer lips. That's whit's gettin tae me. There's words restin oan yer lips jist like after a kiss. Ah'm certain, feel it under ma chin, like a lump ae crust that willnae gang doun. It's a secret ye needed yer auld ma tae ken. An aw night an aw day ah've been strokin ma fingertip ower this wee patch oan yer heid, bitin ma tongue, haudin a feeling doun like a thump in the belly. Is this whit the secret's oan? This wee patch under yer bonnie hair? Ye've got stitches in yer heid, son. An they werenae there when ye said yer last goodbye tae me that night.

Ah count them wi ma nail. Twenty-four. Rusty broon caked roun the threed.

Somewan's come in the room. They're movin aboot wi a bottle. Ah hear them light the Tilly, then shuffle fae the cupboard tae the sink.

'Will ye hae a wee drink ae somethin?'

'George?' Is that his haund oan ma back? Ah put ma pipe doun.

'Ma, it's me. Yer confused. Ah'm nae Dad.'

He hauds a mug towards me, cannae look at his wee brother.

'Ah'm nae wantin that. Tak it awa.'

He puts the mug oan the flair beside ma chair an he pulls up another an sits. Ah can still see ma Jock's shadow oan the wall, fainter noo wi the light oan.

'Ye ken the funeral's sorted, Ma.'

Funeral. Duncan speaks oan it aw gentle, lookin intae ma lap. His voice sounds mair like Jock than hissel. Ah nod, rummle ma rosary roun ma pouch again. Eleven o'clock in ma kirk. The boys sorted it aw atween them. They chose a grave Jock would like, a place where he can see the herons on the loch. It's a braw spot fer a picnic, a wee wander. Aw up in the sky he wis, ma Jock, wi his birds when he wis wee, an his planes.

'Ma? Curly's got his things taegither fer ye.'

'Good. Good.'

'Will ye nae keep anythin? Wan ae they wee wooden planes he did?'

'Nae a thing mair. Ma Jock should be at peace, so the rest's tae go.'

240

'Aye, that it can,' Duncan laughs. 'Ye ken he's got aboot five hundred cigarette cards an a great pile ae comics under thon bed ae his, wee brother.'

Duncan puts his haund ower his mou an it's quiet again. Too quiet.

'Hunners, eh? O ho! Ho! Ha! Ma Jock. Aw yer treasures.'

Ah reach ower an haud Jock's haund, ma dear clever boy's haund.

'Ah can still smell the polish aff his shoes,' ah say tae Duncan.

He did them that night, afore he left. He left the lid aff the tin an the brush oan his bed an it wis me put them back in the shoebox. Ah cannae stop the tears ony mair.

Duncan leans ower ma chair an puts his arms roun his auld ma. He's a strong man. Same build as Jugs. Different fae Jock. Different aw thegither. Ah feel his breath oan the top ae ma heid an bury ma face in his coat. It has the smell ae the whisky. But ah'll no blame him fer that. Nae the day.

'Ah miss him, Ma,' he goes, his words aw broken. He willnae let his bairns see him like this, but wi his ma it's different.

'Think ae the bairnies,' ah tell him, wipin ma eyes an giein him a pat oan the sleeve. He says nothin. He's haudin his breath in. 'Whit's in thon cup, Duncan?'

He sounds relieved an reaches fer it. 'A dram, Ma. Dae ye want it? Help ye rest a wee bit.'

'Aye. Gies it here.'

'We've gied some tae the girls. They were sair fae greetin.'

Ah nod an tak a swig. It burns aw the wye doun, burns sae weel ah cannae feel ma breath hurtin me nae mair. 'Thon's whit the doctor ordered,' ah say. An ah let ma eyes rest back oan ma sleepin son, fine man that he wis. Ah wipe ma een again, an ah think ae thon wound. Twenty-four stitches. Nae doctor's ony good tae us now.

'Ah wonder wha put thon stitches in his heid,' ah whisper. 'Ye've seen them, have ye nae?'

241

Duncan nods. He's pourin hisself a dram an aw. 'We'll find oot. Dinnae think ae that.'

But ah dae think ae it. Wha held the needle? How did he get hurt? Did he hae an accident? Wis he at the hospital? Who wis the last wan tae care fer him?

'Ah hope she wis a bonnie lassie, the wan that stitched him,' ah say, wipin the wet strands ae hair aff ma cheeks. 'Ah hope she wis kind tae him.'

Ah jump at a sudden knock oan the door. Ah'm waitin fer news. An maybe that's it come. Some answers. Duncan opens it.

'Look who it is,' he says, an he opens the door wide. Ah look up, hopeful, but it's jist Big Mary. She's come tae visit her auld auntie, then. Poor lassie. There's nane left now tae marry her roun here. She's nae the bonniest tae behold, nae very glamorous, ah'll grant ye, but she's awright oor Mary, nae a bad sort. Aw she's wantin is a wee family. Her mammy wis Agnes, the sister born after me, an her daddy wis a McAllister. They both passed younger than the rest ae us, wan wi hert troubles, the ither wi pneumonia. Aw her sisters married, an her wan brother wis a piper, mauded in the war. So she's the last, and that's a terrible, lonely thing.

Big Mary's gonnae heid south now, she says, and ah think it's a gye shame fer her, aff awa by herself. Thon's the greatest sadness fer oor fowk, bein aw alane. Pity ma Jock nivver saw past her appearance. But he wis still a boy. After his feet failed the test fer the services we aw thought he'd settle doun. We had hopes fer the pair ae them. But he held fast tae his dreams; planes an pin-ups an aw that poppycock they play at the picture hoose. He wanted tae bide happy ever after.

'Ta fer comin by,' says Duncan. Big Mary tiptoes across the room like she's late fer a church service. The flairboards creak under her boots onywye.

Her face is aw red an she's tryin tae haud in the tears as she looks fae Jock tae me. She hugs a biscuit tin close tae her bosie, like it's a bairnie. She doesnae say a word, but when she touches the coffin her voice breaks oot, suckin in a sob. She kisses Jock's haund, gies him a lingerin look, then straightens up an blows her nose. Ah lower ma eyes.

It's a song an dance death. Fowk hae been in an oot, coverin the wireless an the organ wi clouts, bringin me pieces in biscuit tins, funeral organisin, wantin tae ask me aboot stone inscriptions an this an that, bringin their condolences, payin their last respects. Whit church will we haud the funeral in? Ma's Catholic wan, or Duncan an Curly's Baptist wan? Cause the minister there's a fine sort. Or shall we jist gang tae the Church ae Scotland like abody else? Aw the same tae me. Oor family belangs tae aw the different churches, when we go tae those places at aw. High in the mountains, next tae a bonnie burn, that's where ah feel close tae God. An fer Jock it wis by the sea, watchin the birds like his daddy. It's whit's in yer hert that counts.

They're worried. They dinnae like tae say, but ah ken that wi no wages fae Jock they're wonderin how we can keep the rent up. The Bissaker an Jugs an Duncan were ootby talkin oan it, the council maybe puttin us in wan ae them new hooses. Nae thegither, though, aw in the wan hoose like we are here. The council wouldnae dae that, nae fer the likes ae us. There's too many ae us, an it's aic too much bother. So we'll be separated. Maybe ah dinnae want tae stay here onywye. Ah lost George in this hoose, an now ma boy's gone an aw, another wan. Oot oan the road we'd hae moved. We'd hae built a wee cairn first, tae let ither fowk ken it wis a place somewan passed, jist so they didnae pitch ower it. An then there'd be the burnin fer Jock. A great fire would be made ae aw his belongins tae set him free fae this world.

Then aff we'd go.

Ye hae tae let the mauded rest in peace. Ah cannae haud ontae them. Ainly a few bitties can be kept tae treasure for ever.

Pipes aff the musicians, a rosary like ah got aff ma mither, or a wee photie.

It's later in the evenin when there's an almighty crash ootside the front door. Ah throw ma haunds up, go tae the windae an pull back the curtain. Wha the Deil's makin a noise like that wi ma Jock in here? Is it some news? Ah'm aw ready tae gie somewan a tellin, but aw ah see oot there's a boy, fallen aff his bike oantae the cobbles. Ma temper melts awa.

'Curly,' ah breathe at the bottom ae the dancers, nae wantin tae shout. She appears in her doorway, a wee haund in hers. 'Leave the bairn up there an watch him a moment,' ah say. Curly pushes the quine back intae her room, closes the door an starts doun the dancers. She's quiet, light oan her tramplers, almost like a ballerina.

Ah go oot the front door an stroll up tae the gate. The lad's still dustin hissel aff, trickle ae blood runnin doun wan knee.

'Are ye all right, son?' ah ask. 'Whit a wallop ye gied yersel.' He's leanin his bike oan the wall ae oor gairden.

'Sorry,' he says. 'Sorry fer disturbin ye, Mrs Whyte, at a time like this.'

'Eh. Were ye wan ae Jock friends, lad?' ah ask, thinkin whit's this tounie after? Maybe he worked wi Jock at the station.

'No,' he says. 'I'm a reporter fer the *Courrant.*'

He hauds oot his haund. Ah swallow. That wis the paper ma Jock read, written by country fowk that nivver had a good word tae say aboot us. Ah willnae shake his haund, but this lad's jist a young thing, must be jist oot ae the school. Ah look him up an doun, hook ma thumbs ower the waist ae ma skirt.

'Whit is it yer wantin?'

'I'm very sorry, Mrs Whyte, and sorry about the noise oot here,' he says again, goin red in the face. 'We were wanting tae report what happened. If you didnae mind speaking tae me. Just the facts.'

244

Ah think aboot it fer a minute. The facts. Ah put ma haund in ma pocket an feel ma rosary. The boy waits. He looks me right in the een, this loun. He's fair-haired, nae like ma Jock. But there's somethin in his face that reminds me ae ma son.

'The kettle's oan. Come inside. Ah've pieces comin oot ma ears an aw. Perhaps ma son Duncan'll tak a look at the brakes on thon bike ae yours.'

The loun smiles an ah tak him inside. Curly opens ma door as we go past an ah see him keek ower her shoulder fer a glimpse ae the body, wonder if he's ever seen wan afore. Ah lead him intae Jeannie's room an gie him a buttery piece, pour him a cup ae tea.

An these are his facts. Ah cannae get through them wiout a muckle good greet. But this is whit ah tell him.

Jock wis a healthy boy. Twenty-two years ae age. He wis a good boy, a clever lad jist like his faither had been, an nice tae his family. The bairns loved him. He wis nae fond ae the drink. By faith, his brothers are, but ah tell ye God's truth, nae him. Jock worked at Elgin train station, but his dream wis tae be a pilot.

He went oot oan the evenin ae February twenty-fifth, nineteen fifty-five, an it wis cauld that night. Afore he left he asked his sister-in-law, Martha, tae sew a button back oan the waist-coat ae his uniform, which he'd need fer the followin mornin. He wis aie smart an handsome fer his work. He came in ma room, said 'Cheerio, Ma,' an then he went oot. He didnae say where he wis awa tae, but ah didnae like tae pry. Ah dinnae ken if he wis seein a lassie or whit.

That wis the last time ah saw ma boy alive. Later a neighbour said he'd seen Jock get lifted. He'd ainly been quadded wan or twa times afore, a good few years ago an aw. Jeannie an Wullie went up tae see aboot bail, but the police said he would hae tae be carried hame in a stretcher, he wis that bad. So they came awa. Ah couldnae sleep. At four in the mornin twa policemen came wi Jock's wee dog. They said ma son passed awa in cell number twa ae the jail. It wis a terrible thing.

Duncan went tae Dr Grey's Hospital. He'd tae gie them Jock's name. They kept him a lang time up there, far too lang wiout him haein his family roun him. We're sittin up wi Jock here now, keepin a candle lit.

He's still a handsome loun, except fer the twenty-four stitches in his heid an the bruises oan his chest. The funeral's the morra's mornin. An they're daein an inquest oan whit happened, but nae fer a month.

Inquest, ma arse, ah think tae myself. But thon's the facts. An somehow ah ken it'll be the ainly wans we'll ever get. Ah dry ma een, an when ah can see again, the wee blond reporter looks like his buttery piece stuck in his throat. But ah'm finished talkin, so he swallows, an scribbles his facts doun in his notebook.

✳ PEACE ✳

Wee Betsy, 1955

I must be a wicked lassie. The worst thing in the world happened. It was the middle of the night when a manny came to the door. I heard them hammering loud on the knocker. I thought it was strange for somebody to turn up so late, but then it could've just been Jugs, or one of Uncle Wullie's friends. Sometimes they're too drunk to walk home. I'd been having a good dream, tucked up all toasty next to Mammy. So when Jeannie's feet creaked on the floorboards downstairs I just rolled over, hoping I'd be able to go back into the dream. Jeannie made a strange noise, like a fish bone was caught in her throat, and then she started crying. I felt sick.

I did things to Uncle Jock that weren't nice. Just the other day he came upstairs to have a cup of tea. He was sitting on the wee sofa smoking a ciggie, and I was watching him while I gobbled up my dinner. A wee flame fluttered onto his shirt. I saw it burning, like an orange star near his collar. It didn't go out. Uncle Jock was reading a book to Rachel, who'd already finished her tea. He was doing silly voices and making her laugh.

'Uncle Jock there's a bit of ash on your shirt and it's still on fire.' That's what I should have said. But I never did, cause I'm a sly fox. That's what Daddy calls me, sly as a fox that one. I liked the feeling of knowing what was going to happen next. The way the Batchie Woman knows. I narrowed my eyes and stared so hard at the wee flame I forgot to eat, just sat there with a wicked glint in my eye till Mammy told me to stop dithering. A hole scorched through Jock's shirt.

'Oooyah! Owie! Nipped me,' he said, startled out of his silly reading voice. He made a show of it, thumping his chest like a monkey to put the flame out and saying 'Ooo, ooo, ooo!', and everyone laughed, even Jock. But it was his best shirt, he said so after, and now he's gone and I hate that I did such a wicked thing.

I did other bad things too. I took some of his comics without asking, and I looked in his drawer once to try and find out if he had a girlfriend. I burnt his boot by putting it into the fire, and Granny said he was already cursed, even before that happened.

It's the funeral today. Near the grave there's a tree with rust-colour branches. Granny thinks it's lucky, but I can't see anything special about it. It's a stupid tree like all the others. Daddy says not to listen to my granny at the minute cause she's been fretting and not right in the head. She cries and talks about Jock and Francis and Granddad as if they were still alive, and I'm supposed to be giving her some peace, which is what she needs.

Peace is where Mammy says Jock is at now. As if peace was really a place. At Peace. Not too different from being at Lossie, at school, at the baths, or at the sweetie shop just down the road. But it's more like in *Journey into Space*, when something goes wrong and the crew are lost out in the universe. At least it's meant to be a nice place. I read the gravestones next to Jock's. A lady in the one beside him isn't at Peace, she's at Rest, another place people say you go when you die. I'm not stupid. I know it's just pretend.

There are names and dates on Jock's gravestone. Lots of people brought money to pay for the letters and numbers. I count the dates. Jock was twenty-one. He was nearly twenty-two. I know that because he wanted to go on a train on his birthday, and I had already made him a card with the number twos drawn out, and with different colours and patterns inside.

The grass round the hole is soft and thick, sparkling with

raindrops and cold sunlight. It smells of the picnics we go on in the summer when I run round with bare feet and have to mind the thistles. Coiled up bits of leaves have blown into small piles near the graves and the tree trunks. They would have been nice colours once, but now they're all the same brown, brittle and dull with holes in, like the wings of dead moths that we find in the rags. Wee bits of the brown leaves break up and fly away in the wind, right up over the tree tops. Other bits sink into the soil and help to grow the grass and the trees they fell from. Above us the branches already have new buds, all there cause of the dead things in the earth. We learnt about it at school.

Everyone is being nice to me and Rachel. Miss Webster came to visit already, and brought two yellow cakes, one each. I wanted mine straight away and Mammy gave it to me on a plate while she was talking to my teacher. I took a first mouthful of the treat, but it tasted too sticky and sweet. I got a choking feeling, like I was eating fur or feathers. The icing stuck to the roof of my mouth and I had to close my eyes tight to not cry. But it would have been bad manners not to finish. I gulped it down, forcing it bit by bit. Miss Webster said we could come back to school when we were ready. Granny's finally got rid of the beasties in our hair. But we might go to a new school now. Daddy says we're moving on. I said thank you to Miss Webster, anyway, forcing another bite of cake, which made my heart sore. That was what they said happened to Jock. Something was wrong with his heart. Granny doesn't believe them, and I don't either. Jock loved everyone. There was nothing wrong with his heart.

Behind Jock's gravestone, the minister's making a speech about understanding and forgiveness, the Lord God Almighty and lambs and sinners. I'm a sinner now so I can't look him in the eye. Instead I stare down into the muddy hole, wondering if I'll spot a worm. I keep a watch on Daddy, the Bissaker and Jugs, who are holding one side of the coffin. I want to make sure they are all all right. On the other side are three cousins I don't know. Daddy said folk came from miles away after other relatives spread the news on the road. I never knew we had so many relatives. In the crowd I catch sight of Big Rachel, the lady with the long red hair who gave me the special toffee, but most of them are strangers.

The coffin wobbles on its way down. I watch it disappear into the neatly cut gap in the grass. Lots of people are crying now, holding handkerchiefs over their faces so no one will see. I don't want them to be crying, especially not my daddy. Big Mary howls the loudest, and I wish she would shut up. She hardly knew my Uncle Jock, even if Granny wanted them to get married. Jock didn't love her. But there was nothing wrong with his heart.

A man in a black suit comes round with a velvet bag and everyone puts their hands in. I wonder are they giving money, like you do for the people at the showies? Will it be for us? But then the man shakes the bag in front of me.

My fingers touch something cold and wettish at the bottom. I pull my hand out again quickly. It's covered in earth, all grubby in the grooves of my palm and itchy under my fingernails. Mammy scrubbed my hands this morning till they were sore and pink, and now I'll look like I've been tattie hauking in my Sunday best. I see the dirt on my skin and want to greet again. It reminds me of ripping up the grass in the park that night, and the secret I told the policeman. No one knows about that.

I'm waiting to be told off for getting clatty, but Mammy takes a whole fistful of the mud and divides it in two. She gets me to hold my hand out and gives me half, telling me not to drop it on the ground this time. It goes into the grave! I don't want us to bury Jock ourselves, but one by one people throw handfuls of earth down onto the coffin. Granny goes first and Daddy has to help her away again cause she looks like she might throw herself into the hole. Then him and the Bissaker and Jugs go up. The earth hitting the wood makes a horrible wet noise, a slapping, chopping sound.

Mammy pushes me and Rachel forward and I peer over the edge. The top of the coffin was clean and covered in flowers before, but now it's dark with mudpies. I hold my fist tight and look up at Father O'Brien's stern face. I think he remembers me from Sunday School. Mammy whispers in my ear to throw my earth into the hole now, to stay near to Jock for ever. I hold my hand out over the coffin and uncurl my fingers. To stay near to Jock for ever.

For as long as I can, I look at the little grains of earth scattered over the coffin, searching for the ones that were mine. They'll be there till the end of time, next to where Jock is sleeping. Before I turn away I have to say sorry for another thing, the wickedest thing of all that I did to Jock. I have to make it better quick, cause I know I'll be pulled away from the grave any minute, just like I was pulled away from Granny's door when Jock was in her room.

He was in there for days! I saw him through a crack in Granny's door. He was lying on the table. Mammy said he was sleeping peacefully and I wasn't to go in. I wasn't to disturb him. Only the adults were allowed. He was under a blanket and Granny was rocking next to him in her chair. Jeannie was doing the fire and making them all tea, and Daddy was sitting on Granny's bed with his head in his hands. Mammy caught me peeking and she pulled me back up the stairs. She shouted at me, shouting in a shooshing voice so they wouldn't hear in Granny's room, where there needed to be peace.

Earlier today they opened the door so I could kiss Uncle Jock goodbye. He was still on the table in the coffin, but the blanket was gone, and under it he was wearing his station uniform. The button was back on his waistcoat, the one my Mammy said she would mend for him. No one had their head in their hands any

251

more. They were all standing up now, gathered round him in their best clothes. Granny's eyes looked swollen and red. Mammy had her head down, like us in assembly when we say 'Let us pray.' Rachel was staring at me and Nancy was being hushed in Big Ellen's arms. Daddy and Jeannie and the Bissaker and Jugs and Annie were there too, all waiting for me and beckoning me over. But I stayed in the doorway. Uncle Jock looked pale and cold.

Rachel did it. Mammy lifted her up and she kissed him on the hand. They even made Baby Nancy kiss him on the forehead, and they put a lock of her precious golden hair into his pocket. But I was tall enough to reach Uncle Jock all by myself. I was his favourite because we listened to the wireless together. And I said no.

Someone takes my hand and gently pulls me away from the grave. I can't see my sisters or my mammy any more cause my face is tight and sore as knots that won't undo. I don't even know if there are tears on my cheeks, but the cold's stinging them and my chest feels like it's been squeezed empty.

The lady holding my hand says she'll take us with her now. She puts an arm round my shoulders and holds something out for me to take. That's the first thing I can see that isn't a blur, the hanky clasped in her fingers like a white lily. I take it and the lady presses me to her side and strokes my hair back. I'm still standing there frozen, just holding the hanky, so she puts it up to my face for me.

When I can catch my breath I look up. It's Big Rachel, Nancy in her arms, and Wee Rachel walking on her other side. There's no toffee today and I'm glad. I'm fed up of sweeties. The sun in Big Rachel's hair glows the same orange as the spark from Jock's cigarette. I stay right by her side and let her lead me away from the grave. The path through the woods crunches under my shoes; the bushes rustle; we see a fox. A sly fox that one, I think, and have to swallow. Wee Rachel finds a pretty feather stuck to some bark. Maybe it's a heron's. She draws it again and again along her cheek.

The things I never had time to say to Uncle Jock start to sink, like the dead leaves that feed the trees. I feel them hardening in the pit of my stomach with the other things I can't ever tell.

Big Rachel takes us to the budgie house. It's down a street near the gasworks where we get our cinders, just past a place called the Order Pot, where Granny says they used to drown witches. I've only been to the budgie house three times before, twice when my wee sisters were being born and once when Granddad died. The budgies belong to an old lady who Big Rachel calls Mrs Mellor. They have a room all to themselves at the back of the house, where they swing on pine cones and bells hanging from strings, flap their sherbet wings, and stare out of the window at the rolling thunder clouds and the railway line to Lossie.

Mrs Mellor's been expecting us. She calls us darlings, and when we go inside there's a sponge cake on the table and four places have been laid with a proper china tea set. But before tea we have to look at the budgies. Mrs Mellor is very proud of her wee birdies. My favourite ones are purple with speckled black bits on their heads. I'd like one to come and land on my hand, so I hold it out and pretend I have some food, but none of them are fooled. Wee Rachel leaves the feather she found at Spynie for them to play with.

We sit at the table and Mrs Mellor asks do we want to listen to some music? I don't really, but Rachel nods her head, and Mrs Mellor puts a record onto the gramophone. It's an old song that goes 'Mairsy doats and dozy doats and little somethingorothers'. The words make Rachel giggle madly and she has to hold onto the seat of her chair not to fall off. Big Rachel strokes her hand down my back and we smile at each other just a bit, cause my wee sister's so silly.

I like the plates we eat off at the budgie house. They are so clean and pretty, with roses painted on them, and the knives are always shiny bright. They make everything taste nicer, and I get quite hungry watching Mrs Mellor cutting the cake and scraping the spare butter icing onto the rosy pattern of one of the plates. I decide I do want a piece, and soon I'm licking the icing off my top lip, listening to tiny teaspoons clinking round the teacups and the jingling and chittering of the birds in the next room.

Mrs Mellor's house has carpets and soft chairs, and always smells good. It's the nicest house I've ever been in, like houses in the pictures. Big Rachel helps her keep it clean.

The best thing of all about the budgie house is that Mrs Mellor has a television. When we've finished our cake Big Rachel says she'll get to work now, and she takes our plates away and starts washing them up. Mrs Mellor sends us into the front room with apples cut into slices. We sit on the carpet with our backs leaning against the settee, comfy except that the carpet is rough and itchy on my shins. I pull my kilt down and my socks up as high as they will go. We share the apple and watch *Muffin the Mule*, *Andy Pandy* and a programme about a zoo before Big Rachel comes through and says it's time for us to say thank-you-very-much-for-having-us to Mrs Mellor.

The television is switched off. It makes a popping noise, and then the light of the screen gets further and further away, shrinking till it's just a wee white hole in a world of blackness. It's quiet in the room without the cheerful voices from the programmes, and I feel like something from inside me has been sucked into the little white square along with Andy Pandy. I look round the room for something to think about, something nice. Mrs Mellor has a collection of glass animals on the windowsill, and porcelain girls with lipstick smiles dancing in pretty dresses, but they're so still it's like they're just pretending to be smiling. So all I can think of is Uncle Jock.

I wish we could stay at the budgie house a bit longer. Last time we came home from here we had a new sister, but this time we'll have one less person to say hello to. While we were watching television, Uncle Jock's things were being taken away and burned. That's what Granny said they would do this afternoon. Make a bonfire of all Jock's things. She said it's a wonderful thing that means he can go away, to Heaven or to Peace, or wherever he has gone. He won't have anything left to hold him back. But we won't have anything to hold onto either. I think it's sad. His comics and his aeroplane books, his wallet, the pictures off his wall, his pillow, the letters he got from his penpal in Belgium, his tools for carving, even the favourite shirt with the cigarette burn through the shoulder, all that will be gone when we get home, turned to ashes and dust.

Back at the Lane, I don't go into the house right away. I can hear Granny crying from outside. Instead I drag my feet up to the drying green to see where the fire was. I want to be by myself, except for the doggie. I find Rascal at the green too, lying on the grass. I sit beside him on the edge of the blackened bit, as if it was still ablaze and we were going to sing a campfire song. I rip up weeds from the edge, get up and kick my toes into the dirt. One. Two. One. Two. One. Two, I say. One. Two. One. Two. One. Two.

I throw grass into the black circle and over Rascal's head. He tries to catch it in his mouth. When I'm tired of the game I lean over and press the tip of my forefinger into the dust, draw a snail swirl. And right in the middle I find something. There's one thing that's left, saved from the flames. It's a sooty pebble with a hole in it, which Uncle Jock wore round his neck. He must have meant it for me. When I pick it up I feel like I'm holding Jock in my hands, all of who he was, still alive, as if it was a flying saucer and he was inside.

I put my hand in my coat pocket, wrapped over the pebble, and I turn it over and over as I climb to the top of Lady Hill, following Rascal, my heart getting bigger and bigger. There's no noise from the scrap yard today. All the men were off work to go to the funeral, even the bosses.

It's getting dark fast, but I'm not scared. Rascal's with me and so's Uncle Jock. It feels like I'm holding his hand. The gulls have gone to sleep. No one else is up here except for two old tramps with a bottle in a paper bag. I sit on a ruin and hold the pebble in front of my face like a pirate with a precious stone. I imagine myself in a red velvet ball gown, one of Mrs Mellor's bright green budgies perched on my shoulder, a telescope in my hand, a skull and crossbones fluttering above me. Pretty Polly! Pretty Polly!

My hands are blackened with ashes from the fire dust. I don't mind, though. I'm plundering the seven seas for diamonds and rubies! Pieces of eight! Pieces of eight! I squint through the wee hole in the pebble, moving it round so through it I see the moon, then the mountains, then the Fifth Duke of Gordon's head (Make the gent walk the plank!), then the roof of our house, then a steeple with a cross on top.

As I'm scanning my ocean for the cathedral tower, there's a flash of light. Buried treasure! We're rich! Let's drop anchor and sleep in the caves with the tinkers. We'll live happily ever after!

I hold my hand steady and peer through the hole at my treasure, flashing lights blinking on and off, on and off over the High Street. It's the flicks. C.I.N.E.M.A., the lights spell. On. Off. On. Off. One. Two. One. Two.

This is what Uncle Jock wants me to see.

CINEMA* *CINEMA* *CINEMA

Dawn

Maeve said it was going to snow but Dawn hoped she was wrong. The last thing she needed was blocked roads. Anyway, at this time of year it would be a weird thing to happen. Not right. September for Christssake. But to Dawn's surprise the weather man thought there was a thirty to forty per cent chance. He told them so as he did his wizard's swooping sidestep over the top half of the map. Good odds for Maeve. Much stranger things had happened with infinitely small odds. One day she'd explain all this to her, the tiny chances that things always came down to.

It had snowed the day she left Warren. Her burns were dressed in bandages, and were still sore, but she'd managed to put everything she'd set aside into a suitcase. She'd been preparing for a while by then. She'd been collecting valuables she could tuck away without much notice, jewellery mostly, that and anything else that fitted into matchboxes. She'd thought she'd not have much time, when the time came, so she'd only prepared small things.

But there were two surprises the day she left. First, she had plenty of time. Warren didn't try to stop her. He actually smiled, a daft smile like she was off to get him something he needed from the corner shop. Later, that's what she thought of when Mother asked if the wounds on her wrists had been a mistake, a strange sort of accident. Warren was such a nice boy. His mother was one of Mother's best friends. Dawn could be clumsy, after all, and she was full of stories, so prone to exaggeration.

Dawn saw how wrong Mother was now. She'd never been one for tall tales. She'd never believed in magic or fate, or lucky charms or the kelpies, or any of that stuff. Not ever. She knew when something was real.

For years her ribs had throbbed where he'd got her with his knuckles and sent her to the floor. He'd held her down with just one hand, and forced her against the Valor, an old one they'd got second-hand. It would've been fine except that she'd turned it up just after breakfast when she'd taken the bins out. The wind had chilled her to her core. Back inside she'd needed to warm her hands and she'd turned the thing up even though he'd told her not to. It's like a bloody furnace in here already, he'd said. She'd hated the sound of his voice, and turned it up even more, liking the crack of the dial each time it was notched up a setting. Breaking bones.

She'd never forget the pain of the burns. The screaming was like it wasn't part of her, and she didn't remember that any more. She only remembered thinking the neighbours would hear and come to stop it, and later wondering why the bastards never did.

When he pulled her to her feet he was close enough to kiss. He had her by the collar, almost bloody strangling her with one hand, the other making a fist over her. She watched a ribbon of saliva curl over his bottom lip, saw the shimmer inside it from the Christmas fairy lights. She tried to hide her face, waiting for the fist. With her head down she noticed a drip of slether on the toe of one of his favourite loafers. He buffed those loafers till they shone, bright enough to reflect his face. It took strength to polish shoes properly, he always said. A man's strength.

Mummy! Snow! Maeve shouted from the window.

The snow. That was the second surprise that day. She was wearing heels. She'd got her bag together without once looking out of the window, and she'd shut the front door firmly behind her. She hadn't slammed it, just pulled it quietly to till the lock clicked and it was final. That was when she'd noticed the snow. There was no going back to change her shoes.

Maeve was calling her. Dawn got up from the sofa to switch off the telly, and bending down she felt a twinge. Another wound from him, just above the left kidney. He'd given her old bones. The twinges were always a sign of the cold weather coming back. Time to start saving for Santa Claus.

December the twenty-fifth, one week after she'd left him. The blood hadn't come straight away. She found a dark stain on her white underwear, and Shirley took her straight up to the hospital, poor thing, the second time in a week. But the baby she'd waited years for would hold on. It was just getting comfy. They went home in the evening and sat in front of the films till bedtime. Dawn wasn't really watching. She was too busy imagining it inside her, small and round and suspended, full of secrets, a Christmas orb in red velvet.

That was the real magic.

The phone calls from Warren began on Boxing Day. At night he came to the house drunk and screamed at the door. He fell down the icy steps and lay groaning on the lawn, but they didn't let him in. They kept everything locked and worried he would smash the windows or freeze to death on the ground, so his body would have to be chiselled out in the morning. The fear of it kept Dawn awake all night. Shirley insisted she should leave, as soon as she was fit enough and the snow had melted. And eventually that's what she'd done. Shirley had called a friend in Glasgow who'd given her a bed there for a while, just till she found a job and a room of her own.

It wasn't snowing outside the kitchen window at all.

It will be!

Maeve insisted. She'd already put her woolly hat on, and Dawn realised she was to play the game. She gave the air an exaggerated sniff, but the air hadn't changed. A whole summer and it was still the same smell in the flat. Nearly four decades of talc, dry-cleaned tweed, cardboard, roast tatties, and bloody pot-pourri. She sniffed again.

You're right about the snow, she lied. It's on its way. Are you all packed?

Maeve didn't reply. She rested her head on Dawn's hip. Her thumb was in her mouth. She'd started doing that recently, and Blue Scarfy seemed to have disappeared.

Let's get your boots on, Dawn said.

Dad was waiting at the window, looking into the sky, worried the weather wouldn't hold for their journey. Dawn left most of the cases in the car. She'd handed in the keys at the estate agent's and packed everything she owned in just under an hour. She was wearing the old wool coat, Lolly's favourite shade of blue, and in the pockets there were matches, Marlboros. She'd taken her cassette tapes, the scruffy old child's slipper, the photos, and Shirley's locket with the black curl inside. Maybe it was her own baby hair, or even better, maybe it was Jock's. She could have it tested for DNA. It gave her butterflies just thinking about that. She'd seen it done on the telly. A scientist would look through a microscope and shout 'We have a match!' And that would be it – she would know. Case closed.

She was keeping the locket safe inside a box of Scottish Bluebell matches. That box was the first one in her old collection, a reminder of the first night she spent with Warren in their house with the lucky red doorstep. That was a good memory, one she'd give to Maeve.

They'd arrived late at night. The place smelt of unwashed towels and cigarette smoke which wasn't hers. She didn't start that habit till later. Their bed was a mattress on the floor and she could hear there were mice but it was too dark to see. The light bulbs had gone and there were no spares. Warren went out to scrounge a bulb off a neighbour. She loved his excitement about the place. He'd been on about doing the garden, saving up for a three-piece, even a nursery, for Christssake! When he came back he handed her a paper bag full of candles and that box of matches. Scottish Bluebell Brand. She liked them because they had blue tips and because they were from him. They might have even been the reason she took up smoking.

Later that night she filled the bath and watched the reflections of the candle flames flickering on the water and on the shiny white tiles. He washed her hair, lifting it gently through the water, feeling its weight. He said he'd never seen anything so black. She wore it right down to her hips in those days, an inky spill right down her spine.

You coming in, then? We've a roast on, Mother said. All packed?

All packed.

Maeve had been forgiven and they took her into the kitchen for orange squash. Dawn found Linda upstairs in their old bedroom. She knocked on the door and popped her head round. Her sister was on the bed with the family photo albums open.

Oh, it's you. I was just looking at some of these.

Linda looked better, not as orange as usual. Dawn sat beside her. You not working in the shop right now?

Work's fine. I read a thing on the beds in a magazine, though. They reckon they found a link with skin cancer. So it's just one a week now.

That's good, Dawn said. It only felt strange to say that because she meant it now. Her sister wasn't half as bad as she'd remembered.

You're away tomorrow, then?

Aye, long as it doesn't snow.

Linda went to the window. Her cigarettes and lighter were on the sill. It was raining.

Typical bloody weather, she said. Summer's over, eh?

Dawn looked at the family pictures. They were all together in one old shot, just the four of them, so Shirley had probably been behind the camera. Mother had lifted Linda, just a wee thing, out of the pram, and Dad had his arms tight round Dawn. She was smiling, just for the camera but you couldn't tell. She didn't remember where they were or why the photo was taken.

Can I take this? she said. For Maeve.

Linda nodded. You'll be coming back, though?

Maeve wants to, Dawn said.

So?

Yeah. Probably. I never did get to Lossie beach. I was meaning to visit.

Next time, then.

Yeah.

Dawn turned the page. Wedding photos of her and Warren.

Linda stubbed her fag out on the flat roof. She cleared her throat and closed the window. Take whatever you want.

Aye. Maybe a few of Shirley.

Fine.

Linda sat on the bed and Dawn passed the album back. Linda tapped at it for a while with her nails.

Look at the hairstyles on us, eh? And Mother in that hat, oh Christ!

Dawn sniffed. Warren looks happy.

He was, Linda nodded. And don't worry, he won't find out about her. They've promised nae a word.

Thanks.

You should tell Maeve.

She already knows, Dawn said. I've shown her pictures. She doesn't understand yet.

That's good.

Linda turned more pages. They were all full with photos of her: birthdays, Christmases, holidays on the West Coast. They went to France one year. She was learning French at school so they whisked her off to Paris. She was pictured standing by herself in front of the Eiffel Tower, one of its monster iron legs criss-crossing the sky behind her.

The seventies, Linda said. Flares were in.

Flares and sunglasses. Linda had always had great clothes.

Nothing happened with Warren and me, Linda said suddenly. You know that, eh?

It's okay, Dawn said.

Not that it couldn't have, mind. He didn't half try!

They laughed.

I said he wasn't my type, Linda said.

Dawn needed a smoke. She'd left her packet in the car. Can I?

Course.

Ta.

Here, Dawn said. I've got something for you from Shirley's place. She went to her handbag and pulled out the silver dog with the bell inside it. She pushed down the tail. *Bzzz.*

You remember it?

Linda laughed. Jesus, yes! No one could forget that thing. Thanks. I'll put him in the shop.

Dawn thought she might tell Linda about Shirley and Jock. Not yet, though. It would be too difficult for Dad and Linda would hate her for that. What was the point? They were getting old, just like he'd said in his letter. She saw it more and more in the way he walked and in Mother's hands, slower at the knitting than they used to be, dropping stitches. She was even getting muddled. Dawn- Lindy- Dawn- Lindy- Dawn, she'd say.

The story was for herself. Later it would be for Maeve, when she was old enough.

✳ TELEPHONE ✳

Wee Betsy, 1955

Big Ellen's bairn was born on April the fifteenth. He's John, after Uncle Jock, which made everyone happy and also a bit sad.

I wonder if Uncle Jock's baby's been born, but I'm not allowed to ask or talk about it any more. Mammy and Daddy said it was an unkind thing to make up, and I got told off for telling lies. I'm especially not allowed to talk about it today. As soon as Mammy has Nancy and Rachel ready, we're going to visit the new baby Jock. If I talk about Jock's girlfriend today, Daddy'll drag me out the door by the lugs. If I mention all this nonsense in front of Granny again he says he'll spill my blood. And Mammy's on his side. She said if folk hear the way I'm going on they'll call us baby snatchers as well as beggars.

Now that we don't live with Granny and Big Ellen any more we have to put on our nice summer dresses to visit. Visiting's not the same as running down the dancers to say 'Hello'. We have a new house now, a house with no stairs at all. I like it cause it's at Lossie, up a hill near the beach. Rascal's come with us and I walk him on the sand every day. He chases up and down, barking into the wind and jumping in the sea. The first time he did it I was scared he would drown cause the waves were so big, but it turned out the clever doggie can swim like a fish. The bad thing about the new house is it used to be a place for soldiers to sleep. It's made of metal, and when Rascal barks at night it echoes. It probably wakes everyone in the other houses too.

Daddy likes it here cause we've got a round roof, the same shape as the tents him and Mammy used to live in, only bigger.

We call the house 'The Tin Can'. It's very noisy in the rain, and Mammy says we'd be better off if the roof *was* canvas. She says we'll be hot stew in the summer and ice blue in the winter.

I'm out playing in the garden with my new pal, Jimmy Starbuck. He also lives in a Nissen hut, and Jimmy Starbuck loves *Journey into Space* even more than I do. He pretends his tin-can house is a spaceship. He has a bonnie red bicycle he said he'd let me have a shot of, but now I'm in the saddle he doesn't want to give me the handlebars.

'Let go!' I shout and push at him.

'Put your foot there first,' he goes, kicking at the pedal.

'I know!'

Daddy's making the front of our hut nice, a proper garden with a fence and flowers like the big houses in the West End of Elgin. To the side is a lawn, and this is where I am playing with Jimmy Starbuck and the bicycle.

'Okay,' he says at last. 'Mind yourself.' And he steps back so I can turn the pedal.

And at that exact second Mammy goes and roars on me from round the corner.

'Wee Betsy. Where are ye? We've tae get the bus. NOW!'

That does it. The handlebars wobble off to the left and I go to the right. It's like trying to stand up in the scrap cart when Hughie the pony's pulling over the bumpy bits on the road.

'Oooeeaa!' Starbuck shouts. I think I catch a peek of him out the corner of my eye just as I fall. He's wearing his hands on his ears, something folk do quite often in the tin-can houses. The red bicycle slams into the side of our metal house, and there's a shuddering clash. A thousand dustbin lids clattering down a staircase.

Mammy appears.

'What in the name of Heaven?'

Inside Daddy has dropped something on the floor that's circling and circling, faster and faster, and then it stops. It'll be one of the tin plates Mammy got. She likes them cause he can't smash them when he takes a drink.

Rascal howls before it's finally quiet again. Mammy can't speak. I've a grass stain smeared down the front of my new white frock, and a bloody knee to boot. I like the wounded bit, though. It's shiny and red like the paint on the bicycle, and soon it'll make a really big scab.

Daddy's the first to find his voice again. He shouts, 'FUCK-RAT! WHAT THE HELL?' from somewhere inside the Tin Can. A pissed off sardine. Jimmy Starbuck's behind me, trying not to laugh.

I've told Jimmy Starbuck about Jock's baby and *he* believes me. The only things he doesn't know are that I wanted Jock to marry Miss Webster, my old teacher, and how I told the toby in the park about Jock's baby and the girl from the cinema. I haven't told him about that. I've meant to lots of times, but I always change my mind at the last minute. Anyway, we've decided to be spies. I'm going to search for clues while I'm back in Lady Lane today.

Mammy's still angry.

'I didn't mean it,' I say.

She drags me back inside to change as quick as I can so we don't miss the bus to Elgin.

'Bye, Starbuck,' I shout.

There's a surprise in store when we arrive in our old house. Big Ellen and her bairn have moved into our old room upstairs, and we find Maggie Marbles McPhee sitting at Granny's table drinking a glass of milk. Everyone sits, except Daddy, who stands at the window.

This house reminds me of my uncle Jock, and I don't want to go in his old room. But I do wonder what it's like in there now, and if *someone* is sleeping in his bed.

They start talking about the new bairn. It's resting up in its

267

cot. No one even mentions why Maggie McTootie's sitting with us at *our* table. I'd almost forgotten she knows the secret too. She was under the bridge with me. She could open her gob and tell them the same story. I hope she doesn't, though. I'm not wanting Maggie Marbles on my side. Then I'd really look like a maddie.

Granny's joshing with Daddy that Big Ellen's had a boy and all he's ever had is girls.

'I dinnae see any louns at your hoose. Nae yet. O ho! Ho! Ha!' she says.

Mammy's sat next to Granny, who chuckles a bit, reaches over and rubs Mammy's tummy. She better not start playing music. She's done enough harm already. But I'm not allowed to talk about that.

Maggie's finished her milk. She asks Big Ellen if she can check on the baby upstairs, and Granny tells her aye. She pushes back her chair and runs off like she owns the whole house.

'That's whit ye hae tae worry about,' Granny whispers when she's gone. 'A wee quine like that in a hoose full ae mannys.' She speaks like she doesn't want me and Rachel hearing, and nods to the back where the McPhees' place is.

'You've taken Wee Maggie, then?' Mammy goes.

'Aye. That lot are aw away fer the summer. She's better aff here wi me, ken? She's nae a wee quine any more, even if she acts like it. Those brothers ae hers, ken? They're affae trouble. She's good-mannered, that quinie.'

'Ye talked her father intae it?' Daddy says. He's been acting like he's not been interested in the gossip, staring into the street. I saw him wave to Uncle Jock's pal, the shoemaker from the top of the Lane. He was passing by, swinging a bag in his hand, probably on the way to the shop.

'I tellt thon McTootie that wi yous all gone I could use a young pair ae haunds roun the place. Couldnae refuse an auld wifey, could he? Ho! Ho! Ha! The lassie's better aff here. Four boys in that house, and each as baa-heided as the next.'

Daddy doesn't ask about it any more. He's brought a paper. He looked all important on the bus with it rolled up under his arm, and now he slaps it open on the table in front of Granny.

'You seen this, Ma?'

'No,' she breathes. 'What does it say?'

Everyone's looking at me.

'Will you read for your granny, Wee Betsy? There's my clever one,' Mammy goes.

The paper's swivelled round and they slide it in front of me. Page twenty-one. I clear my throat and sit up straight, but for some reason my heart's thumping like footsteps on the dancers. Last time they made me read it was the article about what happened, and I couldn't do it.

But this is all right. It's just a dead toby called Munro, an auld manny. So what? When I'm finished reading, I look up. They're nodding their heads and chewing their lips, just like folk do at the pictures when the film ends. The paper's folded up and no one speaks about it afterwards, but later I notice Granny cuts it out and keeps it for her tin.

Maggie Marbles isn't the only surprise. The other one's on the bairn. Me and Rachel go upstairs and find Big Ellen and Maggie standing over the cot. They're reaching in, tickling his tummy. It's the first time I've seen a baby boy with no clothes on. All the ones we've had in our family have been wee girls. He's got a thingie between his legs pointing up at us like an extra thumb. I can't stop looking at it till Big Ellen covers it with his nappy.

'Do you like him?' she says.

'He's all right,' I go, still thinking of the thingie, but I don't want to ask about it. The bairn's got thick, black hair like my toy monkey. It's growing right down his neck. Sloe-black is what Maggie and Big Ellen call it. They say it's really special to be born like that, and a few people get it in our family, but I didn't. Rachel strokes the baby's hair. He's got a face more like the McPhee twins than anyone else.

269

I don't look at Maggie the whole time cause I want her to think I've forgotten about Jock and the baby. I don't want her blurting it out like it was *her* secret all along. The three of us follow Big Ellen down the stairs, and everyone in Granny's room makes a big fuss of the bairnie. We have tea and broken biscuits, some of which Granny spits into the bairn's mouth like she used to do with Nancy. I think it's disgusting. I try and forget she did that to me once too.

When we've all finished Mammy says she'll send us to the pictures for a treat. I think she means just me and Rachel, but Maggie gets a coin pressed into her hand too, and the three of us are packed off up the street. This is my chance to do some spying! Now I'll have something to tell Starbuck. I'm so looking forward to seeing Jock's girlfriend in the ticket booth that I don't even care what the picture is. All I have to do is dawdle a bit behind so that Rachel and Maggie Marbles aren't in the way.

We're in the queue, and I'm still wondering what I should say to her, thinking the words out in my head, when the man in front says, 'Thank you, miss.' He's got his ticket and I'm next. I look up to see her, and my heart sinks into my belly. It's not Jock's girlfriend at all.

'Three for *Bambi*, please,' I go.

'What? Speak up.'

'Three, please,' I say again. I push the coins over the counter. The girl looks at me a bit funny, but she takes the coins and gives me a smaller one back. She rips off three yellow tickets from the roll.

The next day, back at The Tin Can, Jimmy Starbuck calls round. He wants me to tell him what I found out as a spy. His bicycle's leaning up against the fence, and it looks even more beautiful in the sun. Two cans are hanging off the handlebars, connected by a long bit of string.

'Come to the beach and I'll tell you,' I go. I stare at the red

270

bicylce and the flashing silver handlebars with that funny invention hanging over them. I want another go on it. We walk down the path to the beach, Starbuck wheeling the bicycle beside him.

'Well?' he goes.

'She's not there any more,' I tell him.

After that I don't know what to say, and he doesn't either. I don't want to think about the baby. We walk over the dunes, where it's hard to push the bicycle cause the wheels sink in, and when we get to the smooth wet surface near the water he puts the bike down.

'Seen one of these before?' he goes. He unwinds the cans on the string off the handlebars. 'It's a telephone.' We try it out, me shouting into one can and him shouting into the other, the two joined by the long string.

'One! Two!' I shout into it. 'Onetwo, onetwo.'

The waves are crashing so loud I can't tell if it works.

'Hello, Lunar 142. Landing Control, please.'

'Here,' Starbuck says, hoisting me in with the string. 'Have another wee shottie of the bike, if you like.'

And this time it feels good. I already know I'm going to get it right. To start with, Starbuck holds the back while I ride along, struggling to find my balance. I'm all unsteady, Skinny Malinky on his long lanky legs. But then it starts to feel smooth, and Starbuck lets go without telling – I'm riding all by myself! The waves and air skim past and my pal's cheering behind me.

'Bring it here a minute. Look at this,' he goes.

I get off the bicycle and tuck my hair back. My cheeks are cold and wet, just over my ear where I flick my finger. It's as if I've been greetin on the bicycle, but I haven't. Or maybe I have. I'm not even sure. Starbuck takes the pedals and does a big circle on the bicycle, right round where I'm stood. He speeds up, then spins out in a straight line. I hear the smooth running of the wheels while he sticks both arms out. No hands!

'I want to do that!'

He starts laughing. 'You'll fall, ye ninny, you just learnt to go!'

But already I can see myself. I'll go right along the whole beach, just like that, with no hands.

'Get on the front,' says Starbuck, nodding to the handlebars.

I sit myself down and stick my arms out while he pedals. I'll just get the hang of it first.

'It feels like flying, doesn't it?' Starbuck says, and he tucks his head down and pedals a bit faster.

Dawn

It was still dark. The road in front was long, lit with cats' eyes and patterned with the shadows of trees. If she followed it far enough north they'd reach the emptiest moors and the most silent mountains, the places with no names in their own language. Or she could head south, take them back to the city where all the lines in the map drew together like veins, a heart. The direction wasn't important.

She'd read the inquest report Big Ellen had stuffed in the old bag. She'd crept out to the car for it in the early hours of the morning, and she'd sat in the front seat reading till the sun came up. Fifty pages of words, but only a few things stuck in her mind now.

The witness list was long and all their statements were typed in a blurry ink with a wide margin down each side. She found Dad's name and stared at it for ages, the dark smudge over the 'H', the name of a man in a black uniform who she didn't really recognise.

CONSTABLE GORDON HENDRY.

Mostly she thought about Jock's shoes. All the witnesses in the report had mentioned them – the way he kept having to stop because they fell off all the time. They were black slip-ons with a worn heel. A size too large. It was probably because of those shoes that he'd tripped in a close off High Street, in the middle of the brawl to which there were no witnesses. He'd cut his head on the cobbles, and was later found in the gutter by a policeman. The police called for assistance. They put his shoes back on for him, put him in the car, and took him to hospital for stitches.

Later, when he'd been patched up by the nurse, they arrested him for drinking.

What if his shoes had fit? Dawn wondered. Would everything be different?

In court there had been two questions to Dad. She had memorised them.

```
Q. Did you have to strike any blows?
A. No.
Q. Did you have to draw any blood from him?
A. No, hardly touched him.
```

Dad. Would he have known something else and kept his mouth shut? Maybe. Dawn could believe that.

Constable Munro was the other policeman on duty that night, but he was dead before the trial. He'd died from asphyxiation, the court heard, probably a heart attack. He'd been walking his dog through Cooper Park and was found in the morning, his body stiff on the grass and his uniform wet with dew.

There was no mention of Shirley. A girlfriend was talked about by Bruce Topp, a witness for the defence, but the court was informed that the girl was unable to testify. There was no name in the report. No one seemed to know who the girlfriend was, or consider it a detail of any relevance. No one was found guilty, after all. Jock's death was explained by a deficient heart combined with the cold weather, the strong likelihood he had been involved in a fight earlier in the evening, and the amount of drink he'd had.

At the Halfway Café Dawn stopped the car and they walked up the gloomy track towards Big Ellen's. She wasn't surprised to find the site deserted. The only signs of anyone ever being there were the black rectangles of burnt caravans and some new graffiti on one of the prefabs. The windows had been broken and

274

the sides were scrawled with mustard paint. Dawn walked over, the dirt crunching under her feet.

SCUM

They turned back.

Where are we going? Maeve said.

You choose this time.

Dawn popped a cassette into the player and turned the volume up. A favourite came on. Maeve had the map open on her knees, her eyes closed. She was spinning a finger over it.

Every moment was the centre of the compass. They took the small roads and drove till the places flashed by too fast to name. And then there were places that had no names at all, places with no people left to name them.

They reached the mountains. They were high, the peaks jagged, grazed with scree and topped with a whip of clouds. Right at the top there was a sparkle of snow. Maeve would never make it that far in her wellies, but Dawn had an idea. Somewhere on the map there was a tiny cable car symbol.

By the time the sun was high over the land, they were travelling upwards in a red cabin with the number 21 painted on the outside. Dawn pointed at the number, but Maeve was too excited to reach the snow, and she didn't care.

Above them the sky was a great expanse of blue, crossed with the long white trail of a jet plane.

ACKNOWLEDGEMENTS

From the beginning, *The Tin-Kin* had the feel of a big family project. I really want to thank my family, all my aunts, uncles and cousins, for supporting the book, and for offering help and calm refuge whenever it was needed. I owe special thanks to Mum and Dad, for their belief in everything I do. I am so lucky to have you. Another special thank you to my cousin Debbie, for trawling the net with me, and for squelching through muddy cemeteries with a buggy, all in the name of genealogy!

Distant cousins and friends who generously shared histories, photographs and enchanting stories include Frances, Linda Gall (née Williamson), the Wilson family, the Williamson family of Williamson & Co. Scrap Metal Merchants, and in Australia, Peter Evans and Clementina Whyte Evans (née Cameron).

Thank you kisses for Christopher Dooks, for truly inspiring me, and for making me laugh every day. Salmon and olives for our cat, Gus.

Thank you to my friends: to Tricia and Dave Eddie, for their energy and for sharing their local knowledge; to Alison Irvine, Kate Dowd, and John McGeown, for suggestions, understanding and good company; and to Robbie Leask, for 'Ellie's Literary Elation' – a joyful fiddle tune.

I am so very grateful to Professor Willy Maley at the University of Glasgow, who read the first scribbles that became this novel, and whose passion for a story that 'had to be told' gave me the confidence I needed.

I would also like to thank the following wonderful institutions: The School of Scottish Studies at Edinburgh University, Elgin Local Heritage Centre, The Saltire Writers' Group, The Taransay Fiddlers, and The Crusty Climbing Club.

Early on, the New Writing Ventures Award opened doors, and also gave much needed financial support, not to mention huge encouragement. A big thank you to everyone at the New Writing Partnership, and to all the writers of 2006.

Euan Thorneycroft at A.M. Heath does a brilliant job as my agent. I really am grateful for the hard work he does and the encouragement he gives me. Finally, a huge thank you to everyone at Duckworth, but particularly to my editor Mary Morris. I feel as if she stepped right into Lady Lane, spent a summer with my 'family', and was very kind and very good to them.

ABOUT THE AUTHOR

Eleanor Thom was born in 1979 and currently lives in Glasgow. She won the New Writing Ventures Award in 2006 with a chapter of *The Tin-Kin*, her debut novel. Eleanor is a graduate of the Masters in Creative Writing at Glasgow University, and an Honorary Writer in Residence for the French Department. She was recently awarded a Robert Louis Stevenson Fellowship.

✷